D0654648

Also by Terri Brisbin

A Highland Feuding miniseries

Stolen by the Highlander
The Highlander's Runaway Bride
Kidnapped by the Highland Rogue
Claiming His Highland Bride
A Healer for the Highlander

Discover more at millsandboon.co.uk.

A HEALER FOR
THE HIGHLANDER

Terri Brisbin

MIX
Paper from
responsible sources
FSC   FSC C013604

is book is produced from independently certified FSC™ pap
to ensure responsible forest management.
For more information, visit www.harpercollins.co.uk/green

Printed and bound in Spain
by CPI, Barcelona

MILLS & BOON

First Published in Great Britain 2018
by Mills & Boon, an imprint of HarperCollins*Publishers*
1 London Bridge Street, London, SE1 9GF

© 2018 Theresa S. Brisbin

ISBN: 978-0-263-93320-8

I lost two of the most important women in my life
this last year—my sister and my mother-in-law.
They were both amazing, strong, loving women
and I will miss them terribly.

To MaryAnn, my sister, who fought valiantly to live
but died with grace. Mar, I miss you.

To the other Theresa Brisbin, my mother-in-law,
who gave me her eldest son to marry and who was
one of my very first readers. Mom, I learned so much
from you and appreciated your help and guidance
all these years. You've earned your rest, lady.

Acknowledgements

I want to thank the Editorial staff at Mills & Boon for
all their support, patience and understanding as I wrote
this book. Thanks to Linda Fildew, my editor, for always
being kind and having my back, and to Bryony Green for
understanding the difficult challenges and losses that life
has thrown at me these last two years.

Thanks to my agent, Pam Hopkins, who calmly answered
my panicked calls and emails as I wrote this book. And
for her guidance and support while I struggled to find the
story that grief had almost destroyed.

And a special thanks to Susan Zen-Ruffinen, my stalwart
companion, who travelled with me to Scotland to find
all the Clan Cameron places. She became my research
assistant, my videographer (on some hysterical travel
videos!) and allowed me to take any turn-off on any road
in the Highlands and Islands except one—Bealach na Bà,
over the mountains to Applecross! Next time, Susan!

Prologue

*The Lands of Clan Cameron,
Loch Arkaig, Scotland
—the year of Our Lord 1358*

Anna Mackenzie watched as Malcolm walked to the edge of the falls and began the long and dangerous climb down the slippery rocks. She tried to stop herself, but she ran to the edge when his head disappeared and she kept him in sight until he reached the bottom. He turned and waved to her before moving off into the forest towards the village and keep near the loch.

Sighing as she wrapped her arms around herself, Anna closed her eyes then and allowed the memories of the last hours to surround her once more. They had laughed and run and kissed... and loved. She loved him more than her own life.

For Malcolm, the only son of Euan Cameron, had braved the rumours and stories about the witch of Caig Falls and come to find the truth. And he'd found Anna, not her mother. She sighed again for they'd found love. It mattered not if she was the daughter of the 'witch' and he the son of the chieftain. It mattered not if they were young. It simply mattered that they were in love and would be together. They made vows to be together and he'd given her a sign of that promise which she carried now close to her heart.

After several moments, the sound of footsteps behind her shook her from her reverie and she turned to find her mother there in the shadows staring at her. How long had she been there?

'Anna, I need your help,' her mother said. Had she seen Malcolm there? From her tone, Anna could not tell. Her mother did not wait for her agreement or refusal, but simply turned and walked back into the forest.

She followed her mother back along the hidden path to the garden she tended in a sheltered place in the thick growth of trees there. Though she could see it plainly, no one else, not the villagers who came searching or Malcolm ever seemed to find it. Until he did.

'We must finish picking the last of these,' her mother said, pointing to several rows of herbs and other plants.

'You have plenty of that already, Mam,' Anna said. 'We dried it just a fortnight ago.'

'We will need more,' her mother said, walking over and picking up one of the baskets that always waited there. She held it out to Anna and motioned for her to begin.

It did not make sense. There was a timing to harvesting the plants and herbs that Lara Mackenzie depended on for healing and treating ailments and afflictions. No one knew that better or more accurately than her mother and yet, here she was, picking things ahead of their time.

Anna did her mother's bidding and, over the next hours, they gathered everything that was at or near readiness. A strange wariness filled Anna as night came and her mother continued to gather and sort and wrap all the plants and herbs they'd collected. When her mother sat at the wide, worn table and just stared into the dark corner of the cottage, Anna went to her and finally asked the question that had haunted her all day.

'Are we leaving here, Mam?'

'Aye, on the morrow.'

The few and simple words tore Anna's heart apart. Her hands shook as she thought on the possibilities facing her now. Had her mother discovered her secret? Her secrets? Anna had been so careful not to bring Malcolm close to the cottage or the hidden garden. What did her mother know?

'Why? Why would you leave this all behind? Where will we go?' Anna stood and walked to the window. Resting her hands on the shutter, she stared past the rough wood and out at the forest surrounding their dwelling, waiting on her mother's explanation.

'Ye've been caught, Anna. Are ye three months gone now?'

Anna's hands slid down over her belly in a movement she could not stop. She did not want to turn to face her mother and see the disappointment and disapproval in her gaze. But when she did she saw sadness, a touch of pity, but mostly the glimmer of love there.

'Aye, Mam. Or close to it.'

'When were ye going to tell me, lass?'

Anna swallowed against the tightness in her throat. She'd never kept secrets from her mother...until Malcolm. Keeping the knowledge of him and their love felt right. Or it had before this moment. 'I would have told ye, Mam. He... Mal said he would tell his father and then we could...'

'Malcolm Cameron, the chieftain's son?' Anna nodded. 'Ye thought to marry him? The chieftain's son would marry the penniless bastard daughter of the *witch* of Caig Falls? Ye ken better than that, Anna.'

Her mother's words forced her to see the harsh and stark situation as it was—not as she'd hoped or pretended it could be. It was much more romantic to believe his promise that they would be together and the vows they'd made to each other. To believe that the child they'd made would be welcomed by his kin. To believe that she would be, too. Anna let out a sigh, releasing all the pretences she'd built around the sad truth of the matter.

Her mother walked to her and gathered her close. 'All will be well, lass.' They stood in silence for a few minutes until her mother released her, clutching her by the shoulders and searching her face. 'My kin will take us in until we sort this out.'

Anna nodded, fighting the tears that threatened to overwhelm her. 'I want to tell him before we leave.'

'Nay. 'Tis too dangerous. If he kens, he will do something foolish and we will face more trouble than we could manage. I have seen this before, Anna. If a woman is called a witch, which is what Euan Cameron will do to me before his clan if it suits his purposes, she dies. Our only choice is to leave. Leave now. Leave quietly.'

Anna would have argued and protested, but

the stony expression in her mother's eyes told her she would fail to soften or sway her decision. The happiness she'd felt, the sense of love and anticipation, fled and a deep despair filled her. Her child would never know their father or their kin. Anna shivered as a wave of dread passed through her. Somehow, in that terrible, sad moment, she kenned she would never see Malcolm again. Never hold him. Never love him.

The next days and weeks passed in a blur as Anna and her mother packed and fled the glen and their home above Caig Falls for the north. Her mother's kin, the Mackenzies, did take them in and her child, a boy, was born among them six months later. When word reached them of Malcolm's death at the hands of Brodie Mackintosh three years later, Anna remembered the portent of it she'd felt that day.

And she mourned his death and the end of all the possibilities they'd shared. Mayhap one day she would return to Cameron lands and give her son, Malcolm's son, the opportunity to be part of his father's kith and kin.

Mayhap one day...

Chapter One

*Achnacarry Castle on Loch Arkaig
—spring, the year of Our Lord 1371*

Davidh Cameron stood at his laird's back, listening and watching as the chieftain of their clan heard grievances and pleas. As the man who led the warriors of the Clan Cameron here on their southern lands, it was his duty to attend these hearings. But, more than once, he glanced up as someone or another arrived in the hall and approached in haste.

He let himself relax only when he saw that it was not someone from the village. When his laird stopped in the middle of speaking to a man and looked at him, Davidh understood his actions had been more apparent than he'd hoped.

'Ye can go,' the laird said, nodding towards the doorway. 'This does not need your attention.'

His stomach clenched then, as he realised his inattention had been noticed and acknowledged. Davidh leaned closer to Robert Cameron's ear.

'They will send word if I am needed, my lord. I will see to my duties here.' Davidh waited for a reply and, when none came, he stepped back to his place behind the chieftain's chair.

He did not wish to shirk his duties. As commander of the clan's warriors, his place was at his chieftain's back during his official meetings and when he travelled or carried out other duties. The last thing Davidh wanted was to be absent when he was needed by his laird.

The business of the clan went on for some time and yet Davidh found himself distracted. What if Colm worsened? What if his breathing became even more laboured than it had been last night? It seemed that the boy failed more with each passing day. What would he do if the worst happened? How could he survive if he lost his son after losing his wife and more recently his own parents?

The last years seemed to be filled with only death and destruction for Davidh and his kin. The only good thing that had happened was the ascension of Robert Cameron to the high chair of the Clan Cameron. Thankfully, the laird's brother Gilbert had ruled for only a few short years, but those years had driven their clan to the brink of a bigger conflict with not only their long-time enemies the Mackintoshes, but also the larger Chattan Confederation. And Gilbert had managed to target his brother in his attempts to undermine Robert's possible claim.

In the end, it had been a Mackintosh raised as a Cameron who had brought Gilbert down and had placed the clan back on steadier ground with the powerful Mackintoshes and even with the King. In the last year or so, Robert had established himself as a fair chieftain with a good sense of how to oversee his people. The self-serving and utter ruthlessness of Gilbert had been followed by a man content at stewarding his clan's lands and people while safeguarding them, too.

The sure and steady footsteps across the stone floor broke into his thoughts and Davidh looked towards the person who approached. His worst fears filled him, making it now hard for him to breathe. Colm? Without waiting for the woman to reach the dais, the laird motioned to him.

'Go.'

Davidh was down the steps before Margaret, the blacksmith's daughter, could reach him. 'Is he worse then?'

'Aye,' she whispered.

The worried expression on the lass's face told him more than he wished to know. Davidh ran then, leaving the girl behind and not waiting for her to catch him. Colm could be... He could die this time. The words of some remembered prayers began to flow in his thoughts as he forced the pleas to the Almighty to replace everything else.

Colm was the last person he had and he could not lose him.

Not the boy. Dear God, not the boy.

He did not remember making his way out of the keep or yard or through the gates and village. Davidh found himself at the door to the blacksmith's cottage and he stopped. Fear kept him from reaching up to knock. Fear paralysed his own breath and made his heart pound within his chest. How could he face the death of his son if that was what awaited him inside?

Davidh tamped all the fears down as he had for months and years and knocked before lifting the latch. Slowly, as he offered one final prayer up, he opened the door and looked for his son. Colm lay on a pallet in the corner near the hearth. The boy was almost lost in a cocoon of blankets and all Davidh could see was the pale face and bluish lips that spoke of a recent attack. He stared now, trying to discern if his son lived or had died.

'Come in,' Suisan whispered as she opened the door wider for him to enter. 'He is sleeping now, puir wee laddie. Exhausted from…well, ye ken what he faces when the spells come on him.'

Aye, Davidh understood the terrible attacks that stole his son's ability to breathe and the racking coughs that strained his muscles, leaving behind bruised ribs from the ferocity of the spasms.

But Colm lived. He'd survived another attack of the breathing disease that had struck him down on a more frequent basis in the last few months. And no tisane or poultice or brew from the last healer had helped. Colm worsened with each bout and Davidh understood that, one day, he would not make it through.

This day, though, Colm lived.

'I would not have bothered ye this time, but I feared…the worst. I have never seen him like this.' She nodded at his son.

'I thank you for caring for him, Suisan.'

The stout woman nodded and then gathered her own daughter in her embrace when Margaret arrived there. Davidh stood over his son, watching and assessing every breath the boy's frail body pulled in and let out. Running his hands through his hair, Davidh wondered how much more Colm could endure.

'Margaret, take this to yer father,' Suisan said. She released her daughter and handed her a small sack. It seemed a strange thing to do, but Davidh watched as the girl obeyed without question. When they were alone but for his son, Suisan walked closer to him. 'I want to suggest something to ye though I have only rumours to go on for now.'

'Go on.' Davidh shrugged. 'I have always heeded your counsel, Suisan.'

'There is talk of the witch's return to Caig Falls.'

Of anything the woman could say, this was completely unexpected.

'The witch?'

'Aye, ye ken the stories that have been told for years of the witch living above Caig Falls.'

'I ken the stories, but have not heard mention of her since...' *Since he himself was but a lad and his best friend Malcolm claimed to have found her.* 'For a long time now.'

'She was not a witch, but a wise woman, ye ken. She disappeared some years ago and has not been heard of since. But, a few days ago, one of the lads climbing the falls fell and a woman saw to his injury before sending him home.' Suisan stared at him then. 'I think she has returned.'

'You think she could help Colm?'

'Ye have tried everything else in yer power to try, Davidh. Why not see if she can?'

Suisan knelt at Colm's side and smoothed the blankets over his frail form. He'd been ill for so long that he was smaller than most lads his age.

'I will seek her out.' Davidh smiled and nodded. He felt better knowing he had some kind of plan. The possibility that something or someone could help his son lifted his spirits for that moment and gave him purpose.

'If ye have duties to see to, I can still tend him.' Suisan stood then. 'Come and join us for supper. Ye can take him home for the night then.'

Davidh watched the shallow rise and fall of Colm's chest for a short time. It seemed even and strong enough for now and every hour that his son did not struggle for breath was a good one. Davidh nodded at Suisan. 'I should return to the castle.'

'Go then!' she said, waving him out. 'I suspect he will sleep most of the day now.'

Davidh returned to the keep, knowing that Suisan would take good and thorough care of Colm. But, with his sister married and moved to Edinburgh, his father and, more recently, his mother deceased and Mara gone these last three years, he realised this was not a solution to his problem. What he needed was a strong and healthy son.

Anna Mackenzie stood at the top of the falls, a short distance from the cottage she'd reclaimed, and stared down to the bottom. Memories washed over her, memories made more bittersweet by the knowledge that she would never see

Malcolm again. Oh, she had not fooled herself into thinking that being here would be easy, but she owed it to her son...to their son.

Could she do this? Could she live here as her mother had all those years ago? The similarities she noticed over the last few years between her mother's life and hers were a bit unnerving. Especially as she stood here now while her child explored the hillside and area around the cottage. Had it truly been ten-and-three years since she had stood here in this very place and dreamed of a future with the man she loved?

Suddenly she felt much older than her years.

Iain came around the cottage and she watched his approach. A pang of guilt rushed through her as she realised he was a handful of years off the age she'd been when she'd met his father... and loved him. Iain kenned little about Malcolm other than the barest of details she needed to tell him to pacify his growing curiosity. That interest had spurred her on to return here and seek out his father's kin. She owed her son and his father at least that.

Anna waved the boy over to her side and pointed down to the bottom, near the pool that gathered in the waters of the falls.

'They call that the "Witch's Pool". Many have tried to climb that path along the edge to reach the top.' Anna traced the path with her extended hand, showing it to her son. 'They never see the true path that begins over there in that copse near the large rock.'

'And my father did?' Iain asked.

He was at that age between childhood and manhood and hungered for knowledge of his origin. He needed a father, someone to guide him on those final steps that she could not. She'd refused a few offers of marriage since his birth, always knowing deep inside that she wanted him to know his own people. She'd always known that this day would come. Smiling at him, she nodded as she noticed that he'd gained another few inches and now stood taller than she did.

'Aye. But not before trying the slippery one a few times.'

Iain's laughter rang out through the trees and she once more noticed the resemblance to his father. Was it there or had she just made herself believe she remembered so many little details about the short relationship? Did her memory reveal things in the way she wanted to see them?

'Look, Mam.' Iain pointed into the distance at the road that led to the falls from the loch to the south.

A man rode towards the falls. She had wondered how long it would take for her presence here to be revealed when she'd helped the lad days ago. Here was her answer. She let out a sigh and shook her head. Now, they would come as they had before, some seeking the witch while others came simply for the challenge of climbing the falls.

When the man slowed on the road and glanced up at the falls, Anna drew her son back into the shadows of the thick forest here at the top. They could not be heard over the crashing waters of the falls, but if the light fell just right through the trees, they could be seen. And she did not wish that yet.

She had tasks to finish, plants to sort and the weeds to clear from the garden before she would be ready to begin offering her services to the villagers here. Her mother had taught her the knowledge of herbs and plants before she'd passed two years ago. Anna had been content to remain among the Mackenzies until that day, then the restlessness began. The news of the Camerons' recent upheaval and new chieftain only confirmed her decision that it was time. Gilbert Cameron's reputation as a ruthless man had kept her away, but his demise and his older brother's installation as chieftain drew her here.

It was time.

'Have a care, Iain,' she warned as her son walked away. 'Until we know if we are welcome here.'

Her son nodded and then crept off into the

forest, exploring as lads did when they found a new place. No doubt he would bring home some fowl or rabbit for supper in his explorations. His hunting skills along with his ability to accept and to adjust to new situations surprised her, but she thanked the Almighty her son had them. It was easier to move as they must and not have to deal with a resistant boy of his age.

Anna returned to the cottage and began the daunting task of cleaning it. Once cleaned she could organise the rest—the plants and supplies. Time sped along as she accomplished many of the tasks she must before day's end. The crunching of twigs and leaves outside her opened door warned her of Iain's approach.

'Good day.'

Anna glanced up to find a tall man standing at her door. His height and breadth almost blocked it completely as he stood there outside. As she walked closer, she realised he was crouching down to look inside the cottage door, which was too short for him.

It was the man they'd seen below, walking along the road. The plaid wrapped around his waist and over his shoulders identified him as a Cameron. From the dryness of that garment, she realised that he'd not climbed the falls to get here. That meant he knew the other path to reach this place. And that did not bode well for her and her privacy or security.

'Good day, sir,' she said.

Anna wiped her hands on the apron at her waist and pushed the loosened strands of hair out of her sweaty face. She must look an utter mess with her dirty gown and face. While he… was dangerously attractive.

The man had gathered his long, dark brown hair back away from his face which allowed her to see its masculine angles. And his intense eyes that were the colour of the darkest wood in the forest. And his strong chin. He was the most attractive man she'd ever met, here on Cameron lands or in the north on Mackenzie lands. She swallowed to ease the nervousness at that realisation as her throat tightened and tried to speak past it.

'I did not mean to interrupt you,' he said, stepping back as she approached him. 'I have heard that you are…' He paused then, as though not able to utter the word that most used.

'The Witch of Caig Falls,' she said.

Chapter Two

'I was about to say healer, but if you would prefer the other…'

She'd blurted out the reply before he could finish his sentence. He guessed it was not the first time someone had called her a witch. Davidh watched as her green eyes widened for a moment and then they sparkled as she smiled. Her full, pink lips curved into an enticing and intriguing one as he wondered if she considered the name a curse or a compliment.

She laughed then and he could not look away. The smudges of dirt across her face did little to hide the freckles on her cheeks. And the curls that had escaped her kerchief showed strands of fiery red and copper amidst the other shades of brown. His hand lifted to pull more of the locks free and Davidh struggled to stop himself.

'Nay, healer is preferred since it is truer than the other.'

Davidh was not convinced. Mayhap she was bewitching him with some spell as she stared at him now? His mouth went dry as she stepped closer and he forgot to move back to allow her to pass. Her body brushed his as she walked away from the door and he turned to follow her movements. Something within him woke, a feeling unfamiliar for it had been so long since he'd noticed it last.

She intrigued him. She appealed to him in a way he could not describe. She aroused him.

''Tis the healer I came seeking, but I expected someone…older. Are you the one who saw to Tavish?'

'The lad who fell and twisted his ankle? About two-and-ten?'

'Aye. That one. He sang your praises to his family and to others. That is how I discovered you were here.'

'Are you ill?' She leaned in towards him and took in his measure, glancing over his body and then staring once more into his eyes. 'Have you a fever?' She lifted her hand up as though to touch his forehead and paused, her hand waiting there a scant few inches from his skin. 'Your pardon,' she said as she dropped her hand back to her side.

'I have no need of your services,' he said. His choice of words was ill made and he shook his head. 'My son has been ill for some time and nothing has helped him.' Davidh shrugged, fighting the urge to beg her for any help she could offer.

'I have not unpacked my supplies yet, but tell me of his symptoms so I will know if I can help him.'

He could not help it—he let out a loud sigh of relief. Something in her expression gave him confidence that she could indeed help his son.

'His breathing becomes laboured often,' he said.

It took a few minutes for him to describe all the ways his son had suffered over the last year and how he seemed to worsen by the week. She nodded as though she recognised these signs and symptoms and he found himself studying the way her brow gathered when she asked him to clarify something he'd said. She was methodical in a way the village healer was not. Her questions made sense to him as she tried to understand his son's illness.

'Can you help him?' he asked when he'd finished.

'I have my suspicions about the cause of his illness, but I must see him to be certain.' She glanced around the small clearing in which this secluded cottage sat and then back towards the falls. 'Can you bring him here on the morrow?'

Now Davidh looked at the surrounding land and wondered if it was possible. This small area of woods and clearing around the cottage was like an island in the middle of sheer rock cliffs on one side and a large river that rushed around the other and fell, forming the falls. Oh, aye, he'd followed the path that Malcolm had told him of all those years ago, but he would have to carry his son to bring him here. Shaking his head, he looked back to the woman.

'Nay. I see no way to get him here in his condition. Even using the hillside path that I did.' She looked startled at his reminder of how he'd arrived there, but he did not let that deter him. 'Can you not come to the village and see him there?' As her expression turned into one of refusal, Davidh knew she would not come. 'I can pay you in coin for your inconvenience.' He would give her every bit of coin or valuables he might own if she could help his Colm.

''Tis not about payment. I have not yet asked the chieftain's permission to be here. To offer my herbs and skills to his villagers. So, to visit your son before I do so would offer an insult he could not ignore.'

Once more relief flooded him. This was not an obstacle. He could bring this woman to Robert and make her known to him easily.

'Then I would take you to Robert and see you

given permission to live here among us.' The words came out even as innate caution raised within him.

Robert trusted Davidh's judgement and would accept this woman on his word. He searched her face for any sign of danger and found only sympathy there.

'You could do that?' Her gaze narrowed then and she studied his face more closely. 'I do not even ken your name or who you are.' She glanced away then, as though thinking on something, and turned back to him. 'I did not mean that to sound as rude as it did, especially not when you have just offered help to me.' A scant smile eased her mouth.

'I did simply invade your home without an introduction and never asked your name either,' he said. 'I am Davidh Cameron and I command the Cameron warriors for our chieftain.'

The effects of his words were immediate and surprising. Her green eyes grew wide and fluttered several times at his words. Then those eyes filled with tears for a moment before she glanced away. Strange, that. Davidh searched her face for some sign of familiarity, but there was no way he could have met this woman and forgotten her. A moment later she seemed to pull herself out of whatever reverie she'd fallen into and looked at him with clear eyes.

'Forgive me for my refusal to help you, sir,' she said softly as she curtsied before him. 'I did not understand who you are and I meant no insult to the chieftain or his man.'

This part, this obeisance, still unsettled him, but Davidh understood that, in his new position of service to the new chieftain, it would be something to which he must accustom himself. He was in a position of honour and a certain level of power and others who wished to gain entrance or favour with the chieftain would attempt to go through him to get it. He nodded at the woman.

'I took no insult from your words, mistress. I suspect Robert would not take insult from your coming to the village first, but others might on his behalf.'

There were always some who protected the chieftain's dignity or just wanted to toady up to him to gain advantage for themselves. She waited with a look of anticipation in those lovely green eyes and he lost his thoughts for a moment. When he wanted to speak, he realised he did not know her name either.

'What are you called?' He finally forced out the words. He wanted to know what name he would whisper when he brought her to mind when she was not there.

'I am Anna. Anna Mackenzie.'

'Lately of…?'

'I have lived with my mother's family in the north.'

'What brings you south? Here?'

Though he was being less than hospitable and was questioning the person who possibly held his son's life in her hands, Davidh could not forget his duty to his clan. She glanced away, staring off in the direction of the falls, and then back to meet his waiting gaze.

'I have been learning the healing ways since I was but a wee lass and showed some skill in them. I have always wanted a place to call my own. A place to hone my skills and to help the ill and injured.' The seriousness of her words gave him pause.

'You make it sound like a calling.'

She smiled then and he nearly let out a gasp. No woman before had caused such a visceral reaction within him as this one did. In a short time, she had him uneasy and aroused and curious. This was not good. He had many things that needed his focused attention and anything, anyone, who took his mind off his responsibilities was not good.

'My mother often spoke of it in those words,' she, Anna, said. 'Some people were called to certain stations or places in their lives. She was called to be a healer and it would seem that I have been, too.'

'We have a healer in the village, but he sees more to injuries. He kens little of concoctions and ways to heal other than what most ken.'

'Then who has been treating your son?' she asked, stepping closer to him. A breeze rustled through the clearing and Davidh inhaled an enticing scent. A soap mayhap that she used? So taken by it, he paused a bit too long and she noticed.

'We had another, a woman, who was here for but a few months, before leaving with her husband to his village. Morag left me a goodly supply of the syrups and medicaments that Colm needs. But now Old Ranald sees to things.'

She muttered something under her breath before she nodded.

'I will come in the morn, if that is convenient for you,' she said.

'Come to the gates and tell one of the guards to send to me when you do,' Davidh said. 'I must get back now.'

He'd spent too much time here and the sun was beginning its journey down to night. Even using the path Malcolm told him about would be treacherous come dark. And the one that went down along the falls was dangerous at any time of the day. Only fools and wee lads were stupid or proud enough to try it.

'On the morrow, then,' she said as he nodded and turned to leave.

'How did you ken about that path to get up here?' she asked.

'I have known it for a long time. I just had no need to use it until now.' He stopped then and faced her, for the loud rushing of the falls would make hearing his words impossible if he walked closer to them. 'My old friend Malcolm told me of it.'

He did not know her at all, but the expression on her face alarmed him, nonetheless. 'Mistress, are you well?' he asked.

'Aye,' she said, waving him off. 'I would prefer that no one knew of it.' He understood that a woman living alone far from the village had reason to wish for privacy…and for safety.

'I will share my knowledge with no one, Anna,' he said, seeing her worry ease and her face brighten. 'On the morrow, then.'

It took him less time to reach the bottom of the falls and the horse he'd left tied there in the shade. And, for the first time in such a long while, Davidh felt hope rising in his heart.

His son would not die.

This woman, this healer, this Anna Mackenzie, would help his son and Colm would grow up to be the man that Mara and Davidh had dreamt of at his birth.

His son would not die.

The chant was familiar to him, but now he allowed himself to believe it could be true.

Anna barely made it back inside and to the table before the tremors began. Even her teeth shook as she grabbed on to the wooden chair next to it and lowered herself down. She prayed that Iain would not return now and see her like this.

Davidh Cameron. The commander of the Cameron warriors. Counsellor to his chieftain. An influential man. A powerful man. One who could ease her path or make her life a hell.

Malcolm's closest friend.

Memories flooded her mind then and she gasped at their strength. Malcolm's voice as he explained about their boyish antics together. Defending their decision to tease Malcolm's sister by putting a dead bird in her bed and the repercussions of that act. Speaking of their plans for the time when Malcolm was chieftain and Davidh would be his man. Malcolm revealed that Davidh had helped and protected him many times.

They were closer than true brothers could be.

Malcolm was gone these ten years now and Anna wondered if his friend yet thought about him. Clearly the man had married and had a son since Malcolm's passing.

A son he'd named for his closest friend.

Funny that, for his friends had called Malcolm *Mal* while this man had called his son the other part—*Colm*.

Would he help her? Not only in meeting and gaining permission from the new chieftain to live here on Cameron lands, but also in helping her son claim his birthright? For just as Malcolm would have been chieftain, so his son should be in line to claim the high seat, as well.

Now, though, a different branch of the clan held it and this chieftain had sons who thought it theirs. Her son would present a threat to that plan.

The sound of footsteps outside drew her attention. These were Iain's and he stepped inside the open door holding out his quarry for the day's efforts. A rabbit. Big enough to provide several meals for them, but not so big as to infringe on the rights of The Cameron.

'A good catch,' she said, pushing herself up on shaking legs. 'I will make stew.'

She knew he watched her as she took the rabbit he'd caught, killed and skinned and began preparing to cook it for supper. Anna tried to calm her nervousness, but her hands were unsteady when she lifted the heavy iron pot on to the hook that would hold it above the fire. Iain quickly came to help her. He took it from her as though it weighed less than a feather.

Her son was growing into manhood.

Her son needed to learn about the important things for the life they, he, would claim among the Camerons if her plan worked. The skills of a warrior and the knowledge of a possible heir to the chieftain and more—things she could not teach him.

But Davidh Cameron could.

While the stew simmered in the pot, she gathered together the supplies she needed to take with her to the village. Then she explained to Iain the tasks she needed him to do while she was away for the morning.

All the while, her mind turned over and over the plan she'd devised before they'd left her mother's people. Now that Davidh Cameron was involved, she saw another way, another possibility, to get what she wanted most for her son.

It would not be easy. It would not be quick. It could be dangerous. Nay, that was not true and she would not be foolish enough to ignore the truth that she knew now.

Davidh Cameron was dangerous, for he would

defend and protect his clan and his son from all who threatened them.

Even if the threat came from his closest friend's lover and her son.

Chapter Three

The clouds gathered as she made her way along the road through Achnacarry village towards the castle. Anna lifted her woollen shawl over her head and tossed the end of it across her basket to protect the supplies she carried. If the chieftain gave his permission, she would see Davidh's son before returning to the cottage.

There was so much work yet to be done and she'd not planned to reveal her presence until she was ready. She could almost hear the fates laughing at her for believing she would control every aspect of her endeavour. If only that boy had not ventured so close… But once he'd fallen she could not ignore him or his injury.

The sigh that escaped her then seemed to echo across the road as she continued on, not wanting to delay this meeting for even a moment more. She nodded a greeting to an old man who walked by her away from the castle. Though she passed by a number of people of all ages along the way, not many acknowledged her. She was a stranger here, for now, so it was to be expected. Would there ever be a place or time when she was not that?

Her life had consisted in segments for as long as she could remember. Her earliest years she remembered not so she would have to accept the explanation her mother had given her. Then, the years spent here, living above the falls while her mother saw to the ills and hurts of those who came to her. A smile came to her face when she thought on the next part—the months with Malcolm.

A few glorious and shining months of love and happiness and hope. Anna would live on those memories her whole life.

Then, her flight north and separation from him and the birth of their son. Iain had only two years when the news of Malcolm's murder spread across the Highlands and clans. Her mother had helped her through that desperate time—and Iain, a sunny, happy child, did, as well. His childhood years seemed to fly by and then her mother's passing drove Anna to make her decision to return here.

To the lands and clan of her son's father.

Anna glanced ahead and saw the guards standing on each side of the large iron gates that allowed entrance to the castle grounds and keep. Would they send for Davidh at her, a stranger's, word? They caught sight of her and moved to block her from entering, as guards did.

'What is your business within, mistress?' the taller one said. His hand on his sword reminded her that she was an outsider and unknown to them.

'Davidh Cameron said to call on him this morn. He said to send word to him of my arrival.'

The change in their expressions and the strange glint in their eyes happened and fled so quickly that Anna almost missed it. It was obvious that they misunderstood her purpose or the handsome commander's wishes in this. Anna drew back the shawl to expose her basket, filled with various jars and containers of medicaments and such.

'He has asked me to see to his son,' she said.

Now sheepishness entered the men's gazes and they nodded and stepped back to their positions on each side of the gate as one, the shorter one, called out to someone within to send word to their commander. Anna expected Davidh to come for her, but another man hastened down the path to the gates instead.

'Come! Come,' he called out. The guards nodded her to go so she walked through the gates, stopping when the man reached her. 'He is expecting you, though the chieftain is too busy to speak to you just now. Come, you can wait inside.'

She had to quicken her steps to keep up with this man and she did, arriving at the doorway of the keep out of breath. But he was not done yet and led her within, down a long corridor towards a noisy chamber. As they reached the doorway there, she heard angry words being exchanged. The man took her by the arm and tugged her to a place by the wall.

'Stay here until Davidh calls for you.' The man nodded at the stool there and walked away before she could say aye or nay.

Anna sat as directed and then glanced about the chamber, the great hall of the keep, and sought out the only one she knew here. She heard his voice before she saw him. There he was, standing at his chieftain's side, involved in some discussion. Well, from the raised, angry tones, it sounded more like an argument, but she was a stranger to the proceedings here and could not gauge if there was true anger or something else.

Studying the various people up on the dais, she could see that Davidh was held in high esteem, not only by his clan's chieftain but also by those who served the laird. Several times as she watched, the chieftain asked for his counsel on the matter and others referred to that opinion in their own statements. This seemed to be about an incursion on to their lands and the question was about the actions to be taken. The discussion continued for some time, and, though not familiar with the particulars of it, it sounded as though Davidh's judgement would prevail.

'Enough.'

When spoken by the chieftain in a tone and loudness that all could hear, the arguing was done. She watched as the powerful man sat back against his chair and nodded. Everyone surrounding him stepped away and waited on his pronouncement. Instead of calling out orders to them, Robert Cameron spoke softly then.

'I will make my decision by nightfall and Davidh will have your orders.'

From their stances and the manner in which they held their bodies, Anna could tell some were not pleased at all by this. Whether they wanted the chieftain to act now or whether they did not wish for Davidh to play such an integral role, she could not tell. But clearly the chieftain's men were not in agreement with this. When the small gathering broke up, Davidh raised his head and nodded at her.

So, he knew she was there. He called not for her, but motioned a servant to his side and spoke to the woman. Anna watched as she picked up a cup and pitcher and made her way down from the dais, along the hall's stone walls to where she sat waiting.

'The commander said 'twill be some time, mistress,' the woman said, holding out the cup. 'Would you like some ale while you wait?' Anna nodded and took the cup. As the woman filled it, she continued, 'There is yet some porridge or bread and cheese in the kitchen if you have not broken your fast yet.'

'Nay,' she replied in a low voice. 'The ale is enough for me.' Anna nodded at the woman who curtsied as though Anna were of higher station than she was. 'My thanks to you,' Anna added before the woman returned to the dais and those to whom she should bow.

Anna held her basket on her lap and allowed her shawl to drop around her shoulders. Tucking her loosened hair back under her kerchief, she waited and watched the comings and goings of the mighty Cameron's hall.

So, this was the place where Malcolm had lived.

She'd never been into the village before and certainly not the hall. Her mother had hidden her presence from the villagers and, until Malcolm had found her by accident in the woods near the falls, no one had known she existed.

This hall was grand and she could almost see

him running the length of it as a lad. He would have sat on the dais next to or nigh to his father, Euan Cameron. As his son and tanist of the clan, Malcolm had been trained from birth to fight and to rule. Her breath caught then as she realised the truth of her mother's words spoken so long ago.

His father would never have allowed their marriage—bairn to be born or not. A son of this great place would marry the daughter of another, not the penniless offspring of a healer. The tears surprised her and she wiped them away. Though it had not felt so, her mother's actions had saved her great pain. Her mother had understood what would have happened if they'd remained.

A leman would be the only place she could claim in his life. Loved, certainly, but never to be at his side except in the dark of night or the moments of privacy they could seek out. And a son born in wedlock would supplant any place their son would have held. Anna reached up and wiped away more tears.

It was strange that this place had caused such a long-overdue realisation, but it had. Now, though, she needed to gather her wits and her control and speak to the current laird to gain a place here. So that her son could claim his place here when the truth was known to all.

'Anna Mackenzie. The chieftain calls you now.'

That man who'd led her inside stood before her now and she glanced up to find everyone in the hall looking in her direction. So caught up in her past was she that she had missed her summons forward.

Anna stood quickly and lifted her basket on to her arm. Following the man forward, she stopped where he pointed and she curtsied to the man seated above her without looking up. She waited until the laird spoke her name, signalling her to rise.

'My commander tells me you are a healer, Mistress Mackenzie.'

'I am, Laird,' she said, without raising her gaze.

'You seem young to be such,' The Cameron said. 'How came you to be here in Achnacarry?'

'My mother lived here some years ago and I wished to return.'

'Your mother?' Davidh asked now. She did not yet raise her eyes, but he came down the steps and stood next to her. 'You did not say your mother lived here.' He moved between her and his chieftain then. 'Anna?'

'I think I understand,' The Cameron said from his seat. 'Your mother was…' She did look at him then and saw that he knew.

'Aye, Laird. She was the one they called the Witch of Caig Falls.' The word echoed through the rest of the hall, not because she'd said it but because those watching whispered it then. 'Though she was only a talented healer and could cast no spells or enchantments.'

'Surely she could not,' The Cameron said. 'She was a God-fearing woman. The rest were just rumours.' He waved Davidh back; his action declared she was no threat.

Had this man, the head of the mighty Cameron clan, just defended her mother against the fanciful but very dangerous claims of being a witch? His eyes crinkled with merriment as he smiled at her. The last chieftain here would never have done such a thing, nor the one before him. Malcolm's father had ignored the threats against her when they began. That was another reason her mother had chosen their time to flee—a woman called witch was living in a dangerous situation and it would take but one incident to spark into a life-threatening one.

'Aye, Laird,' she said now. 'She had the skills of a talented healer. I only hope I can be as able as she was.'

'Well, Old Ranald will be glad to have someone take over those duties from him. He has more skill with a saw and wooden splints than any of the finer healing talents. You will live by the falls? Davidh said the cottage there is fit for living, but remote.' A glance at Davidh who had stepped to her side revealed his nod. 'Will you not live here in the village?'

'My mother's plants yet grow near the falls. 'Tis easier to cultivate what I need there.' Anna glanced around and wondered which of the laird's counsellors would turn against her if she did not agree to his terms. At least one dark, narrowed gaze met hers—the man who'd escorted her in was not happy over this, over her. No need for trouble now, she thought, so, she acquiesced. 'But, if it would please you, I can make arrangements to visit the village each day and see to any needs.'

He considered her offer seriously and for some time. She was almost on the point of giving in and moving to the village instead, but the touch of Davidh's hand on her arm, something hidden from the view of most everyone there, forestalled her from doing that.

'If it would serve you better to live out there, you have my permission to do so,' The Cameron declared. 'And my protection while you serve my clan here.'

'My thanks, Laird.'

'Davidh, come to me after you have seen to your son.'

She released a breath she had not known

she'd held in and nodded. She curtsied then and watched as he stood and left the dais. Though others there turned their attentions away from the dais, Anna could feel their gazes upon her. They were curious about the woman just welcomed into their midst.

'I brought what I think I will need, but I would like to see what you have been using.'

'This way,' he said, leading her back the way she'd entered.

'Who was the man who brought me in?'

'That was Struan, The Cameron's steward.'

She stopped right then and there in surprise. The steward had been sent like a common servant to fetch her from the gate? The steward? The same man who'd stared at her with open dislike in his eyes was the steward and in charge of everything in The Cameron's household here at Achnacarry.

'You sent the laird's steward to the gates?'

'Aye,' Davidh said. 'Robert wished to continue the discussion and you needed to be admitted. Struan was the only one not needed in the hall just then.'

Men could be both practical and oblivious at the same time. Davidh had walked on and she rushed to catch up to his long-legged strides. They left the keep and the yard and walked back into the village. Now, people openly stared as she passed by them. Word would spread about her identity quickly, for that was how news raced through these small villages. Soon, everyone would know.

They turned down a path and she smelled the scent of hot metal and fire and knew the smithy was nearby. Soon, they walked by it and stopped at the large cottage next door.

'This is your cottage?' she asked, peering around him at the dwelling. 'Is your wife within?'

Now, he stopped and turned to face her. His face had lost most of its colouring, making him appear gaunt and frightening. He took a step towards her and she fought not to shrink back away from him. He leaned down closer to her and spoke in a harsh whisper.

'My wife died of fever a few years ago and I have raised him since.'

'I...am...' She could not speak the right words to him now.

'I do not wish to discuss Mara before my son, so I pray you will not mention her within.' His voice betrayed the emotions he must feel. She heard the loss and grief and yearning there and her own heart wanted to weep for his loss. 'This...' He paused then and cleared his throat making hers feel even tighter with the emotions she could see and hear within him. 'This is where Jamie, the blacksmith...' he nodded over her shoulder at the smithy '...and his wife Suisan live. She cares for Colm when I am on duty.'

'I understand,' she said softly.

He nodded, knocked on the door and then lifted the latch gently. She smiled at the efforts he took not to disturb those within. For all his strength and formidable size, he softened as he must for his ailing son.

The good thing about this cottage was that it was filled with light and fresh air. Often, those treating the sick closed the windows and built up the fire which allowed the smoke from the peat and wood being burned to fill the often cramped place. In her mother's opinion, that did more harm than any possible good for most ailments and illnesses. Anna followed Davidh in, smiling at the anxious woman standing next to the pallet.

'Suisan?' she asked. At the woman's nod, she introduced herself. 'I am Anna Mackenzie.'

'From the falls?' the woman asked.

The damn rumours and stories always followed her and her mother before her. 'Aye, from the falls.'

'I am glad he sought ye out. The puir wee lad is not much better this morn than he has been these last days.' Anna had learned early that suspicion was hard to fight and so this unexpected sense of welcome surprised her. 'Let me show ye what the last healer gave us to treat him.'

'I would see your son first,' she said, lifting her head to meet his gaze.

Whether he'd known it or not, Davidh had placed himself between her and his son. The sense of protectiveness about his son pervaded his every action and deed and somehow that made her heart warm to him. It was something she'd never had in her life, so she always seemed to notice it elsewhere.

The chieftain's commander eased his stance and stepped aside, allowing her closer to the small boy lying on the pallet. With his eyes closed, she could not tell if he slept or not. Kneeling down, she leaned in and watched the rise and fall of his chest. Not good. The rasping sounds and the shallow quickness of the breaths were not good.

A quick assessment of the colouring in his fingernails and lips told her more. His eyes fluttered and then opened when she laid the back of her hand on his forehead.

'Good morn to you, Colm,' she said softly. 'How are you feeling this day?'

Anna leaned back and sat on her heels so that the boy could see those he knew behind her. Frightening him would make his condition worse. When he tried to sit up, she slid her arm behind him and used her other hand to guide him do so.

And then he began to cough.

Chapter Four

The boy shuddered in her arms, his body trembling, and his chest rattled as his body fought against the racking coughs. She heard Davidh move behind her and Suisan walked closer, but she waved them off with a nod of her head. 'Wait,' she whispered.

'He needs this.' Davidh thrust a small bottle in front of her. 'The healer said three to four drops when he begins.'

He'd already removed the stopper and she could smell the concoction within the bottle. Juice of the poppy. A strong blend from the smell of it.

'Nay.'

She shifted on to her knees and brought the boy up to sit. With an arm in front of him, she eased him to lean against her and she placed her hand on his back, trying to feel the source of the cough. Anna had seen this before, as had her mother. Poppy was the last thing the boy needed.

'This will quiet the cough, Anna,' Davidh said, holding the bottle out again before her. 'He is in pain.'

Davidh was in pain, that much was certain. She heard it in his voice just as she heard the rattling in his son's chest. She hated to make either of them suffer, but giving that concoction to Colm would calm the coughing even while making it more difficult to breathe.

'Davidh.' Suisan spoke then, whispering to the commander, and his shadow moved away.

Anna listened and watched until the boy's fit eased and he could once more draw in breath. She did notice that he continued to pant, probably afraid that taking in too much would cause another round.

'Now that it has ceased, can you stand up, Colm?' The boy agreed just as his father said nay. After glancing nervously at his father for permission, Colm allowed her to help him up once Davidh nodded. 'Come, I will help you. You may feel better sitting on that chair than lying down when the coughing strikes you.'

Once she'd seen him settled there, she took a small sack out of her basket and handed it to Suisan. 'Would you brew this in a small pot for me?

By the time it cools, 'twill be the right strength for him.'

Then she began her true work.

'Davidh, 'tis better for him to sit up more and lie down less. Suisan, can you leave the shutters in the back of the cottage open like that for most of the time he is here? Smoke, from the fire or the smithy, is not good for him.' Anna glanced at the pallet. 'When he does lie there, he should not be flat. The higher his head, the better.'

She waited until the tisane had brewed and was cool enough for him to drink before saying anything else. Instead, she examined each bottle or jar and asked Colm about the taste. His remarkable sense of humour and resilience showed through as he made faces to describe each one.

'How many years have you, Colm?' She thought she remembered Davidh mentioning his age, but she wanted the lad to speak.

'Eight years.'

'Mistress Mackenzie,' Davidh said over her shoulder.

'Mistress Mackenzie,' Colm repeated. 'I have eight years.'

'Nearly full grown, then?' she said. His face lit up at her words and she saw the same eyes staring at her as his father had. The shape of his face and his colouring was not familiar so Anna knew those traits were from his mother. 'So, you are old and wise enough to understand and follow instructions?'

Colm nodded and took another mouthful of the tea as if to show her how compliant he could be. 'Aye, mistress.'

'Firstly,' she said, meeting his wide and serious gaze, 'is that I want you to lay on the pallet only when you plan to sleep.'

'He is weak…' Davidh began.

She ignored him and spoke only to his son.

''Twill be hard at first because you are accustomed to lying abed, but soon you will feel strong enough to sit up or even stand all day long.' She nodded at the boy. 'What say you, Colm? Will you try this?'

'Aye, Mistress Mackenzie!' From the tears she saw in Suisan's eyes now, Anna suspected that this enthusiasm was something not seen in the lad in some time.

'And I fear I will have other concoctions that you must take. Some will have a terrible taste, but they will help you. Can you promise to do as I say?'

'I will try, mistress. I will!'

Davidh could not stand this any longer. True, his son had rallied in a way he'd not seen recently, but it could not last. Had he made a mistake in bringing this woman to see Colm? Other than her appearance at Caig Falls, her claims of being a healer, and the bottles and jars that seemed to indicate it was so, he had no proof that she'd ever treated anyone successfully. And yet, he'd brought her to his son on what? His gut reaction to her?

As he listened to her voice as she spoke to Colm, her manner of addressing the boy as though he was in charge surprised Davidh. She did not coddle him or order him. Instead she explained and asked for co-operation. It was how he spoke to the men under his command.

This Anna Mackenzie seemed to know what she was about, even if her suggestions and changes so far were completely the opposite of previous advice he'd received. Watching her now, he understood that she had a plan and he waited to speak to her about that. Even Suisan nodded in agreement as the woman instructed Colm on what he would take and when he would take it.

'Now, if you would kindly pour some boiling water in that pan and place it here on the table,' she said, aiming her words at Suisan. 'Colm and I will play a game.'

Davidh walked to the doorway and leaned against the frame, watching as Anna chose some leaves from a sack in her basket and then retrieved one of the thick blankets from the pallet.

She shook it out and folded it in a particular way, repeating her actions until it was as she wished it to be. Curious, he watched without asking any questions—though he had many she would need to answer before long.

Soon, a pan of steaming water sat before his son. Anna crushed the leaves in her hand and sprinkled them over the water. A fragrant aroma filled the cottage within a few moments. Anna tossed one end of the blanket over the pan and then directed Colm to lean over it.

'This is to see how long you can go without coughing. First, take in slow breaths while I count and try not to cough.' Then she draped the rest of the blanket over and around his son's shoulders, creating a tent over the pan. 'Are you ready, Colm?' His son's muffled assent could be heard even through the thick wool over his head.

Davidh could not help it, he found himself inhaling and exhaling to her soft, slow count. As it went on, he waited and listened for signs of distress in his son and heard none. Then it came.

Colm burst out into a coughing fit and Davidh took a step towards him before Anna waved him off. She held Colm's shoulders to steady him and softly spoke to him, telling him how to let the coughs happen and how to breathe to calm them. Rather than escalating into an uncontrollable wave that would see Colm collapsed on the pallet, with blue lips and bruised eyes, this time the coughs subsided and soon Anna was back to counting. He met Suisan's gaze over Anna's head and saw her tentative and yet hopeful expression.

But Davidh dared not hope too much this soon. Other treatments and medicaments had seemed effective in the past, only to stop helping his son. Would these as well? At this desperate point, as long as Colm did not worsen, Davidh would be happy. After a short time, Anna lifted the blanket off Colm and placed it with care to the side of the now-cooled pan.

'How does your chest feel now, Colm?' Anna asked his son.

A smile that made it hard for Davidh to breathe settled on Colm's face and he shrugged. As the boy inhaled, they all waited to see if the coughing had truly been eased by the vapours of whatever those leaves were.

'Better,' Colm said, drawing in a deeper breath than he would have dared just an hour ago. 'It doesna hurt now.'

All three of those observing the boy let out a sigh of relief, even the one who had brought about such a change.

'I must speak to your father and Suisan about what to do and when to use these,' she said, sweeping a gesture over the small collection of ingredients there on the table. 'Will you sit here quietly while I do?' At the boy's doubtful glance, she added, 'I want you to listen so you will know about it, too. Can you do that, Colm?'

The expression on his son's face was the same as the one Mara would have when concentrating on something important. In the set of Colm's chin and the tilt of his head, he saw his wife's face. God, he missed her so. He could not lose their son, too.

'And I will return in a few days to bring more of the leaves and tinctures and see what else might help you.'

'A few days?' Davidh realised he'd not been paying heed to her specific instructions. 'You will not come on the morrow?'

'Nay,' Anna said, stepping back, but not before running her fingers through Colm's hair in an affectionate way. ''Twill take a few days for these to do their work. If they are successful at keeping that cough under control, then I will adjust them as we need to.' She patted his shoulder and walked to where Davidh stood near the door. 'As I have said, I have many things to get organised and ready up at the cottage.' He would have objected, but she shook her head.

'If he worsens...?'

'Send for me and I will come,' she said, meeting his gaze now. 'I think he will not.'

Suisan moved the supplies to a shelf near the

hearth and began preparing for her noon meal. Colm missed little now, watching with an interest that Davidh had not seen in many months. Anna retrieved her basket and put what she would take with her back in it, before taking her leave—first from Colm, then Suisan and then himself. Davidh followed her outside, trying to find the words he wanted to say to her. She stopped after a few paces and turned to face him.

'I did not wish to say this in front of them, but I cannot know if this will make him better. He may never re—'

His hand covered her mouth before he could stop himself. Her lips were soft against his fingers and he felt her gasp before he heard it.

'Your pardon, Anna,' he said. 'Watching him just then, well, I do not wish to hear words of caution. I have been living with his eventual death for so long, I had not realised the weight of it until just now. Now, when he has more colour in his face and is breathing more smoothly than he has in months and months.' He dropped his hands to his side then and shrugged. 'Allow a father a measure of hope before tearing it apart.'

Whatever she was going to say, she did not. Instead he saw the tears filling her eyes before she turned away from him. He'd not meant to drive her to tears, for he'd simply spoken his fears aloud for the first time to someone other than his dead wife or the dark of night.

'I will come two days hence then,' she said.

He stood there on the path and watched her until she disappeared from view on the road through the village and towards the north. He went back inside and spoke to Suisan and Colm for a short while before returning to his duties at the castle. For the first time in such a long while, the sound of Colm's coughs did not follow his steps away.

Anna used all of the control she could pull together not to fall to her knees and sob over this man and his son. Truth be told, she worried that the lad was too far gone to bring him back from the brink of death. But how could she say that to the man who stood there with both hope and desolation in his gaze? He knew. He *knew* how dire the situation was. And somehow his own survival depended on that of his son's.

Nay, he was not ill or stricken by the same lung weakness that assailed the boy, but she thought that his son's death would tear him apart in other ways. Anna stopped now, at the edge of the village, and turned to look back. He'd been watching her, she could feel his gaze burning into her with each step. Now, though, she did not see him there.

She quickened her pace, wanting and needing to put some distance between herself and the village. But the boy and the man were in the centre of her thoughts all the way back to her cottage. And for the rest of the day as she weeded and pruned the unruly and overgrown plants in her mother's plot above the falls.

Davidh and his son remained her concern over the next two days as she prepared concoctions and unguents and even as she and Iain ate and talked. Methods of treating the boy's lung affliction filled her thoughts. She had kept notes on her mother's recipes and cures in a precious book and she consulted it as she prepared her basket for her journey back into town. Though Iain wanted to accompany her, she bade him to wait there, in the safety of the shadows.

The revelation of his existence and his connection to this clan would come, but Anna wanted it to happen to her own plan. Once it did, she would lose control over the one thing in her life that was her own to claim and she did not relish that moment at all.

Chapter Five

'Mistress Mackenzie!'

Colm's excited call greeted her on her approach to the blacksmith's cottage. He sat outside the door, waving and speaking to anyone who passed by him that morn. A collection of others stood nearby, waiting or watching, she could not tell.

'Good day to you, Colm,' she called out to the boy.

Sitting in the unexpected morning sun revealed that there had been some improvement in his condition. His colouring, though not as pale and pasty as he had been, was a scant bit nearer to health than sickness now. A good sign that. Anna reached the boy and he reached out and tugged on her skirts.

'Mistress Mackenzie, I sat up all day except for when I was asleep. Like you told me to.'

Suisan came to the opened doorway then,

wiping her hands on the apron tucked at her waist.

'Good morn to ye, Mistress Mackenzie,' she said, nodding at the boy who was struggling to remain on the stool there. 'He has been hoping ye would give yer permission for him to leave the cottage.'

Anna walked over and slid her hand across the boy's hair and forehead. No fever. 'Well, let me see how he is doing and we can talk about extending his prison walls.'

'I have taken every one of your remedies,' Colm said. 'Even the brown one that smells putrid.' He gagged loudly, showing his distaste for it.

'Is that true, Mistress Cameron?' Anna asked in a serious tone. 'Has he followed my instructions?' The lad's enthusiastic words and manner spoke of his improvement, with or without Suisan's confirmation.

''Tis true,' Suisan said.

'Come inside and let me check your breathing first, Colm.'

She smiled as the boy jumped up from the stool and ran into the cottage. The mistake to avoid would be to let him try too much too soon. Though, watching his increased vigour, she knew it would be hard to keep him from pushing himself.

Colm allowed her to push and prod him and he followed her instructions to test his breathing. He coughed, but it was not the uncontrollable, breath-stealing spasms it had been. This was good. He was not recovered, that would be a long process, but if the various things she'd given him eased the symptoms, she would be happy.

'I think he can be permitted some time outside on the morrow, Mistress Cameron,' Anna pronounced when she'd finished. 'No running, course, but some time with his friends.'

'Truly?' Colm asked. 'On the morrow?'

'Aye. If you promise not to run.'

'Aye, Mistress Mackenzie. Aye!'

Colm's smile warmed her heart and she could see a bit of her own son in his reactions. They were but a few years apart in age with Iain being nigh to ten-and-three while Colm had eight years.

'For now, you may sit outside and speak with your friends. Make your plans.'

The boy was up and outside before she could say another thing. True to what Anna asked of him, he sat on the stool next to the door and called out to his friends.

'So, the vapour has worked then?' she asked Suisan. 'Has he been coughing much?'

'Nay,' the older woman said. 'Some the first night, but less after each dosing or use of the vapour. He did not complain or refuse, nay, he did not. He is a good lad.'

'Better than most others who have asked for my help,' Anna said.

'About those seeking your help...' Anna raised her gaze to Suisan and waited for her to continue. 'Word has already spread about ye being a healer.'

'Those outside?' Anna walked to the doorway and looked past the boy and his friends to see a growing crowd. 'They are to see me?'

'Aye, if ye would? Many have ailments that Old Ranald could not see to. Many have minor things, but I think ye could help a number of others with the things ye grow and make.'

Those waiting noticed her scrutiny and began to move closer. Anna nodded to them and they approached. She recognised a variety of symptoms and ailments as they grew closer.

'Suisan, I would not see them in the road. Can I bring them inside your cottage? Or is there another I might use?'

'Ye are welcome here and mayhap I could help ye a bit? Introduce ye to the villagers and such?'

Within a short time, Anna was speaking to the people who needed her services. Though it took several hours, with Suisan's help, Anna managed to speak to each person who sought her aid. Some could be helped then, but others could not for she had not the ingredients or supplies to do so. A few more days and she would have some of what she needed, but it would be weeks of tending to the plots above the falls before she would be ready.

Colm sat by the door, greeting everyone who came by, but she could see the exhaustion growing in his face. Just as she finished with the last person, a loud voice rang out drawing her attention.

'Malcolm Cameron, what do you think you are doing?'

For a moment, she lost her place and time. She heard the name and stumbled to the doorway, almost expecting to see her Malcolm there before her. Staring into the road there instead she saw Davidh's approach. Anna shook herself from the shock and glanced at Colm, who sat there watching his father walk towards them.

Colm.

Malcolm.

He had truly named his son after his closest friend.

'You are not supposed to be out here!' Davidh said sharply.

'Papa, Mistress Mackenzie said I could.'

Davidh had only been watching his son and

now caught sight of the healer as she stepped into the sun's light. He did not know who looked paler at that moment—her or his son. Crouching down before Colm where he sat on a stool, he studied his face and listened, as he always did, to his breathing. Though pale, he did not struggle to draw a breath.

'Well, if Mistress Mackenzie gave her approval, I cannot naysay her.' He read the relief on Colm's face then. How long had it been since his son had been outside this cottage or theirs? He glanced up and met Anna's gaze then. 'And what else did Mistress Mackenzie have to say?'

'If he rests today and follows my instructions, he may walk about in the village a bit with his friends on the morrow,' she replied.

'From the look of him, he has not done the first.'

'Nay, not yet. This morn, I was grateful for his help with the others who came to see me.'

Davidh stood then and touched his son's shoulder.

'You look tired, son.'

He could see the struggle within the boy. He did not wish to go back inside and yet his strength was fading. Considering that he'd been up and about more in these last two days than he had in weeks and weeks, Davidh was more than willing to listen to the healer's advice. Whatever doubts had initially assailed him had faded in the face of the results in his son.

'Since we have finished our work, I think it a good time for you to rest, Mal-colm.'

She stuttered over his son's name. Oh, she'd heard him use his proper name. But a glance at her face revealed something else or something more was behind her stammer.

'There you go then. Mistress Mackenzie has so spoken and we cannot argue with her. Well, you could, but I suspect that her promise to release you from this doorway depends on you obeying now.'

Colm grumbled as he stood, waved farewell to his friends and walked in slow, delaying steps inside. Davidh fought the smile that threatened to break out on his face since it would ruin the serious attitude he was forcing himself to show. He found he needed to turn away rather than watch as Colm sighed over and over as he lay down on the pallet. It was the short time it took for his son to fall asleep that reminded Davidh of his true condition and need for rest.

'I...' There was so much to thank her for doing, yet the words would not come.

'I have given Suisan something new to try over the next few days,' she said. She blocked his view of his son then, standing closer so her words did not carry inside. 'The vapours seem to be helping.'

'Aye, they have. He barely coughs.' Again, words of gratitude swirled around, but none seemed good enough for what she'd accomplished. 'Anna...'

'The thing is, Davidh, this is only the beginning. The weakness in his lungs will not stop because of a few concoctions or using the vapours for a couple of nights.' Why was she trying to dissemble with her words? To what purpose was it to undermine what she'd accomplished here?

'He has been ill for some time,' he said. 'I understand that it could take time.'

'Or not.'

He heard her words, but he did not want to accept them. That tiny bit of hope that he always carried in his soul for his son had burst into a stronger one just over the last two days. Could he contain and dampen it now? Must he? She reached out and placed her hand on his arm.

'Sometimes it does not proceed as I expect it to and if, if, this does not work...' She paused then and stared out towards the village. 'I do not wish to raise your hopes without making certain you understand the true situation here, Davidh.'

'I am afraid 'tis too late for that, Anna.'

She blinked several times and looked at him. He shrugged.

'I understand the situation, Colm's situation, for I have watched other bairns and wee ones die of things like this.' A single tear trickled from the corner of her left eye and he wanted to reach out and wipe it away. He stepped back instead. 'I will take whatever days your treatments give him. The rest is in the Almighty's hands.'

She walked past him then and he heard the soft groan as she did so. Watching her, he noticed the signs of discomfort or pain in the way she walked now.

'Mistress Mackenzie, are you yourself in need of a healer?'

She laughed then and the sound of it made his heart beat faster.

'Aye, I think I might. Do you know one?'

'Old Ranald is good if you need anything hacked away.' The jesting relieved the tension in him.

'Nay, not that. I just need to walk a bit after crouching and bending for so long. I will not keep you from your duties, Commander.'

'Come,' he said, motioning with his hand ahead of him. 'I am not expected back for some time yet and I can show you the rest of the village if you have not walked it yourself.'

'I would like that,' she said, following him to the road, then walking at his side.

They walked along that main road and Davidh pointed out the important places of their village—the smithy she knew, but the baker, the miller near the stream and the weavers she did not. Word had spread about her and many came out to greet her. Some she called by name which surprised him at first, but she told him that she had seen them just a short while before his arrival.

Davidh guided her as far as the stream that led north to the river that connected Loch Arkaig to Loch Lochy. To reach the falls and her cottage she would follow the river to the mouth of Loch Arkaig, cross the small bridge there and head around to the northern side of the river. The river that rushed over the falls fed back into the River Arkaig. The most surprising thing about the walk was that Davidh found it easy to talk to her. Giving her bits of gossip and explaining the connections between this person and that one continued as they made their way back to the smithy.

'You did not show me where you live.'

He had not time to ponder her curiosity, for a man came running towards them, shouting out his name. Only then did Davidh realise he'd lost all sense of time as he'd walked with Anna. Robert expected him after the noon meal to meet with the steward and Davidh had forgotten all about it.

He could blame it on the sight of his son, sitting outside for the first time in weeks. He could and that would have been part of it. The other part was that he'd been enjoying himself too much and, for that short time, he'd forgotten his duty. He'd forgotten his duty.

Davidh nodded at the messenger and faced Anna.

'I must go.' She nodded. 'Will you be back on the morrow?'

'I will be back in a few days. There is so much to do before I will have enough to help those in the village.'

He wanted to argue with her, but he could not now. Any anger or frustration he felt was his own fault, so he took his leave with a hurried word of gratitude. Davidh cursed silently first, with every step he ran to the smithy to claim his horse and then with every stride of his horse after he mounted and as he rode to the keep.

Never in his life, never since taking command, had he ever forgotten to carry out a task or duty or responsibility. Never. Not even when Colm suffered the worst of his affliction.

But this young woman arrived, bringing help to his son and appealing to him more than any woman before or since Mara, and he allowed her to distract him. From his duty.

This could not happen again.

Chapter Six

Three days passed and Davidh found the sense of distraction growing. Anna had not returned to the village since their encounter which saw him running off to the keep. Though Robert said nothing about his lateness that day, others whispered. And not all of the comments were meant in jest. With things still unsettled among the various factions in the Cameron clan, the last thing he needed to be was less than attentive and less than consistent in his duties.

When the last chief's perfidy and betrayal had been uncovered, the clan broke apart. Gilbert's supporters fled, unwilling to wait for their own guilt to be exposed and to pay for their part in his sins. Though Robert was the legitimate, pragmatic and reasonable choice to replace him, some elders and others well respected in the clan wondered if the man who'd served in silence to protect his own secrets could be trusted to lead them now.

Robert's choices and decisions since taking the high chair were closely watched and examined for weakness or ill judgement. That included his own selection of who to command the warriors while Struan took over as steward. In the months since, and with the support of the powerful chief of the Chattan Confederation, Robert had made progress in re-establishing trust in the treaty that had been put in place between them.

Still, the laird did not need his commander to look unprepared or unready to train and manage all the warriors of the Cameron clan. For the last three days, Davidh had thrown himself into his duties. Knowing that Colm was improving, he remained at the keep from morning until dark.

He worked with his men in the training yard, he assigned guards and others to do needed repairs to the buildings in the castle and elsewhere. Though they might not have wanted to do it, such work strengthened them and their endurance and was a useful way of accomplishing both.

And no matter how exhausted he felt himself, thoughts of the green-eyed healer kept him from sleep. Like some callow youth who'd never had experience with a woman, his mind turned her words and every action over and over again, keeping him from rest. So, on the fourth morning after their walk, Davidh decided to seek her out. With Colm healthier than he'd been for months, he believed the boy could make the journey out to the falls. If he tired too quickly or easily, Davidh would turn back.

With the ready excuse of a lack of those leaves for making the vapours and some coin to pay for her supplies in hand, he walked to Suisan's to retrieve his son. Not ten paces from the door of his house, he almost slammed into a woman walking towards him.

'Good day and my pardon, Lilias,' he said as he grabbed his neighbour to keep her from falling. 'I did not see you there.'

'Good day, Davidh,' Lilias said. She regained her balance and he released his hold. 'Ye seem to be in a hurry this day. Is something wrong with the boy?'

Though he did not have time to waste if he wanted to get to the falls and back before dark, Davidh did not wish to be rude to a woman who had stepped in many times to help him care for his son.

'Nay, Colm is doing well,' he said. Smiling then at the thought of how well he was, Davidh nodded. 'There has been some improvement of late. But,' he said, gazing past her towards the smithy, 'I am taking him to the healer now.'

'Everyone has been expecting her to return here,' Lilias said. 'Is it wise to take him so far?'

There was an unfamiliar glint in Lilias's gaze and Davidh could not tell if the woman was questioning his judgement or just curious. He shrugged.

'That is another reason I go. She has not been seen in four days. The village boys have not caught sight of her near the falls. Robert extended his protection to her and...' He did not lie so much as lead her to believe this was part of his duties.

'Would ye come to supper upon yer return from the falls then? 'Tis been a long time since we shared a meal, Davidh.' Lilias smiled. 'And bring the boy. I have a stew cooking and there will be plenty.'

Davidh stopped and stared at the woman. He'd never noticed the primping and preening before, yet there it was right in front of him. It might have been a long time since he courted or wooed a woman—hell, it had been—but he recognised what she was doing now. As she twisted a loose lock of hair around her fingertips, he understood that she was flirting with him.

'My thanks, Lilias. I do not know when I will return or if Colm will feel up to a visit.' He fought to keep his impatience under control as he reminded himself, again, that she had done him and his son many kindnesses. As had many of the villagers. 'I must go.'

'Another night, then?' Lilias said, stepping out of his path. 'I hope the boy keeps well.'

Davidh nodded and strode away. His horse was at the smithy since Jamie had repaired one of the horse's shoes. Jamie called out a greeting as Davidh walked to the cottage and found it empty. Jamie shouted to him and Davidh looked down the path towards the well near the centre of the village. Suisan and Colm were walking from the well and Davidh could see that his son carried a bucket.

And he did not have to stop and put it down once.

And he talked with Suisan as he walked.

Davidh could hardly breathe himself as he watched this new Colm approach. Every day saw a step towards health. Every day Davidh's hopes rose in spite of Anna's warnings about the true nature of Colm's affliction. He had just been so sick for so long that this improvement, even if a temporary respite from the worst of it, seemed a godsend.

'Papa!' Colm called out as he noticed Davidh. 'Look! Look!'

Colm shifted the bucket into both hands and

began trotting towards him. He wanted to urge him to slow, but the expression of sheer joy on his son's face forced him to remain silent and watch. When his son reached him, half of the water in the bucket had sloshed out. Davidh laughed as he crouched down and pulled his son into a hug.

'Papa, I carried it all the way,' Colm said. Suisan reached them and took the bucket.

'Aye, he did,' she said, never mentioning the lack of water in the bucket now.

'How do you feel, Colm? How is your chest?' Davidh placed a hand on his son's chest and back, a way he could feel the strength or weakness of his son's ability to draw breath.

'I am fine, Papa. Suisan said so. And so did Mistress Mackenzie.'

'Mistress Mackenzie? When did she visit you?' Davidh stood and looked at Suisan.

'She came very early this morn, Davidh,' Suisan explained. 'You'd barely ridden away before she knocked on my door.'

Anna had been here? Had she waited for him to leave before seeing to Colm?

'She said she was in the middle of many things at the cottage, but wanted to bring some supplies for Colm and some of the others in need.' Suisan gestured to the basket sitting by the doorway that now held trinkets and wrapped bits that were payment for Anna's help. The woman shrugged and put her bucket down next to it. 'Colm and I saw that everything was given out.'

He was both disappointed and elated at the same time. That his son was strong enough to walk the length and breadth of the village made that hope within him grow. And yet, Davidh was not pleased that Anna seemed to come and go without seeing him.

'Did she speak of her return? For I had planned to seek her out.' Davidh nodded at his son. 'I thought we could ride out to the falls since the day is a fair one and Colm seems much stronger.'

His son reacted as he thought he would and Davidh had to caution him not to wear himself out before they rode. Soon, Davidh, Colm and the basket for Anna were on their way north, to the end of the loch and on to the falls. He kept the horse from galloping and held his son before him, protecting him from the worst of the jostling along the road.

They rode most of the way in silence, but as they approached the falls Colm began questioning him about them. Davidh spoke of his times as a boy when he and his closest friend Malcolm would try their best to climb the slippery rocks, as Tavish and countless others had, and their failures. When they arrived before the deep pool that captured the flowing water before sending it south to the river, Colm stilled and stared at the falls as they rose overhead.

''Tis a long way down.'

'Aye,' Davidh said. 'Tavish is lucky that he broke only his foot and not every bone in his body. Let that be a warning to you and your friends about the danger here.'

He doubted his words would work any better than those of his own father all those years ago. The boys Davidh grew up with spent every possible moment out here trying to make their way up the falls once word of the witch spread. Rumours tied her abilities to the illness the cattle suffered one summer. Other stories spoke of her curses...and of the love philters she could make.

Malcolm had gone looking for one of those.

'So, how do we find Anna?' his son asked.

''Tis a secret path and I must have your word of honour that you will not share the way with anyone. Not your friends. Not anyone.' Now that someone lived above, it was for her safety as much as anyone seeking her.

With the solemnity of a man taking Holy Orders, Colm nodded his agreement. Davidh lifted him down to the ground, dismounted and tied the horse to a tree there. Then he crouched down and told Colm to climb on his back—it would be the easiest way to carry him up the steep path. Soon, they were headed to the copse of trees that hid the entrance to the cave and the way up the falls.

It was a slower pace than when he climbed alone, but soon he took the last few climbing steps and stood at the top of the falls not far from Anna's cottage. As he approached it, the door was open and no one seemed to be within. She must be working in the field she called a garden. The last time he'd seen it, it was much too big to be called a garden.

'Anna!' Colm called out over Davidh's shoulder. Reminded that he yet carried his son, he bent down and let the boy off his back. 'Anna.' He scampered towards the woman who was on her knees, digging at something in the dirt. 'Papa brought me to see you.'

She jumped up at his words, quickly rubbing the dirt from her hands and taking him by the shoulders. She knelt before Colm and touched the back of her hand to his cheeks and forehead. She thought him ill. She'd told Davidh to seek her out if he worsened.

'Anna, he is well,' Davidh said, walking to them. 'He is well.'

The worry did not leave her gaze immediately and did not dissipate until she listened to his breaths and studied his face. She stood and shook out her skirts to remove the dirt she'd collected on them while kneeling there in the field.

'When you had not returned to the village, I wanted to make certain you were safe up here alone.' The explanation sounded suspect even to his own ears, but she nodded.

'I saw this one just this morn,' she said. 'But I appreciate having my basket back.' Davidh had forgotten about the basket his son now held out to her. 'What are these?'

'They are...' he began. 'Tavish's mother sent the cheese. The bread is from the baker and his wife. The thread is from Mistress Cameron—the one they call "Peggy". Oh, and Old Ranald said you can have his needles and threads when you come down next since he willna be using them.' It all came out of him in an unstopping burst of words and gestures as he explained each and every little thing in the basket and who'd sent it.

'My thanks for bringing me such treats,' she said, smiling as she held the basket closer. 'Though I could have got these when I visited next.'

'The baker's bread would have been stale,' Colm said.

'They like to pay their debts promptly,' Davidh added.

'Ah. I had not thought on that,' Anna said.

'More than that, they wanted you to have something for your care and kindness to them.'

She smiled then, first at his son, then she raised her gaze to his and he saw tears shimmering there. Had she not thought those who'd benefited from her treatments would respond like this? Mayhap that was not how it was done in the place where she'd lived before? It mattered not, for she was here now and this was how they would thank her. And in other ways.

'Do you need help there?' he asked, trying to change their conversation. The plots of land laid out were covered in overgrown weeds though he knew there must be some plants within the brush and leaves that she wanted to save and cultivate. 'I could send some of my men to take care of the heaviest work.'

For a moment, she looked as if she would refuse. Then, she stood back and turned away, putting her hands on her hips, her lovely hips, and stared out at the work before her. 'But you would have to tell them how to get up here.'

'I could let them try to climb the falls, but I suspect there would not be many willing to do that.'

She laughed then. She turned to face him and let out another burst of merriment that made him smile, as well.

'You jest!' she said, nodding at Colm who

stared at him as though he spoke a language he did not understand.

'Of course I jest. I will have them swear an oath as my son did before showing them the way,' he offered. 'One that will make them shrivel and die if they reveal the truth.'

Now it was Colm who laughed and Davidh swore he would do whatever was necessary to make such a sound a regular occurrence for his son. He wanted the smile that lit his face now to remain there for ever and the pain and suffering never to return.

'You did not have your son swear to such a thing!' She rushed to his side and shook her head. 'He is too young for such a vow.' She mussed Colm's hair up again, something she liked to do each time Davidh saw them together. It was a natural thing to her. As though she understood lads his age.

'You are under the laird's protection, Anna. In truth, no one will bother you or they face Robert's judgement.'

'Very well, Commander. I would appreciate the help for the tasks I cannot see to myself.' She took her basket in hand and nodded in the direction of the cottage. 'Would you like something to drink before you return to the village?'

The words were said with a graciousness and warmth and yet Davidh very much felt he was being told to leave. Glancing around the area, past the cottage and into the forest, he searched for signs of anyone else there. The wind whispered through the trees and the sunlight rippled and threw patterns of light and shadow on the ground. But they were alone.

Colm accepted for both of them and dogged Anna's steps back to her cottage and waited for her to enter. His curiosity was a welcome thing to witness, but Davidh did not lose sight of his son's ease at tiring. Too stubborn to admit to such a weakness, Colm would push himself too much and suffer for it later. A drink to refresh themselves and then he would take his son back to the village.

Just as Davidh ducked to enter, something caught his attention and he turned to see a shadow move quickly towards the other side of the cottage. He stepped back, not certain if he'd seen someone or a creature, when Anna called him to enter.

'I thought I saw someone,' he said. 'Between the cottage and the falls.' She held out a battered cup filled with cold water to him. 'I wonder if any of the lads did make it up the slippery slope.'

'I have not seen anyone. Though some deer have been making their way in from the cliffside. I suspect they are waiting to forage on whatever I can get growing in the field there.'

'Will you need someone to scare them away, Mistress Mackenzie? My friends would do that for you.' Colm turned his serious gaze to Davidh now. 'They would swear never to tell, too.'

Anna handed his son a cup and motioned for him to drink it. She placed her arm around his shoulder as he did and then she squeezed him. 'Firstly, you must be well and strong. So, if you...'

'Drink all the putrid concoctions and rest...' Colm finished her sentence, knowing what was coming.

'Then, your father and I will decide when it is time for you to add your efforts to scaring off the deer.'

'I think we need to get back to the village, Colm.'

'But, Papa...'

'We were a surprise and an interruption to Mistress Mackenzie in her work. Take your leave so she may return to her tasks at hand.'

Strangely, Davidh wished to leave this place and this woman even less than his son did. Something within made him want to work by her side. To come to this cottage at the end of their day's labours. But he forced himself away from such a reverie and back to his responsibility to get his son home now.

'We hope to see you in the village soon,'

he said, walking out first. He crouched down and waited for Colm to climb on his back. She laughed again.

'I did wonder how you managed it,' she said. 'Have a care on the way down. The recent rains have made the path near the entrance to the cave slippery.'

Davidh stood and nodded, wrapping his arms around his son's legs for a better hold. Then he remembered one message he was supposed to pass along to her.

'Lady Elizabeth, the laird's wife, would like you to call on her when you are next in the village,' he said. 'She was very happy to learn that a new healer was in our midst.'

'If you see her on the morrow, tell her I will.'

Davidh walked towards the falls and turned to follow the path down. At the last moment before entering the heavy brush that covered the path from prying eyes, he glanced at Anna.

And she stood staring into the shadows, clearly searching the forest for something...or someone. Then, she startled and ran towards him.

'Davidh. When will you send the men?' she called out to him.

'In three days.' He would speak to Robert on the morrow.

'I am grateful. My thanks!'

Davidh nodded and turned back to the path, while Colm called out and waved to her. As he walked into the shadows of the thick trees, Davidh glanced back.

Anna stood staring towards the falls with a very worried expression on her face.

Chapter Seven

$\infty\!\!\!\infty\!\!\!\infty$

Anna held her breath as she entered the hall of the keep. All around her, servants carried out their tasks of cleaning or preparing for the noon meal. Others, men on the laird's business and those who needed his attention, waited near the dais as Robert spoke to those of more importance.

She'd tended to her own matters over the last two days.

Iain was getting restless and bored, a frustrating thing to be told he must not stray and must not be seen or speak to anyone from the village. She could not keep him hidden much longer. And now that she was becoming accepted, mayhap she would not need to. Still, having others know about him was one thing while having them know the truth was quite another.

The good thing was that his curiosity about the lands around the falls and their cottage kept his interest. Hopefully, he would be enthralled for a few more days. His hunting skills had made it possible to trade with the baker and others for needed household items and other foodstuffs. No one asked how she came by the fowl and hares for they each most likely thought others had paid for her help with the various items.

Today, she was not here to seek out the laird but his wife as Davidh had told her. As lady here, Elizabeth Cameron supervised all the women within the keep and saw to the more domestic needs of the clan. From what Anna had gleaned from Suisan, the lady had taken on much work when her husband took his position as chieftain less than a year ago. Turmoil had reigned for too long and there had been no ladywife to take things in hand.

Nor, Suisan had whispered, would any woman have dared, with the late Gilbert Cameron as husband and laird. Two wives of his had died and a challenge to him over that and his other crimes against the Camerons, his own clan, had led to his death. Now, his once-banished older brother and sister-by-marriage controlled the lands and people here.

As she made her way to the door near the front of the hall, Anna nodded to a few people she recognised. She approached one of the servants and explained her purpose. Anna was directed to a small alcove to wait. Within a short time, an older woman entered from behind the dais. The chieftain paused and greeted her so Anna knew this was the lady herself.

For someone old enough to have three grown or nearly grown sons, the lady retained her youthful appearance and carried herself as one much younger than she must be. Wearing not the costly gown and veil of one of such rank and wealth, but the simple gown of a woman working in a household, she surprised Anna. Regardless of her appearance, Anna dropped into a curtsy before the woman who, now that her husband had given his permission, was in charge of her.

'My lady,' Anna said, lifting her gaze and then rising at the lady's signal. 'The commander said you wished to speak to me.'

'Anna Mackenzie, is it?' the lady asked. Anna nodded. 'We are glad of you settling here, as your mother once did. We are sorely in need of a healer.' The lady then laughed at the inadvertent jest she'd made. 'Even Old Ranald is pleased and relieved to have someone with skills here now.'

'I am grateful for the laird's permission and your welcome, lady. Is there something I can do for you?'

'I have already heard of your work in the village. Tavish's father works here and told us of your rescue and treatment of the lad. My boys managed to get into such trouble when they were that age,' she added. Elizabeth motioned for Anna to walk with her. They went past those assembled there and into a smaller corridor that led away from the hall. 'Just down here.'

They walked down a short flight of stairs and stopped at the bottom. The lady peered down one hallway and then another before leading on to a doorway at the end of the one to the right.

'I found this and had thought to ask a brother from the nearest abbey with skills in such to come, but then you arrived and I thought it must be meant for you.'

The lady lifted the latch and pushed the heavy door open. A torch already burned inside the chamber and Anna stepped in behind the lady. Then she glanced around the room.

Bins and bottles. Jars and sacks and baskets. All sorts of containers lay on shelves before her. Dried herbs hung overhead, lending all their scents to the heady mix that filled the room. A small window high in the wall let in some light from outside and she could see there was an abundance of different types and sorts of medicaments already made, as well as the supplies needed to compound more.

'My lady!'

'A grand mess of things,' Lady Elizabeth said. 'I have not the knowledge to determine if these are beneficial or even safe to use or for what treatments they could be for,' she said as she pointed around the chamber. 'But Davidh tells me you do.'

'My lady, I am not as knowledgeable as a learned brother might be,' she disclaimed. 'I am only familiar with those things my mother taught me over the years. Many of these—' she waved with her hand at the astonishing sight '—are unknown to me.'

Anna walked closer to the large work table in the centre of the chamber and studied what lay there. Several of the plants dried and bundled were known to her, but the rest were not.

'I think your plan to summon a healer from the abbey is a wise one.' Anna shook her head. 'I have not the experience or learning to use all of this.' The lady's eyes narrowed as she stared at Anna. 'Where did this come from? Who gathered and used such a wide variety like this?'

'Apart from Morag who was here but a few months, there has not been a healer other than Old Ranald for years. The previous laird saw no reason for one. So, I think this has been untouched for four years? Mayhap longer.'

So, most of these would be useless, too old and impotent to do much good. But there might be something. If that was what the lady was offering.

'Since your skills will serve our people, I pray you to take whatever you can use from here. And, if you have need of other supplies and such, speak to the steward or to the cook.'

When Anna had made the decision to return here, she had thought to be quietly ignored, allowed to be there, but with little or no attention to her. This response was unexpected and she hoped it was a sign that her true aim would also be successful.

Her son's acceptance into his father's kith and kin.

'You have my permission to come and sort through all of this when you can. It looks daunting to me, but then I do not have the experience that you do.'

The lady's admission of ignorance made Anna like this woman even more. She did not pretend to something she did not know.

'Thank you, my lady,' she said.

Lady Cameron turned to leave, but stopped just before they reached the corridor. Facing Anna, her expression filled with worry and concern, she reached out and touched the younger woman's hand.

'Will Davidh's lad be well?' she asked. 'He has been through so much and so many challenges.' For a moment, Anna did not know if the lady referred to the father or the son. 'Young

Malcolm is special to me, for his mother was my goddaughter.'

As it had the last time, hearing his whole name spoken startled Anna. It was not an uncommon name among the clans, it just had such power over her.

'Davidh was one of the first to stand for Robert. His faith in my husband, though he is young, helped to stabilise things over the turbulence. I hope you can help his son.'

'I will try, my lady. I will try.'

Lady Cameron patted her on the hand and then turned and walked out of the chamber. Anna followed along, impatient to return to her tasks of the day. When they reached the main level of the keep, the lady pointed the way back to the hall.

It would take hours—nay, days—to sort through the contents of that chamber. In spite of the daunting amount of time she would need for it, Anna's hands almost itched to begin that work. As she walked into the yard, she began formulating a new plan to accomplish all that she must. Winter had begrudgingly let go its hold on the lands and she needed to have her plants and field ready for the longer, warmer days of the summer-growing season.

So caught up in her thoughts was she that she walked into Davidh without seeing or hearing him. The shock of contact with his bare chest unsettled her and she lost her balance. Lucky for her, he'd seen her and grabbed hold of her shoulders before she could fall to the ground.

'Your pardon,' she said, stepping back away from him. As she looked up and up to meet his gaze, she noticed his uncovered chest.

'I called out to you, but you did not seem to hear me,' he explained. His chest was the most muscular chest she'd ever seen on a man. Granted, she did not go around gaping at half-naked men, but she'd seen more than a few in the years since she began helping her mother. And this chest, these arms, were some of the best she'd seen.

'I fear I was so overwhelmed by the lady's generosity that I was lost in my thoughts over how to proceed.'

Now she noticed that he'd tied his long, dark hair back into a tight tail. Then she saw the men standing in the yard watching them. All of them strong and powerful warriors. All of them holding swords or other weapons. All of them watching her speak to their commander.

'I have disturbed your training,' she said, with a slight curtsy to him. 'Forgive me.' She began to walk away, but could hear the whispers of the men who yet watched the encounter.

'You did not disturb…the training,' he said.

For a moment she thought he was going to say something else. 'I wanted to make these men known to you, Mistress Mackenzie.' Davidh pointed to three men who stood closest to them. 'They will be helping with your field and planting on the morrow.'

'Mistress,' they each said, nodding at her. She studied each face so she would recognise them.

'I thank you for your help,' she said. Then she turned to the commander. 'And I thank you for your offer.'

'Robert agreed that helping you was a good idea,' he said. Leaning closer, he spoke softer then. 'He and Elizabeth like having a healer back in our midst. As do I.'

'I will be ready,' she said. She would not waste their time once they arrived. Three men would complete the work in less than a day. And with her working at their side, it would go even quicker. 'In the morn then.'

A sense of anticipation grew within her as she visited the village and saw to those who asked for her help. Though Davidh's son said he felt stronger, Anna worried over something she heard in his breathing. Suisan had been very careful in giving him the concoctions and medicaments Anna had made and yet there was just...something amiss. Something she could not identify.

While not wishing to worry the boy, she advised him to limit himself to one excursion in the village each day and only if he was not coughing for all of the morning. Suisan met her gaze with a questioning one and yet Anna could not explain her hesitancy or her concern.

The next day was both the hardest and the most satisfying in such a long time. Not only did the three men Davidh pointed out arrive at her cottage, but he joined them, as well. Better still, the lady sent them along with a huge basket of food for them all. Even though Anna had made a very large pot of stew and had bread from the baker, she realised it would not have been enough for four strong, hard-working men.

Several times during that day, she found herself standing in the shadows and watching the men work. Digging, sawing, raking and more, they were all strong men familiar with physical labour, but her gaze was drawn by just one. His men did nothing that he was not willing to do. She noticed the deference paid to him as commander, but also the easy comradery that existed among them.

Once or twice during the first part of the morning, she noticed Iain skulking closer than he should, but her son understood and stayed back. Soon, she'd promised him. Soon.

Once the work was done and the men gone, Anna understood it was time. Time to put her true plan into motion. To reclaim her son's birthright. To claim his place among the Camerons.

After keeping him hidden since their arrival, she needed a way to bring him into the light and introduce him. A few days later, unfortunately the decision was made for her.

The rains came later that night and it poured down in torrents for the next day. The water collected in the river above the falls and pushed over them with a brutal force that could almost not be contained within the rocky formation or be caught in the pool below. She'd warned Iain not to go near them until the overflowing currents returned to their usual amount and ferocity. Working inside after midday, she was crushing some dried leaves into a powder when Iain came running.

'You have to come!' he screamed. 'Mam, it's a boy!' He was gone before she could ask him anything.

She followed him out of the cottage and towards the falls. The roar of the waters had not diminished since this morning and she could hear nothing over it. Iain stopped near the top and gestured to something below.

God, but there was a boy on a ledge next to the falls!

She crept closer to the edge, trying to keep her balance while not losing her footing. The rocks were slippery and water from the falls constantly poured on to them, making them even more dangerous. Anna managed to lean over and saw her worst nightmare right there below her.

It was a boy, but not just any one—it was Davidh's son clinging to a shallow handhold in the rock. His body trembled and he fought to get his foot into a divot in the rock that could hold him. Far below him, a number of other boys from the village watched in horror as their friend clung to keep from falling to his death.

'Go!' she shouted as loudly as she could. They could not hear her so she waved them towards the village, praying that they would understand that they needed to go get help. When they ran off, she hoped it would come in time.

But Colm would not last long enough. He was already weak and had not the strength to hold on for much longer. She called out to Iain to get a rope and then moved quickly down the hill until she was level with the boy. His face was ghostly pale and his body shivered. Though he moved his lips, she could neither hear nor understand what he said.

Iain returned with rope which she tied around her waist while he secured the other end, tying it to a sturdy tree. She motioned to her son to come closer—the overwhelming roar of the water made it impossible to hear.

'Give me your belt, Iain,' she shouted once he was close enough. She grabbed Iain and hugged him tightly to her for a moment. 'I love you, Iain. Now stand back and do not come any closer to the edge. Be ready to pull me back once I have him in hand.'

Anna reached down and gathered the back of her skirts and pulled them up tightly. After tucking the ends of her skirts into the rope at her waist, Anna formed a loop with the belt and wrapped the length of it around her hand. Then, she began to inch her way to the edge. What had the boy done to get himself to this point? It mattered not for she could do nothing to change it now. She was his only hope.

Offering up a prayer for strength, Anna took the first step out on to the rocks, holding on to the rope. She could not dare to look at Colm as she moved ever closer. She needed to keep her attention on every step she must take to reach him.

It seemed as though it took hours to get close

enough to him to try to grasp him, but soon she stood just inches away. Holding out her hand, she urged him to take the looped end of the belt from her.

'Put it around you,' she shouted. 'Over your head!'

It took several tries before he could grab it and manoeuvre it over and around him. When it was in place, Anna nodded to him as she wrapped the belt around and around her hand, easing him closer to her. Then, with a glance to Iain to begin pulling her off the rocks, she backed up and tugged Colm with her. The belt became crucial when the boy lost his hold and began to slip.

With all of her strength and that of Iain, too, she pulled the belt while allowing the rope to guide her off the rocks and on to the hill next to the falls. She collapsed to the ground, holding Colm in her arms as she tried to catch her own breath.

'Mam?' Iain knelt at her side and yelled at her.

Anna rolled to her side and nodded to her son. Thanks to his efforts and quick response, Colm yet lived. As she studied the boy's face—now grey—she could feel him struggling to breathe. 'We must get him inside now.'

Iain helped her to her feet and they half-carried, half-dragged Colm up to the cottage. Once there, she laid him on the pallet while Iain gathered blankets. She quickly undressed Colm and tossed his wet garments to one side. Within a short time, tea with several herbs that would stimulate his breathing and fight the fever that would come were steeping.

And Anna began what she knew would be a long struggle to save Colm's life.

Chapter Eight

He was not at Suisan's cottage or in their own. He was not sitting by the well or in any of the other places the lads in the village liked to gather. Davidh noticed that none of Colm's usual companions were anywhere he looked in the village either.

The boy had not the strength or stamina to go very far, so they all must be hiding somewhere nearby. After more searching and asking everyone he met along the way, Davidh was convinced the boys did not exist. The only place he'd not searched was the keep, but the guards would not allow a gaggle of young lads through the gates without a reason—or without mentioning it to him as he'd left.

Colm was missing.

He stood outside his house and ran his hands through his hair, looking, searching once more for any sign of them. If Colm had not been so ill until just recently, Davidh would think nothing of the lads disappearing for hours, off exploring as boys did. Still thinking of possible hiding places, Davidh heard their approach and turned to see a pack of boys running towards him. It was their screaming and their faces that struck terror in his heart. The first boy reached him and Davidh knelt down to face him.

'He is on the rocks. Colm is climbing the rocks!'

'Where? Where is he?' Davidh asked, even though he suspected the truth already.

'The Witch's Pool!' another called out.

'The falls!' Tavish said. 'He was trying to climb the falls and got stuck.'

He heard nothing else. Explanations could wait until his son was safe. Davidh mounted his horse and rode like the demons of hell were chasing him. Without thinking, his thoughts fell into the same old pattern.

Dear God, not the boy. I pray you, not the boy.

He did not know how long it took him to reach the road to the north and then to the falls, but he crossed the last few yards before the falls would be visible with his stomach in his mouth. Rounding the last curve in the road, he heard the crashing waters and looked into the pool and then up along the rocks and the falls.

Nothing. No one was there. He jumped to the

ground and ran to the edge of the road nearest the pool. The pool churned deep and wild from the force of the waters pouring into it from above. Glancing upwards, Davidh saw no one on the rocks and no sign of anyone along the hills on each side of the falls.

Thank God!

But where was he, if not here?

Anna's.

Davidh climbed his way up the path that led to the top of the falls and ran the rest of the way to her cottage. Voices within told him she was there. He lifted the latch on the door and pushed it open without knocking. His son lying pale and quiet on the pallet in the corner caught his attention first and he'd taken several steps towards him when she spoke. He glanced over at her while yet walking to his son.

It was not the fear in her voice that stopped him then. Nor was it her dishevelled, wet condition. Nay, what stopped him was the boy, young man, standing at her side there.

He was clearly of Cameron blood, the crooked nose inherited generation after generation declared him so, and yet Davidh did not remember seeing this boy in the village…or ever.

'What happened to my son?' he asked. With a nod at this newcomer, he continued, 'And who is this?' Facing them, he noticed the similarity in colouring to Anna.

'This is my son, Iain,' she said, placing her hands on the boy's shoulders. 'He found Colm clinging to the rocks below.'

Davidh stared at the boy and then at his... mother. Why had she kept him a secret? Where had he been? Ah, the movement he'd seen several times in the forest, in the shadows. The boy had been here all along. He had many questions, but his own son's racking cough stopped everything. Davidh went to his side, but Anna pushed her way there.

'He has a fever and the cough has returned. We got him out of his wet clothing and made him warm. The tea has several herbs in it to help his symptoms.'

Concise and clear, her explanation gave him all the important details, but they left out much of the story he needed to know. Her own garments were soaked and he could feel the damp seeping into his own trews where their legs touched.

'If you will sit behind him and support him, I must get more into him now.'

Davidh picked up the slight body of his son and slid behind him. They arranged him against Davidh's chest, all the while Colm made no sound and did not rouse. After pouring more of the fragrant brew into a cup, Anna handed it to him and they worked to get it in his son. When her hands and body trembled, Davidh realised that she was cold and wet.

'You should get out of those wet garments,' he said. 'I am the one without any healing skills, if you should grow ill.'

'Try to wake him while I do,' Anna said. She walked to the other side of the cottage and into a smaller chamber.

He spoke to his son, called his name and shook him gently, but nothing seemed to work. He was deeply asleep or unconscious and would not wake. Glancing into the shadows, he realised that her son stood there watching everything without speaking a word.

'Iain? How many years have you?' he asked the simple question to get the boy to speak to him. He'd remained hidden for almost a fortnight so Davidh suspected the boy would be wary of strangers.

'Ten and almost three,' he replied. The boy remained there, nothing moving except his gaze which flitted back and forth from Davidh to his mother's chamber.

'My thanks for finding my son,' he said. 'No doubt he would be dead if you had not.' The boy nodded and crossed his arms over his chest. The gesture felt somehow familiar to Davidh, but he did not know why. 'Can you tell me what happened or how he got there?'

Anna entered and nodded at the boy. 'Go ahead, Iain. Tell the commander what you saw.'

'They, your son and others, were gathered around the pool. It looked like they were fighting…arguing. Yelling back and forth and then your son started climbing the falls.'

'I do not understand,' Davidh said. 'He knew the other way. He could have reached the top without going near the water.'

'I swore not to tell, Papa.' The whispered words surprised him. Colm had wakened and heard his question.

'Swore not to tell what, Colm?' Davidh shifted and offered his son a sip of the tea before anything else. 'Tell what?'

'They kenned I had been up here and did not believe I could climb up.' He coughed again and Davidh waited for it to pass. 'I would not tell anyone about the way here. Not my friends. No one.'

Her gasp and her stricken expression told him that she understood. Davidh had made him swear to keep a secret and it had almost killed him.

'I did not tell.'

Colm's body slumped against his chest and, for a moment, Davidh feared the worst. Was his son dead? He looked at Anna who rushed over and knelt there beside him, touching and feeling and listening for his son's breaths.

'He is so weak. I do not know how he held on for as long as he did,' Anna said, sitting back on her heels.

'Tell me the rest.' Davidh looked at Iain, who still stood in the shadows watching him. 'They argued and Colm climbed. How far up was he?'

'About halfway. He made it just above the first pool.'

'God!' Davidh said. He put his arm around his son from behind and held him. 'How did he get here?' The boy across the chamber did not reply in words, just a nod in his mother's direction. 'You brought him here?'

Anna nodded and stood then. 'Aye. With Iain's help.'

'You got him off the rocks? How?' With the falls overflowing due to the recent storms, the thought of any of them in its control was unthinkable. But that she even attempted it for his son... He was the one finding it difficult to breathe then. 'You risked much, Anna.'

'He is just a boy, Davidh. Who would not have done it?' She walked over and put her arm around her own son and he realised that the lad was almost as tall as she was. 'You would have done it for Iain. Or for any child.'

'I thank you for what you did. He would have died there.'

'He was keeping his word to protect me,' she said.

'You did not know that when you went out on those slippery rocks, in those torrents of water.' Davidh eased himself from behind Colm and rose to his feet. 'You could have been hurt or worse.' He walked over to her, fighting with each step he took the urge and need to hold her in his arms. He stood a few inches from her now as he stared into her eyes. 'I thank you for saving my son.'

Had she lifted her chin just then? Would she allow his kiss? Tilting his head, he moved closer. Before he could touch his mouth to hers, everything changed. Iain shuffled in the corner, Colm let out a moan and Anna uttered the worst words he would ever think to hear.

'I have not saved him yet, Davidh.'

Davidh turned to his son and watched as the coughing and tremors began anew. Worse, these spasms were harsher than any since Anna had begun treating him. It was as though the last fortnight had only been an imaginary reprieve and it was over. The coughing had returned as though it had never gone and he rushed to his son.

'Sit him up and support him,' Anna said as

she fetched something from the table. She moved around it, picking up this and that, adding each to a bowl, and then mixing it. 'This will ease the cough,' she said.

'But you said not to stop his coughs with the juice of poppy.' He remembered she thought it was the worst thing to give his son.

'Listen to his cough, Davidh. Listen as he tries to draw breath. This is a different cough,' she said. 'This is a different tincture.' She came over to them and bent down. 'Lean his head on your shoulder and open his mouth.'

It took a few tries, but soon the thick liquid had been placed on Colm's tongue. Together, they coaxed him to swallow it. A second wave of coughing followed and then a third, but, thankfully, each one seemed to calm a bit more until his son was deeply asleep. They sat a quiet watch to see if he had calmed indeed. Davidh dared not move while Anna sat there on the edge of the pallet, not taking her gaze from his son.

Iain looked on from the corner. Only then did Davidh realise he was working with a dagger and a piece of wood. After easing Colm down to the pallet and tucking the blankets around him tightly, Davidh stood and stretched his own muscles that were tight from holding one position for so long.

'You have quite a skill there,' he said, crouching down in front of the boy. 'Who taught you?' If there was a son, mayhap there was a husband?

'One of the men at the Mackenzies' village where we lived. He was a carpenter and liked to carve the extra bits into animals.'

'What are you working on now?'

'A deer. Like the one that sneaks up to the cottage in the morn.' Iain held it out to him and Davidh took it.

'You have the head and neck exactly as it looks. How long will it take to finish the rest?' He handed it back, watching as the boy's fingers moved over its surface as though contemplating the next cut.

'It depends on what chores my mother gives me. On the morrow, I would expect.'

'You have my gratitude as well, Iain. For what you did for my son.' The boy's face flushed at his words and he nodded. 'He would have died there if you had not sought help.' Davidh stood now and nodded to Anna.

'And you also. No matter what the outcome of this, you have done so much to ease my son's affliction over these last weeks. You have my word that I will do anything for you that is in my power to do.'

A sense of peace filled him then and he had

the strangest feeling that his son would survive. He could understand the challenge ahead
of them, but he had faith that Anna would see
Colm through it.

The next two nights and days tried that faith
and his endurance and patience and every other
shred of self-control he thought he had. He and
Anna took turns staying at Colm's bedside and
giving him a series of brews and tinctures and
drops, all in an attempt to end the fever that
burned its way through his son's frail body.

Davidh's own chest hurt in sympathy with
Colm's as wave after wave of coughing came and
went. Just when Anna thought she had the right
measure of ingredients, it would fail. She tried so
many ingredients that he lost track of what had
worked and which had not. But she did not. She
surprised him when she opened a worn, leather-
bound book and scratched notes and amounts in
it each time she changed a recipe.

On the third morning, one that began with a
strong, bright sun rising in a near cloudless sky,
Colm seemed to improve. Or, he seemed to stop
worsening. His breathing came easier and his
colour looked better.

While Anna and her son slept in the other
chamber, Davidh left the cottage for a few minutes. The air, with the chill of a spring morning

lacing through it, was cool and it felt like heaven to him. The cottage had been warm—another change to the way she handled Colm these last few days. Warmth was needed to keep his body from struggling to warm itself.

He walked now, back and away from the falls, to a place he'd found the day before. It was difficult to believe that the river meandering along the sides of the hills there was the same one that became so dangerous just yards further on. A small, calm pool formed in one of the river's curves and that was his destination now. He tugged off his boots, then his shirt and trews and walked into the water gathered there.

The cold of it shocked him at first, but it also brought him fully awake. The water only came up to his hips, so he dipped down, wetting his hair and rubbing his face. A few days' growth of beard would need to be tended. He spent some minutes submerging in the pool and then stood and twisted his hair to wring out most of the water.

He needed to return to the keep and speak to Robert. By now, he was certain someone had told him of the situation and Robert knew him to be trustworthy enough to get back as soon as he could. As he walked from the pool and began tugging his clothes back on, he knew that this was that time. When he approached the cottage,

Davidh found Anna watching from beside the open doorway.

'Tavish's father was just here.'

'Robert sent him?' he asked, as he tied his hair back out of his face. 'Was there a message?'

'There has been a skirmish or trouble of some kind near Tor Castle and you are needed.' He glanced in the direction of the cottage and she stopped him with her hand on his arm. 'Leave Colm with me and see to your duties.'

'You would do that?' he asked. The warmth of her hand on his now-chilled skin spread up his arm.

'Aye. He is in no condition to be carted on your back down the hillside and will need supervision these next days. Leave him with me.' She released his arm and stepped out of the door so he could enter.

'Have you enough food?'

'Aye. And my son can hunt for more when we need it. I have plenty of oats to make porridge.'

He paused for a moment and stared at her. The question that had gnawed at him for days now pushed forward, needing and wanting to be asked. But first...

'If you would like to see to your...needs, I will wait.'

A momentary hesitation vanished and she nodded. 'I will hurry.'

He watched as she gathered a few items and then ran out the door, heading for the same place he'd just been. Even as he sat at Colm's side, his thoughts followed her steps. Wondering if she had a husband that she'd not mentioned. Cursing himself for a fool for even thinking about a woman who was not his to question. A woman who'd saved his son's life.

Colm stirred then and opened his eyes. When he saw that his gaze was clear and not glassy-eyed, he offered up a prayer of thanks that the fever had finally relented.

'Papa?' Colm's voice was hoarse. Davidh retrieved the cup of cooled betony tea with honey and held it out to his son to sip. Colm was able to lift his head off the pillow and drink a small amount.

'I am here, Colm,' he said, brushing the tussled hair out of his son's eyes. 'We must talk when I return.'

'Aye, Papa,' his son whispered.

'For now, you will obey every word that Mistress Mackenzie says and you will thank her for saving your life.' Colm's brow gathered and he looked puzzled. 'You do not remember?'

'Nay. Only bits and not much.' His son swallowed the rest of the tea and shrugged. 'When will you return?'

'A few days. If longer, I will try to send word.

Do not make yourself a nuisance to the woman or her son.' Iain chose that moment to come out of the smaller chamber. 'Mayhap you can ask Iain to show you the deer he carved. Or the horse he is working on now.'

The door opened then and Anna stood there, outlined by the sunlight. Her long hair had been twisted and piled on top of her head. If she let it dry that way, it would tumble down over her shoulders in thick waves when she… Davidh shook himself free of such images and leaned over his son.

'As I said, do as Mistress Mackenzie tells you.' He touched Colm's cheek, trying not to think of how close the boy had been to dying just two nights before.

Davidh gathered up his belongings and carried them outside. His horse was waiting below; he or Iain had seen to its care several times over the last days. After tying the length of tartan around his waist and placing his belt there, Davidh slid his sword from under the pallet and placed it back in its scabbard. He knew she'd followed him outside and she watched as he prepared to leave.

'I will be gone for a few days. This fight with the outlaws is not unexpected,' he said. 'I will send a message if I will be longer than that.'

'We will be fine, Davidh. See to your duties

without worrying about your son.' She let out a breath and nodded. 'I think he will be well soon.'

He turned to go, but knew he wanted to say more to her. She had saved his son's life at the risk of her own. She had dragged him back to her cottage and kept him from dying. He owed her so much.

'When I return, we will talk about how I can repay you for what you have done.'

'I could do nothing less,' she said, clearly uncomfortable with his praise.

'When I return,' he promised in a sterner voice, one he reserved for a misbehaving Colm. She nodded and he turned, but not before asking that damned question he needed to ask.

'Have you a husband? Iain's father?'

A shadow filled her gaze then. 'Iain's father is dead.'

'A Cameron?'

He did not think she was going to answer. The slight nod was long in coming. Then she stared off for a moment before turning that green gaze back to him. 'Aye, he was. But I have no husband.'

He had even more questions now about her son and his connection to the Camerons, but they would have to wait. Knowing that the boy was kin made her return here more understandable.

Davidh walked away then, following the steep

path down through the shadows and trees until he reached the bottom. Looking up past the falls, he saw her standing there. She waved and he lifted his hand to return the gesture. Iain walked to her side then and Davidh shivered. The old ones would say that the feeling was like that of someone picking at your long-dead bones, but Davidh only knew it was a strange sensation that rippled through him as he watched mother and son at the top of the hill.

Chapter Nine

Tor Castle, banks of River Lochy

Davidh stood on the parapet of the castle and looked south and west along the river. The castellan, Archibald Cameron, pointed to the last place where the band of outlawed men had been seen. Robbie, the chieftain's eldest son and the clan's tanist, stood at Archie's side. The lad was strong and learned quickly. He had a good grasp of the balance needed to rule over a clan the size of the Camerons.

'They fade back into the forest by the time we reach them,' Parlan, Davidh's friend and second-in-command, explained.

'Do you think someone is warning them?' Robbie asked. Observant, too, this one.

'Aye,' Parlan answered, turning to face them. 'We have tried approaching from different directions and at different times of the day and they always scatter just ahead of us.'

'Do you know who it is yet?' he asked of Parlan. His friend had been here for more than a week, searching for those behind the recent attacks.

'We suspect that some are those who fled when Gilbert was killed,' Archie offered. 'They were complicit in his crimes against the clan, but were never caught.'

'Colum and Duncan?' Robbie asked.

'Aye, and others, too,' Archie said.

'Many had fled that night while The Mackintosh helped the Camerons sort out the truth of Gilbert's perfidy,' Davidh said.

'What is their plan? What is their aim?' Archie asked. 'Why remain here?'

'To make my father's position and claim an unsteady one,' Robbie answered. 'Many Camerons still question his right to rule, especially considering the revelations and events of that night. These…outlaws sow seeds of discontent and illegitimacy where they can.'

Davidh's estimation and respect for Robbie rose with every assessment the young man made of this situation. Robbie stepped back from the edge of the stone wall and nodded at him and Parlan.

'What are your plans for eradicating them?' the young man asked him.

'I would speak to Parlan and the other men and see what has been done so far. Then I will bring the plan to you.'

The tanist nodded and walked off with Archie, leaving Davidh and Parlan there on the highest part of Tor Castle. Gazing over the side, he watched the river flow by and was reminded of the other river.

'I did not want to summon you here, Davidh.'

'I understand. And I had no doubt you could handle this matter. But 'tis my duty to see to such as this, so I came.'

Parlan motioned for him to follow and they entered the stairway leading down to the lower floors of the castle. The evening meal would not be served soon, so they sat at one of the tables and Parlan explained his previous actions to his commander. Davidh could see no weakness in what his man had done, so their suspicion of collusion, of someone here and throughout the areas involved, must be correct. He asked many questions and was satisfied by Parlan's answers.

The conclusion worried him for a number of reasons. He'd not expected complete and instant acceptance of Robert as chieftain, but this attempt by those elders who yet held the respect of many kith and kin was...dangerous.

'There is enough daylight left to ride to the place that was attacked most recently. Take me there,' he said.

Within a short time, he and Parlan were on their way to the southernmost point on the Cameron lands. Not a true village in size or inhabitants, it was more a small gathering of crofts at the river's edge. They dismounted and several approached them. They recognised Parlan and so spoke openly to him.

After inspecting the storage barn that had been damaged and hearing from the people who'd witnessed it, Davidh was more convinced than ever of the identity of the perpetrators and their cause. Worse, knowing the extent of this threat did make Robert's hold on his high seat less a sure thing than it had been even weeks ago.

They ate supper in an uncomfortable silence that evening. Each of them realised the possible consequences if those who had betrayed their clan were allowed to live and succeed in their goal. Though none of those outlawed by Robert had a direct claim to the high seat, the old ways of choosing a laird still held sway in some areas and clearly these men were attempting to do that now.

The only thing that linked the attacks was the river, so he and Parlan laid plans to place guards at key locations along the river leading north to Loch Lochy and then the river and Loch Arkaig to try to capture some of them. With a little luck, they would see something and report it.

'So, I have not asked and you have not mentioned how Colm is doing,' Parlan said.

'Thanks to the new healer at Achnacarry, he was much improved,' Davidh replied.

'Was?' Parlan drank from his cup and then grew serious. 'Not now? Then why are you here? Robert would surely have given you leave to remain there.'

'Aye, he would have. If I'd have asked for it. But, Parlan, these are dangerous times and the chieftain's commander cannot ignore his duties to tend to a sick child.' There it was—plain and simply put.

'If Gilbert was chieftain, I would agree. 'Twould have been a risk to you and the boy to ask such a thing. But, Robert?' Davidh shrugged then. 'So, what happened?' Parlan asked again.

'He was doing much better. She had come up with some concoctions that seemed to work.' Davidh drank the last of his ale and put the cup down. 'Then his friends challenged him to climb the falls.'

'Dear God, man! How is he?' Parlan sat back

in his chair and shook his head. 'So many who try it are injured. And those are the strong ones.'

'He is well, thanks to the healer. She saved him from falling from the rocks.'

'Who is this woman?'

'Her name is Anna Mackenzie. Her mother lived here years ago—lived there above the falls.'

'The Witch?' Parlan asked in hushed tones. 'Her mother was The Witch of Caig Falls?' His friend laughed aloud then. 'So, is she one as well?' Davidh reached over and punched his friend on the shoulder.

'Nay, not a witch. Simply a healer. A woman with a son of her own, but no husband.'

'That seems convenient then since you are a man with a son of his own with no wife.'

His first reaction was to strike out at such a statement, but he held his fists on the table and glared at his friend.

'Not many could say such a thing and remain upright.' He forced out the words through clenched jaws.

'Not many are willing to say what needs to be said. It has been a long time, Davidh.'

'Spoken by a man who never had a wife to mourn.'

Parlan reached over and put his hand on Davidh's shoulder then. Leaning in so others would not hear his words, he spoke again.

'And she was a fine wife to you and a good mother to Malcolm. But she is gone and you live, my friend.' Parlan shook his head. 'She would want you to live on.'

He wanted to argue that point—his loyalty to Mara almost forced the words off his tongue. But it was the truth. She'd told him exactly that during those last terrible days of suffering. Davidh just did not want such a discussion now. Not when his attention needed to be centred on his chieftain and his clan.

'Leave it.'

Parlan held his cup up and a servant filled it. Though Davidh had not asked for more, his cup was filled, as well.

'So, where is Colm now?' his friend asked. 'Now that Anna Mackenzie saved him from the rocks.'

'Do not jest, Parlan. He nearly died. She could have.'

'Your pardon,' Parlan offered. 'I asked because, in spite of the seriousness of this news, you seem…well, calm about him.' Parlan took a mouthful of ale and swallowed it, shrugging. ''Tis your custom to worry and fret over the boy every moment he is out of your sight. Yet you have not mentioned him at all until I asked you.'

His friend's words explained exactly how he had felt ever since Mara died and Colm became his sole responsibility. Well, he'd had help from his parents and his sister, but he had been on his own with his ailing son for a long time. Neighbours had stepped in, his chieftain had been accommodating and others helped as they could.

'Anna offered to keep him with her until I return.'

Parlan just grunted then and Davidh found his silence more unnerving than his custom of bold truths. He leaned back in his chair and stared at the man he trusted more than any other. They were kin and they were friends, but Parlan could be frustrating and infuriating at the same moment when he wished to be. As he was now.

'Say what you will,' Davidh urged.

'So, this woman, this healer comes to Achnacarry, treats your son and then saves his life twice more. A widow with a son. And you leave your son in her care to come here.' Davidh nodded. 'You are suspicious of any stranger who passes through Cameron lands. You question the presence of anyone you do not recognise. And yet you leave your son with a woman who arrived when? A few weeks ago?'

'What are you saying?'

'I want to know why you trust this woman and what you're willing to do to make her stay in Achnacarry?'

Davidh stood then and walked away from

the table, ignoring the knowing laughter of his friend. He'd been given a chamber to use this night and he went there. He did not sleep much because the questions Parlan asked turned over and over in his thoughts, too.

As he rode along the river on his way back to Achnacarry, he thought he knew what he could offer her. The boy's father had been a Cameron and he knew that had played a part in her return to Achnacarry. By the time he reached the village, he was clear on what he could offer her.

Anna watched as Colm tried to follow Iain's directions, but the boy had not the skill that her son did. Iain made it seem an easy task while Anna understood that it was not such a thing. It was no different from her own ability to create recipes from the herbs and plants and other ingredients and know that they would work for this ailment or that complaint. And yet, the younger boy did not give up easily.

She was not worried over his ability to carve wood. The thing that pleased her was that he had regained enough strength to sit outside and try in just the three days since his father had left. He looked at her then and she smiled back at him. That he was alive was an undoubted miracle.

The sun finally broke through the thick layers of clouds that had kept the morning grey and cool. Cocooned with a thick blanket, Colm faced no danger of catching a chill, so they remained there, next to the cottage. A pot of savoury soup boiled over the fire for supper and the aroma drifted on the breezes around them.

Even taking care of the boy had not stopped her from making great progress in getting her stores of supplies in order. He had a quick mind and, once he could get up off the pallet, he liked to help her in mixing and compounding the recipes. He'd not been taught to read, as her Iain had been, but he could do his sums well and kept track of the ingredients and amounts needed as she measured and mixed.

The other ability he had was his knowledge of all sorts of gossip about every person in the village of Achnacarry. In just these last few days, he'd told her more about his kith and kin than she'd known about the Mackenzies and she'd lived among them for more than a decade!

'Mistress Mackenzie?' She glanced at him and waited. 'I do not think carving is something I will do well.'

He held up the pitifully shaped creature and she could not identify it. It resembled nothing she'd ever seen or imagined. 'Nay,' he said, shaking his head sadly.

'I think your skills lie elsewhere, Colm,' she said, putting down the garment she was mending as the boys worked on their carvings. She stood and walked to his side. 'Your skill at numbers is far better than mine.'

'I think my father will be disappointed in that. He wishes me to be a strong warrior like he is.'

'Your father will not be disappointed, Malcolm Cameron.'

They all turned at the sound of that deep voice and found Davidh standing there watching them.

'Papa!'

Colm jumped up and ran to his father, who opened his arms to the boy. She saw the surprise and delight on Davidh's face as his son moved so assuredly towards him, without help. He wrapped his arms around him and lifted him from his feet, all the while whispering something to him. The boy nodded or shook his head in reply to the questions he was being asked.

Davidh's gaze met hers and something changed in that moment between them. He looked at her differently somehow, as though he had only just realised she existed. That was just fanciful thinking, but something was different. It made her skin feel too tight. It made her flush with heat.

'Good day, mistress,' he said as he put his son back down. 'His improvement is unexpected, considering his condition when I left here.'

Colm ran to her now and she placed her hands on his shoulders.

'Aye, a greatly improved Colm,' she teased. 'But he did as you commanded and obeyed my every order. He even drank the putrid syrup without complaint.'

'Aye, even that one,' Colm admitted. Iain laughed then, for he knew that the boy had indeed complained at every dose. That could remain their secret.

'How is your carving going, Iain?' Davidh asked her son. 'Did you finish the deer and the horse as planned?'

'Aye, sir,' Iain said. He walked over to the commander and held out those two and another he'd completed over the last days.

'This is amazing,' Davidh said. He examined the carvings closely, especially the newest one—a falcon in flight. First glancing at her, he turned to her son. 'You have captured every feather as though it was alive.'

Her heart swelled with pride. She could see that this man's praise affected Iain, as well. What would Malcolm have said if he could have seen his closest friend with his son?

It made her question her own decisions from the years past. Once she knew of Malcolm's death, had she made a grave error in not accepting a proposal of marriage when he'd been a bairn? Should she have done so to provide a father for her growing son?

There had been two and Anna had been tempted, but feared giving up control over her life. Neither would have been a love match, but she'd not expected that. Each one would have been for the sake of expediency and would have given her son a father. Now watching them, heads bowed together, as Davidh asked about his method and technique, Anna doubted herself.

'Papa? Am I coming home with you?' Colm asked.

Davidh walked to where she stood and he crouched down so that his face was the same height as his son's. She'd noticed he did that when speaking to the lads. ''Tis up to Mistress Mackenzie. What say you, mistress? Is my son well enough to return with me?'

'If you are not opposed, I would keep him this day and night and bring him back to the village on the morrow? A few more doses of that syrup are needed to make certain—' Colm interrupted with a gagging sound and a scrunched-up expression on his face. 'To make certain the cough is controlled,' she finished.

'He will need to endure that whether here or at our cottage?' Davidh asked. The hope of escaping the noxious brew disappeared and his son let out a huge and loud sigh. She nodded her answer and the boy groaned which made her and his father laugh aloud.

'Are you hungry? We will be eating supper soon,' she said to him. She wanted him to stay.

'Since I have made my report to Robert on the way here, I can stay.' Colm looked pleased by this. Even Iain seemed happy about it. And Anna knew she was.

While Davidh spoke with both of the boys, she went inside to prepare the rest of the supper. The conversation while eating was entertaining to her, for she saw even another facet of the commander as he described his journey to Tor. Iain and Colm sat enraptured as he spoke about not only the journey there, but the castle and the weapons he had and the men who fought for The Cameron and the clan.

Soon, too soon, the meal was done and it was time for the commander to return to the village. She observed him out of the corner of her eye as he took his son aside and spoke to him on some serious matter. The boy did not say anything, but the sombre gaze told her he was being reprimanded.

He needed to be, for he had placed himself in grave danger. She understood the playfulness of lads his age and their need to challenge themselves and each other...within bounds. Since he had been trying to honour his word to his father and to protect Anna, she found it difficult to be too angry with him. And she was glad that his father, and not she, would have to take him to task for his actions. When Davidh patted his son's shoulder and nodded to him, Anna waited for his approach.

'His friends have been punished for their part, so I needed him to understand his part in it.'

'He is just a boy,' she said.

'Aye. I did plenty of foolhardy things at his age, but none put others in danger as he did.'

'Are you certain of that?' she asked. Malcolm, her Malcolm, had told her stories about their antics and excursions—especially the ones they never revealed to anyone else.

'Why?' he asked. He smiled then, a wonderful mix of male guilt, boyish anticipation and lack of fear. 'What did Colm tell you?'

'He spoke of everyone else in the village and clan, but little of you.' She laughed at the way he frowned, as though disappointed not to be the centre of his son's words. 'I just know lads well enough to know you must have done some bad things when you were growing up.' She did not want to think about the person who'd revealed their secrets right now.

'I was a challenge to my mother,' he admitted.

'Colm seems to understand the seriousness of what he did.'

'Aye.'

He stared at her then without speaking, his dark eyes bright and intense from across the small space. She sensed that he wished to speak to her about something else.

'Before I go back to the village, I would speak to you about a matter…of importance to both of us.'

Chapter Ten

Her stomach tightened then and a tiny bead of sweat suddenly tracked down her back as she followed Davidh out of the cottage. His tone neither threatened nor insulted her, so she could not think of a reason to be afraid of this encounter.

And yet she was very afraid.

Had he discovered the truth about her son? She thought not, for he would have reacted differently to her jibe about his own childhood if he knew her connection to Malcolm. Davidh stopped a short distance from the cottage and faced her. He stared off behind her and she realised he was as nervous as she!

'When you said that Iain is a Cameron, I understood that he must be part of the reason for your return here. I mean, that you brought the boy back here to meet his kin.'

'Aye.'

'I even understand why you kept his presence

here a secret. It is not always safe for a woman alone.' Davidh took a step closer. Anna clutched her hands together to keep them from shaking. 'So, I have an offer for you.'

'Offer?'

'Proposal.'

'Proposal?'

He shook his head then and laughed. 'This is more trying than I thought it would be.' Her face must have given away what kind of offer she thought he was presenting. 'Nay, not an offer like that.'

'So…?'

'I told you I wanted to do something to show my gratitude for your help with Colm. I have asked Robert—'

'You discussed my son with the laird?' This was not good, she could feel that to her bones. This was too much attention paid to Iain too quickly.

'He is the leader of our clan. He is responsible for the welfare of every Cameron.' He gave her an incredulous glance and she realised that he had complete and utter faith in his chieftain to do the right thing for his people. 'We know it is not what you had planned, but I wondered if you would consider moving into my house in the village?'

'Your house?' This was yet as clear as a muddy lake to her.

'You could use it as your own—it is large enough to do your work in the main room and there are two other chambers. You could have use of it.'

'And you will live where?'

He let out a loud breath and shrugged. 'Let me begin this again.' He pointed at the stool she'd left there earlier and she sat.

'Robert has always offered me a chamber in the keep for me and my son. But, since I have the house in the village, I have always preferred that Colm live there. Now, though, if you would like, you could have use of it and we would move to the keep.'

'Should Colm not stay in his own home?' she asked. Anna appreciated his offer and it was tempting, but not at the cost of putting a boy, a sick boy, out of his own home.

'We can speak more on that. I suggested this because it would be a way to introduce Iain to his kin and kith.'

'You would do this? Offer your house to us?'

'You gave me back my son when he should have died, Anna. Twice—thrice if we count your original treatments. 'Tis the least I can do for you and your son.' She stood, but he motioned for her to stay.

'I have spoken to Robert of Iain's skill with knife and wood and he suggested that the boy could apprentice with the carpenters in the stables, the keep and the kitchen.'

'A house. A place in the village. A skill and work. That is what you are offering me?'

Then he gazed at her and, even in the growing shadows, she saw that strange unfamiliar glimmer she'd witnessed there a short while ago. It was as though he wanted to say more, or say something else, but did not. But there was the promise that he would say it…soon. Her body shivered in awareness that the promise was not simply words, but more.

'Aye.'

One word, spoken in a husky voice filled with hope and promise and…desire? Anna shook herself free of this foolish direction of thought.

'I must think on this before I give my answer.'

He nodded and she thought him done speaking until he stepped closer and lowered his voice.

'There is another reason for moving down to the village.' Now his tone was one of his position—commander, protector, confidant of the chieftain. 'The outlaws appear to be using the river and lochs to move between their attacks. A woman alone here much of the time would be…at risk.'

And a choice target—she understood the

words he did not say. She shivered then, at the threats that had faced her mother before her and her now.

'I will give serious thought to this, Davidh. And I thank you for the generous offer of your house.'

A house. Not a cottage as he'd described it previously. Well, he'd not truly mentioned it during the tour of the village and the only part of the village they'd not visited had been the place where several stone buildings sat. She'd thought them storehouses, yet could one of those be his house?

The strangest thing about this offer was what came next.

He nodded, spoke his farewells and took his leave of her, heading down the path to the falls and below. Anna watched his every step and did not move after he'd been gone for several long moments.

Would he accept whatever her decision was?

This man, who held the power to order men, nay, everyone save one in this clan, to do his bidding, had given her a choice in this matter? He must know that few would consider not doing whatever he bade them do. Especially women. She'd witnessed the deference to him from those in the village, but the women they'd passed or met had other emotions in their gazes.

Admiration. Approval. Liking. A need to please him. Even frank wanting. The things one saw in the eyes of those looking on a man who held the trust of their laird.

They were not hard to identify if one had lived in a village, among closely knit kith and kin. One where powerful men made the difference between existing and living. Or living in some measure of comfort.

Where those men were accustomed to being obeyed and not questioned. Whether this newest laird was less brutal than his predecessor or not, this second offer was not something to ignore or refuse lightly. And not without specific reasons that the laird and his man would accept and not take as an insult.

Not a few times, she had recognised the other emotions directed at her.

Surprise. Curiosity. Jealousy. Each one of those was a danger to her, to her son. Women might not rule clans, but they held certain power and wielded it in a different way from the power and the ways of men. Yet, women and their powers were no less dangerous. Indeed, it had been village women who'd caused the most trouble for her mother here all those years ago.

Their rumours. Their veiled accusations and questions. The suspicions they raised and voiced.

Anna shook her head to no one but herself

then. She'd understood the mistakes her mother had made here and had pledged not to make the same ones. If she moved to the village, and it was looking as though she must and she should, she would handle the challenges in a manner unlike her mother had.

Regardless of the dangers, this offer was exactly what she'd hoped for when she'd planned to bring Iain back to Malcolm's family. Better still, it would put him in the centre of things and give him the opportunity to learn so much.

Anna entered the cottage to find Colm asleep on the pallet there. Iain sat at table, working on the few adjustments to the falcon. Davidh had only seen the three carvings, but Iain had dozens more in his trunk. She sat next to him as he held the bird up to check it. He nodded in satisfaction and placed it there before them.

'We must speak,' she whispered to him as she threw a glance at the sleeping boy. 'The commander and the laird have invited us to move to the village.'

Her son's face brightened and guilt pierced her heart. Her aim had been to keep him safe, but the result was it had kept him isolated. So, while she visited the village and met people, he'd been hidden away here on his own.

'Can we?' Iain asked.

''Tis not how or what I had planned for our life

here and yet I think we must.' Anna shrugged. 'The commander has offered the use of his house to us. And promised to see to your training as apprentice to the carpenter.'

Excitement bubbled within him. This was an amazing opportunity and it would give him everything he'd ever asked of her.

Kith and kin.

To know his father's people.

A chance to hone his skills and learn a craft.

Iain had no idea of her final goal for him and the true reason for her bringing him back here— and he would not for now. First, she would allow him and the Camerons to learn about each other. Then, they would be in a better position to make his claim.

Without realising it, and while thinking it was to show his gratitude, Davidh Cameron had handed her the perfect opening for her plan. More so than that, by introducing and sponsoring her son to his laird and their clan, he would be seen as supporting Iain's position when the truth was out. A pang of guilt shot through her as she nodded to her son. A strong warning, but not strong enough to turn her from her goal— Malcolm Cameron's son taking his rightful place as heir to the chieftain.

As his father had been all those years ago.

And if it meant deceiving the commander to

attain that, she would regret using him in this manner, but would not turn away from it. The guilt would be hers to bear while the high seat would be her son's to inherit.

She bade Iain to sleep for the next day would be a busy one. Though her son fell right into sleep's grasp, it did not take her. So, she spent the next hours organising her thoughts on the best way to move all of their belongings and her supplies and plants. The only variance between this time and her move from her mother's village was that she was not even fully settled in here yet.

Anna did not begin packing, for on the morrow she would take Colm back to the village and inspect the house. No matter where she lived, she would need to tend to the plants and herbs she'd just planted here. Now, though, instead of living here and visiting the village, she would do the opposite.

'Wait, Colm.' Anna rushed after the boy who insisted on running down the road into the village. 'You must not run!' she called out.

He slowed then and Anna caught up with him, taking hold of his hand and waiting for Iain to reach them. Now people called out greetings to her and Colm while scrutinising her son. They would know him soon enough. They walked towards the ever-present smoke rising from the smithy and found Suisan working within.

'Mistress Mackenzie!' she called out. 'Malcolm Cameron!'

The woman grabbed Colm and dragged him to her ample bosom, rocking him and murmuring words in his hair. The boy allowed it, probably due to his father's reprimand about worrying one and all by his reckless behaviour. The boy did not fight it and Anna understood the genuine affection between this motherless child and the woman who cared for him.

'So, are ye moving to the village after all?' Suisan said, after releasing Colm. The blacksmith's wife leaned over and glanced behind Anna. 'And who is this fine young lad?'

'Suisan, I would make you known to my son, Iain.' She tugged Iain in front of her. 'Iain, this is Mistress Cameron. Her husband is the blacksmith there.'

'Mistress Cameron,' Iain said as he nodded a slight bow to the woman.

'Well, no mistaking him for anything but a Cameron,' Suisan said. 'His colouring is yours, though.' The woman waited and Anna knew she hoped for more details about her son, but Anna just smiled and nodded agreement.

'Colm!'

Anna turned at the call and saw the same

small gathering of boys who'd been waiting at the bottom of the falls. Davidh's son looked out the door and she saw the hesitation in his manner.

'They are waiting for you,' Suisan said. 'Go. Speak to them.'

Colm raised his serious glance to Suisan. 'Papa told me they had been punished for...what happened.'

'Aye, they have. 'Tis over and done now. Go on with ye,' she said once more. 'Take Iain with ye, too. He looks about their age.'

A pointed look at Anna and she understood the woman wanted to know more about him. Iain followed Colm out and Anna watched as Davidh's son made him known to the others. After nothing more than a moment's awkwardness, they fell in together and all she could hear was a garbled burst of chatter. Turning back to Suisan, she shrugged.

'Iain has ten-and-two years,' she said.

'And ye have been gone from here for how long, Mistress Mackenzie?'

'Just so.' That was all she would say.

'Davidh was not certain ye would accept the offer. Have ye then?'

'Aye, Suisan. Iain and I will move to the village.'

'Into Davidh's house, then?' The woman

crossed her arms over her bosom and narrowed her gaze.

'Aye, into his house, once he moves into the keep.'

The woman let out an exasperated breath and shook her head. ''Twas not the arrangement I had hoped for, I will tell ye that much.'

She'd no idea the blacksmith's wife was also a maker of matches. Or that she had some plan in mind for the two of them. Unfortunately, no matter how appealing the commander was or however much she might be willing to consider some other arrangement, he would never forgive her for her deception once it came to light.

'My only question is whether he'll permit Colm to stay with us rather than moving him to the keep.'

'You would do that? Care for his son?'

'He has offered to help my son,' she said, nodding. 'How could I not at least offer to do so for his?'

Suisan grew quiet then and Anna faced her.

'He is not well, is he?'

There were ways to answer this question— one his own father had not dared ask yet. Anna could give hope and allow one and all to think the boy was recovering. Or she could give the truth and voice her own fear.

'Nay, he is not.' Even spoken softly, between just the two of them, the words sounded harsh.

'And will he recover?'

'I think not.' The silence spun around them as Anna watched the lads outside. A soft sob drew her attention then. She touched Suisan's arm. 'That does not mean I am not going to fight the affliction with every tool at hand. I will.'

She brushed the unexpected tears from her own eyes and stepped out of the door.

'Come now, Colm. You must show us the way to your house.'

The boys followed and it took little time to reach the road that led out of the keep and past the large stone buildings there closest to the gates. Colm brought them to stop before the larger of the two.

'This is my papa's house, Mistress Mackenzie. This one.'

As she and Iain stood there in surprised silence, Anna wondered what she had got herself into with this offer.

Chapter Eleven

A casual comment from one of the warriors about the healer broke Davidh's attention to their task. The man had seen her in the village.

So, she was here. He wondered if she'd made her decision since they spoke last evening. By now, she must have. Was she still in the village? Davidh glanced up at the weak sun above and guessed it to be nearing mid-afternoon. She would still be seeing to people and most likely not return to the falls until nearer to supper.

He was out of the gates before he knew he'd taken a step. Then, as he turned to go to Suisan's to see how Colm fared, he glanced towards his own house and noticed smoke rising from the chimney of the hearth. He walked closer and heard the voices from within. Had Colm allowed the other boys inside, disobeying his rules? Why was he not with Suisan? He strode up to the door and lifted the latch.

Anna stood in the middle of the main chamber and the lads, all of Colm's friends along with Iain, sat in a circle around her. They all turned in unison to glare at his interruption.

'Papa.' Colm frowned and waved him in. 'Mistress Mackenzie is telling us about a stone up the glen that tells the truth. And you interrupted her!'

'I...' He stepped inside and closed the door. Leaning against the door frame, he nodded for her to continue.

'As I was saying...' Anna began her story once more.

Davidh did not know which impressed him more—the lively manner in which she told her story or the way she drew the lads into it. As she explained the story of the large boulder that seemed alive on a certain day each year, those listening never looked away from her.

Though he'd heard the story before, he found himself drawn into it now. He even called out his suggestions when she asked questions. The lads seemed to fall under her spell and, by the time she'd finished weaving the tale, they all believed that the stone could tell the truth when asked questions.

She chased all but Colm and Iain out then and he noticed how they obeyed her without hesitation or delay. Soon, the noisy chaos had ebbed away and he turned back to see her standing in the middle of the main chamber.

'I have not heard that story in years,' he admitted then. 'And when I did, 'twas not that good in the telling of it.'

''Tis Iain's favourite,' she said. 'Is it true that the stone exists? I have heard it lies in the glen on the way to Ben Nevis.'

Davidh smiled. He and Malcolm had searched for many weeks to find the truth stone after hearing the story of it. And they'd found what was purported to be the actual rock of the tales.

'I have seen it with my own eyes,' he said. 'My friend and I walked many hours to get there and we did see it. It is about this—' he motioned in a huge circle with his hands '—this big. And though it is too heavy to move, some there said they had seen it wobble in answer to questions put to it.'

'Where is it, sir? Close by?' Iain asked.

'Closer to Tor Castle in the south,' he said. 'Though it has been many years since I saw it. If my duties permit, mayhap we could go there and look for it.'

Their two sons yelled out, Colm with an excitement and vigour that was unexpected. Then they ran off into the chamber that Colm used as his own.

As Davidh looked around the house, the other

thing he realised he'd not seen in years was… life. Even now that the boys had gone, their excitement yet lingered here. Davidh looked at the one responsible for the change.

Anna had not moved anything in the chamber and somehow it felt like a different place. She'd brought laughter and the lads back in and she'd not even told him of her decision. If she could do this in a few hours, what could she do in days or weeks or…?

'You did not tell me you lived in such a place as this.'

He smiled then. 'In truth, I have not lived in one place for several years. I have spent days and many nights at the keep or seeing to my duties. Colm has been shuffled from place to place as others have seen to his care. This has been ours since Robert took control and made me his commander. But I have not called a place home since Mara passed.'

'Colm's mother. She died several years ago?'

'Aye. Then my parents this last year.'

'You have a sister?'

'Aye, my sister Aileen returned here briefly to help me. Apparently, Colm did tell you about everyone.' His son had not been so talkative in… for ever.

'Except you. He left your secrets intact,' she said. 'If he knows them at all.'

'Speaking of your secrets...' Her gaze narrowed for a scant moment and then she blushed, a becoming pink flush rising in her cheeks, at his reference to her son. 'Have you made your decision about the boy? And living here?'

'We must talk about that.' Anna motioned to the table and brought a pitcher and a cup there. Filling it, she handed it to him as she sat across from him. 'I do not feel it would be right to push you and your son from this house.'

'You are not—it was my offer.'

'Aye, but the result is the same. You and your son will not be here in the village. And you'd said you wanted him to live here.'

'Did I say that?' Davidh asked. He tried to think back on their words about this. 'Aye. This, though, would work better.'

Anna stood then and walked to the door leading to Colm's chamber. She tugged the door closed a bit and came back to face Davidh.

'I will only move here if you and your son remain in your house. I can see to his care just as I have these last days.' Anna sat again and he studied her face as she spoke. 'He will be no more burden than your offer to help my son will be.'

'So you seek to make this measure for measure? You will see to my son in exchange for me helping yours?' Even as Parlan's words floated in his thoughts, Davidh nodded his agreement to Anna's demand.

'Then, aye, I accept your offer and will move here,' she said. Then she huffed out a breath and looked exasperated. 'And I just sorted out my stores and supplies up at the cottage.'

'More moving, I think,' Davidh said. 'How did you get everything up there?'

'There is a very narrow path along the river next to the hillside. We have a small cart that we pulled along there, moving everything from the larger wagon that brought us here. But I will not move everything down here at once. It will be easier to bring some things down when I come into the village. And some of the plants and herbs growing up there will need to be tended and dried.'

'If you need help...'

'Nay, you have helped so much already. And you have your duties.'

'Ah, duties.' He shrugged. 'This is timed well, for I expect to be sent off on an assignment.'

'Well, then.' She pressed her hands on the table and stood. 'On the morrow, I will begin bringing our belongings down.' Davidh stood as she called to Iain and prepared to leave.

They exchanged a few more words about her move and her needs and expectations for tables and places to work and then she was gone. He watched as the two walked down the road towards the other end of the village and he smiled.

For the first time in so long a while, Davidh felt relief pass through him.

Each day over the next several brought more of the woman and her son and their belongings into his house. Each night when he arrived at the house, sometimes long after dark, a hot meal was waiting for him. When he returned from his duties and three days on the roads around Loch Arkaig and the surrounding Cameron lands searching for the outlaws after another attack, he found that Anna had taken over his house completely.

Now, as he stood observing the men under his command in their training the next morning, Davidh considered the changes to his life and realised something.

He was not displeased about it at all.

Once his own duties allowed him to be here at Achnacarry more than he was on the roads and rivers around it, he would fulfil his part of their bargain and see to Anna's son. The boy was skilled in working with wood and his intricately carved animals impressed Davidh more each time a new creature appeared in the boy's collection. His skills would be a good addition to those of the village's and keep's carpenters. And give him and his mother a place in the Cameron Clan since his looks alone claimed his place there.

'Davidh?'

He startled when he heard his name being called and looked up to see the Lady Elizabeth standing near the fence and strode over to her. Robert was not with her, nor anyone else save her maid. He bowed to her when he stood before her.

'Forgive my lack of attention, my lady.' He met her gaze and recognised the merriment there. 'Have you need of something?'

'Has Mistress Mackenzie settled in the village?' the lady asked. Davidh glanced towards the village and his house and nodded.

'Apparently.' Whether his tone was somehow unwarranted or inappropriate, he knew not, but the lady's laughter informed him she thought otherwise. 'I mean only that the speed of it was a surprise to me, my lady. Once the decision was made, 'twas handled quickly, it seems.'

'Well, you must admit that you were away for three days of that time.' The lady's eyes twinkled again and Davidh wondered if he was to continue as the target of her teasing manner. 'It takes an organised woman less than that to settle in place.'

He had no reply so he simply nodded and shrugged at the lady's words. Anna had made her place in his house, that was certain.

'And the sooner she is settled in, the sooner she might be able to see to the stillroom.'

'Ah, there is your motive for asking,' he said, laughing as he realised the lady's true aim. 'You wish that chamber seen to.' Lady Elizabeth smiled then, an enigmatic one that gave him the feeling that she had several reasons for asking after Anna.

'Aye,' she said, laying her hand on his forearm. 'But, I pray you, do not press her to see to it until she is ready. Truly, I think there is little to be salvaged there, but Anna will be a godsend in getting it organised so we ken what we will need to do next.'

'Well, I will speak to her when I see her. She was up and out before I rose this morn.' But not without leaving a freshly cooked pot of porridge waiting for him. His mouth watered again at the thought of it.

'I will let you see to your duties, Davidh,' the lady said.

He bowed as she took her leave of him, walking towards the keep with her maid trailing behind her. He did turn back to his duties, to the men there practising their skills, and it took little time for him to realise that all his men were present. Including the two or three who he'd assigned to help Anna when she was up at the cottage or needed something heavy moved. He called them to his side.

'Did Mistress Mackenzie ask for your help this morning?' To a one, they shrugged or shook their head in reply. 'Have any of you seen her about her tasks since this morning?'

'Nay,' Eonan said. 'She said she was seeing to the last few things herself this morn.' The others nodded in agreement.

'She is there now?' he asked.

The reports of the outlaws had continued and their movement grew closer to Achnacarry. Not near the village, but some outlying places had seen some evidence of their growing proximity and boldness and the knowledge weighed on him now.

Eonan shrugged as did Micheil and Donald. With a nod he sent them back to their training groups and tried to get back to his own duties. He walked the yard for some time, watching, calling out suggestions, appraising the efforts and skills of the warriors under his command. Soon, though, Davidh could not keep his thoughts here on what he was doing, for they drifted from the yard to the cottage at the top of the falls.

Was Anna up there now? Was her son with her? Though young, his presence might prove a deterrent if stragglers or strangers happened upon them. But with the outlaws that were proceeding with destruction and attacks on their minds…

Whether by design or not, Athdar, his training commander, called a halt then and the men dispersed from the yard. With a nod to his friend, Davidh left, too, but his path took him first to check on the lads, then to the falls.

The burning in his gut warned him there was no time to waste.

Chapter Twelve

Anna pressed back against the boulders as much as she could, hoping and praying that the men did not turn their attentions in her direction. Positioned as she was—only in an alcove in the face of the rocky hillside and one that was open to the fields—she held little confidence that she would not be seen. Of all the days to wear a gown of a brighter hue than her usual work gowns. This one would give her away to anyone looking rather than helping her to blend into the surrounding colours.

The three men argued once more among themselves, keeping their gazes away from her. She knew not what their purpose was when they entered the glen from the path along the hills, but finding her cottage and the well-tended garden changed their intentions. There had been almost nothing left within the cottage, but something had caught their interest.

She realised they'd grown quiet and Anna ducked down as far as she could, watching for a moment when escape might be possible. Unfortunately, to move from this shelter and get to either the path down or the other way out, she would expose herself to the men. Only when the three began to slowly shuffle off in different directions, did she understand the danger that she was in.

'Weel, now, what do we hiv here?' one said as he met her gaze and took a step towards her. 'A sweet treat for us before we head back?'

Anna glanced around her, looking for anything she could use as a weapon. The only thing she carried was the small knife she used to cut branches or blooms from the plants she tended and that would do little damage to these men. The crackle near by startled her and she looked up to see another of them approaching from the direction of the falls. The third one stepped closer and blocked her path to the garden and fields.

Trapped.

Escape…impossible.

Anna tried to stay calm, but her hands shook and her knees trembled.

'I want her first,' the one blocking her escape to the falls said. 'Ye had the other ones before I got 'em and I want this one.'

'Ye can have her,' the biggest one said, nodding his head and licking his lips in an obscene gesture. 'When I am finished wi' her, ye would no' want her.' His huge hand slid down below his belt and she looked away as he fondled himself.

She drew the knife from her belt, even knowing it would do little good, then bent down and picked up a rock she could use to slow them down. Her mouth went dry as they moved closer and the realisation of what was to come filled her thoughts. Pushing the terror back, she struggled to think of a way out. The idea came from where she knew not, but it was the only thing she could do. She lifted her head and called out in a loud voice to them, putting as much courage and confidence into her words as she could.

'Hear the Witch of Caig Falls!'

Silence met her words, but at least they did not move closer to her.

'I call on the spirits of the air, earth, fire and water—heed my call!' She slid the knife in her belt and dropped the rock, raising her arms out before her. 'Heed my call!'

The winds, thank God, moved just then, rustling through the trees around her and she nearly laughed at the stark expressions on the men's faces. Knowing she must get out of the alcove to even try to outrun them, she took a step forward.

'I call on my powers to rise and protect me!'

When they stumbled back away from her, Anna slowly slid her feet along the ground, trying to make her movements easy and gliding. 'I curse you all. You will suffer my wrath.'

'She's the witch who lives here!' the man closest to her yelled out. 'I dinna want to swive a witch!' Shaking his head and waving his hands at her, he stumbled back.

Anna took advantage of the moment and ducked and ran, trying to get past them before they could...

'Witch or no,' the big one said, grabbing hold of her arm and pulling her back, 'I will swive her.' He tossed her to the ground, the impact forcing the breath from her body.

'I will curse your...manhood and make it shrivel,' she forced out, pointing at that part of him.

'Curse it all ye like, witch,' the big one said, crouching down closer to her as he used his knee to trap her gown and keep her there. 'My manhood is just fine as ye will find out.'

As he slid his hands down to lift the plaid he wore and she knew her gamble had failed, Anna began to scream and struggle to free herself from his hold.

Then, after a moment of terror, he disappeared from above her and she could move. Scrabbling away, Anna slid back towards the rocks as someone intervened to save her from attack.

Davidh.

Davidh Cameron had saved her.

Anna watched in grim amazement as he knocked the largest man off his feet and then beat him into the dirt. Drawing his sword, he fought off the other two as they charged him with theirs. He moved in a graceful yet deadly dance, drawing them closer and then striking them down. They were dead before their bodies landed in the dirt. She could not take her gaze off Davidh as he defeated the three of them without pause and without a word.

Now, the three vanquished men lay silent and only the sound of his heaving breaths betrayed his exertion. And he still did not look at her. His right fist clasped the hilt of his sword and he held the weapon as though ready to face more foes. She had not noticed the smaller, yet still deadly, dagger in his left hand until now. Then he did turn, but instead of looking at her, he searched the area around the cottage and back into the gardens and fields.

'Were there only these three?' he asked, sliding the dagger into his boot and holding out his hand to her. She nodded in a jerky movement and reached out to take his help. Her legs wobbled as she gained her feet and he did not rush her.

'Did they come from the falls or from the stream?' he asked. His voice was calm. Too calm. She dared a glance at his face and the cold stare shocked her.

'The hills along the stream,' she said.

'Come. We must return to the village.' He guided her towards the cottage and then stopped. 'Can you make it to the path and wait for me there?'

He moved away before she replied, but he was the commander now and expected obedience to the orders he issued. She stumbled a few steps before her legs would obey her own commands and Anna tried not to look back. The racing of her heart made her want to run, run away, run fast, but she forced herself to walk, concentrating only on the sound of the falls and trying not to allow the fear to overpower her now.

A glance over her shoulder revealed him checking the three men who lay motionless on the ground there. Anna stopped and watched him then. He walked away from the two and towards the biggest man. A shudder tore through her as the possibilities of what could have happened had Davidh not arrived struck her. As he raised his head, looking around the clearing for something, he caught sight of her.

'Have you rope? Something to tie him with?' he called out to her.

Pulled from her helplessness, Anna nodded and ran back into the cottage. She'd not emptied it of all supplies—indeed, the necessary things used in the garden and fields remained there for use. Anna grabbed a coiled length of cord and took it to Davidh. His expression gave her pause.

'Come. 'Tis safe now.'

Only then did she realise that she stood but a few yards from him and that her hands shook. And her body trembled. The shudders paralysed her. The sight of the three men—two of them in darkening pools of their own blood and the other one unconscious there—made her stomach roil. Now unable to draw in a breath, her vision clouded and sweat poured down her face and back. The strength in her legs seeped out then and Anna began to tumble down.

'Anna.'

Davidh's strong arms surrounded her from behind and kept her from falling. He whispered her name over and over as he held her against his chest. Anna closed her eyes and tried to let go of the fear.

'Take in a breath,' he whispered against her hair. She shuddered in a shallow breath. 'Now, push it out with all your might.' She failed, for her breath trembled as her body yet did. 'Come now, lass, count as you draw a breath. Good. Now push out for the same.' Again, she could not control her body, but soon his soothing voice and warm embrace helped her to do as he said.

'Again,' he ordered in a soft yet commanding tone. 'One…two…three…'

Anna listened to his commands and obeyed them. When she noticed his heated breath as it tickled her ear, she knew she was recovering from the shock of the last minutes. She pushed up to stand on her own and, damn it, she noticed that he yet held her in his strong, warm embrace.

And in that moment, Anna did not want to be any other place in the world.

She closed her eyes, savouring the feel of his strength, his hard-muscled chest against her back, his breath now on her neck, the enticing scent that was his alone. It had been so long since she'd allowed anyone, any man, this close, and in that single moment, she did not want him to let her go.

Then, the cold truth of the situation struck her and she stepped away from him. Her body shivered as the day's cool air whirled through the inches of separation between them.

'Let me see to this and I will take you back to the village.' His calm, cool words reminded her that he was treating her no differently from how he would treat anyone he dealt with.

Anna held out the rope that was yet clenched in her hand and nodded. His movements now were swift and practised as he bound the outlaw who lay unconscious on the ground. In all her years, she'd never been accosted like this. Oh, some men had pressed their attentions with ardent enthusiasm, but none had ever attempted to take her against her will.

The shiver that coursed through her made her understand that the terror had not left her, no matter that she wanted it gone. She turned and walked to the opening in the hillside that led down to the road. Anna heard Davidh's approach and faced him. He took her hand and guided her down through the pathway along the falls. At one point, he slid his arm around her waist to support her. When they reached the bottom, she expected him to release her, but his arm remained around her. A few more paces and they stood at the road where his horse waited.

'Anna...' he began. Instead of releasing her, he turned her to face him and slid his other arm around her. 'Are you well?'

Before she could answer, he slid his hand up to cup her cheek as he stroked her with his thumb. Anna wanted to say aye, to say something, but the words escaped her when she met his gaze. His brown eyes darkened to almost black as he stared at her.

'I feared I would not get there in time,' he whispered. His hand slid around as he entangled his fingers in her hair, caressing the back of her scalp and sending tiny sparks of pleasure down her spine. 'I heard your scream…'

Anna watched until the very last moment, as he tilted down and touched his lips to hers. Then, she closed her eyes as he kissed her. It was madness. It was hot and possessive. It was…something wonderful and she leaned into him and gave herself over to it.

To him.

Davidh rarely felt terror. And, if he did, he did not admit to it. Even in the thick of battles or attacks, the excitement and danger of the challenge made him feel alive. But the sound of Anna's scream as he reached the top of the path had made his blood freeze in his veins. After killing the second and third outlaw, he'd turned and planned to kill the one who'd been standing over her. He'd gained control over his rage at the last moment and realised that a live outlaw could give them knowledge about the others who plagued their lands and clans.

The sight of her, lying on the ground, fighting for her life, overruled his usual battle calm. He'd never lost control in a fight before, yet seeing her there, terrified and screaming, tore it from him and he could only think one thing—destroy them. And he nearly had.

If not for her glancing over her shoulder, he would have thrust the bloodied sword into the fallen outlaw's gut. Her distress and the panic in her gaze stopped him and gave his self-control the chance to reassert itself. Then, his duty as commander took over as he tended to her and then secured the man so he could deal with him later.

Only now, as they reached a safe place, did he allow himself to take in all of her. Her braid had come undone and long, curling locks of auburn hair lay strewn wildly around her heart-shaped face and shoulders. Her forest-green eyes met his gaze and he wanted to lose himself in their depths.

Lose himself in her.

It was such a strange concept to him that he had no defence for it. Nothing to stop him from…kissing her.

Davidh raised his hand to her face, waiting for any sign of hesitation that would stop him. Instead, she lifted her cheek against his palm and a sigh so soft he doubted she heard it escaped her lips. He followed the sigh down and touched his mouth to hers. Sliding his hand into her loosened curls, he slipped his tongue into her heated mouth when she opened to him.

Sweet. She tasted sweet. Davidh lost himself in the pure delight of her mouth, sweeping his tongue deep in to savour the essence of her. That would have been the end of it, if she had not leaned her body against his and let out a soft moan.

Her full breasts pressed against his chest and his flesh responded against her hip. She opened more to his questing tongue and he delved deep into her mouth. Needing to possess her, Davidh slid his hands down over her shoulders and wrapped his arms around her, bringing her soft curves even nearer to him. When Davidh realised that her hands clutched his arms and pulled him closer, he turned the one long kiss into two and then three. Only when she lifted her lips from his to take a needed breath did he stop. She had not hesitated in accepting or taking those kisses. Drawing a breath in sharply, he leaned his forehead down against hers while they each caught their breaths.

For a long moment, they stood in that silent embrace. The amount of need racing through him shocked him. He wanted her to never let go. He wanted to kiss every part of her and explore her body endlessly. He wanted…

He would never know what sound gave him pause, but one did and he knew this moment was done. He gathered his wayward self-control and eased his hold on her. Easing a scant foot back from her, he still held her shoulders until she nodded and stepped away.

'Anna... I...' he stuttered out, but had no clue what he should be saying to her just then. Apologies? Explanations? Anything? She stopped him with the touch of her fingertips on his lips and a shake of her head. He chose to follow her example and nodded towards the road.

'My horse is there. Come,' he said, holding some branches out of her way. 'I need to send some of the men back here.'

He climbed up on his horse and held out his hand to help her up. She slid behind him and grabbed hold of his belt to steady herself. When Davidh felt she was ready, he touched his heels to the horse's sides, urging him to ride on. Many thoughts raced through his mind then, plans and arrangements and warnings to be seen to and dealt with now that the outlaws had ventured so close to the village.

And he spent the minutes riding back to Achnacarry doing that—until Anna shuddered behind him. Her body stiffened against his back, once and then twice. He drew up on the reins to stop when she whispered for him to go on. Davidh reached around with one arm and pulled her to sit before him. Then, after settling her across his thighs, he kicked the horse to a gallop.

'Hold on,' he ordered as the horse sped down the road.

He felt her hands slide around his waist, securing herself. Davidh ignored the warmth of her body against his. Well, he did until she leaned her head down on his chest and rested against him.

And, in that moment, something between them changed. More so even than in that kiss a short time ago. Something had shifted within himself and it unsettled him.

As he spied the first cottages of the village ahead of them, Davidh put all these thoughts aside to concentrate on his duties to his clan and chieftain. There would be time enough to sort the rest of this out later.

Chapter Thirteen

He'd ordered her to stay with Suisan and to summon the lads there, too. He'd commanded her in an unfamiliar voice to do several other tasks and then he rode off as fast as he could make the horse move towards the keep. Anna heard his voice calling out to villagers as he made his way to his chieftain and the other warriors.

And though his imperious attitude should have bothered her, it did not. What did make her uncomfortable was that kiss. Well, if truth be told, it was not the kiss so much as how much she had wanted it and wanted more than just a kiss. The safety of his embrace was dangerous to the purpose that had brought her to Achnacarry. The very thing she'd been ignoring these last few days. Anna turned now as a small group of men, riding hard and kicking up dust, passed her as she yet stood where Davidh had left her.

'Ye look pale as the moon,' Suisan said.

Standing now at Anna's side as another group of riders rode through the village, Suisan held up a small cup to her. 'Ye look like ye could use this.'

Anna watched as Davidh approached, riding this time at the chieftain's side. Though he appeared to slow as he grew closer, he stared at her and nodded as they continued on.

'Drink, lass.' Suisan nudged her and pressed the cup in her hand.

'Are you the healer now?' Anna asked as she lifted it to her mouth.

From the smell, it was some strong spirit used to fortify the body and not a concoction for healing. She swallowed it all and grimaced against the burn that spread down her throat and into her belly. Then a warmth spread through her bones and blood and the shivering that had begun anew eased.

'These outlaws grow bold,' Suisan said. 'And ever closer.' The older woman turned a keen gaze on Anna then. 'Were ye harmed?'

'Shaken about a bit and frightened,' Anna admitted. 'But Davidh got there…'

Before it could happen. The words were not spoken, but Suisan's knowing nod told Anna they were thinking of the same thing.

In a short time, word of the attack had spread as had the new orders from the chieftain—no one was to leave the village without permission or an escort. Both her Iain and Davidh's son had been spending much of their free time exploring the forests along the banks of Loch Arkaig as lads their ages did. She let out a breath she did not know she held in when the boys approached. Anna sent them off on some tasks to keep them occupied and, as she crossed her arms over her chest and rubbed her arms, she faced Suisan.

'So, who are these outlaws? They seemed to have no particular intentions in mind other than mayhem and stealing what they could find.'

Suisan entered her cottage and returned a few moments later carrying a woollen shawl. Anna accepted it and wrapped it tightly around her shoulders. Though she acknowledged to herself that the continuing shivers were more about the shock and terror that had yet to seep from her body than the coolness or warmth of the air around them.

'Some of those who supported the last chieftain,' Suisan said. In a shocking move, she turned and spat in the dirt at her feet. 'He betrayed the Camerons and is better off dead. May he…' she paused and spat again '…never rest in peace!'

'Suisan!' Anna whispered loudly. 'Never say such a thing.' Anna lifted her hand to make the sign of a cross over herself.

'Ye didna ken the man and the evil he did,

even against his own clan,' Suisan explained.
'When he was killed, those who supported him
either left on their own or were exiled by the new
chieftain. I have heard talk that these outlaws are
those and others trying to cause upheaval for the
laird and his family.'

Anna listened to the words and tried to piece
it together with what and with whom she knew.
The current chieftain was a younger brother to
Laird Euan who'd ruled when Anna's mother
lived here. Gilbert, as Suisan said, had laid
claim, as he was eligible to do, though Robert
was older and with a better claim. The reasons
for that became clear when it was discovered by
Robert's stepson that Gilbert had been plotting
with their enemies to take power to satisfy his
own greed and not for the good of the clan. A
battle of honour had ended Gilbert's life and the
high seat was claimed by Robert.

Neither Robert nor the now-dead Gilbert had
true claim to that rulership, Anna knew. Iain,
Malcolm's son, was the direct heir and the one
who should be leading the Cameron Clan. Or be
in line for that seat now. As Suisan continued
telling her the tale of how and when it had all
played out, all Anna could do was think of Malcolm and the unfairness of his missed chance to
rule over his clan.

Soon, the lads returned from their tasks and

Anna decided to return to Davidh's house instead of being in Suisan's way. As she watched her son, she knew she must press on with her promised plan. Iain must stop being a guest and take his place, his rightful place, in the Camerons. He must be allowed the chance to regain his claim to his heritage. And to do that, she must become a part of this village. Not a guest or visitor.

And she must gain Davidh's fuller co-operation.

Not just his protection because his laird had granted it to her. Nay, she needed his personal protection to assure success for her son. There were several ways that a woman could gain such protection from a powerful man. Anna needed to decide which she would pursue and then how to accomplish it. His kisses revealed one such path. But could she, who prided herself on never using such means to serve her aims, take that road?

She reached Davidh's house and stood staring at it as the boys passed her and ran inside. Right now, this was an equal arrangement—her help with his son for his with hers. Knowing his dedication to his duty and his loyalty to his people and his chieftain, he would not forgive her this deception—well, this omission as it was now.

All it took was one glance at Iain to remind her of her purpose and the rightness of it. He deserved…all of it. A life with his father's family and a chance to inherit the rights that came from his name. Anna pushed on and entered the house.

Even without the items she'd gone up to the cottage to retrieve, there were many things to accomplish today. But first, she added water to the kettle, tossed a few crumbled leaves in it and waited for it to boil. The fragrant aroma of betony filled the chamber and that scent began to help her relax, allowing the tension that yet controlled her to ease.

As she sipped the brew, Anna paced around the large room. The lads were in Colm's chamber. Iain was teaching, or trying to teach, the young boy to carve animals as he could. Her son showed great patience with Davidh's son, more than she had most times she was trying to demonstrate a recipe or procedure with the herbs and plants she used.

An hour or so passed as she returned to the tasks waiting for her attention. There were a few moments when the terror of this day faded and she seemed to forget the danger and the possible fate she'd faced. Caught up in the flow of memories and her attempts to ignore them, she did not hear him come in. She was alone in the large chamber and then she was not. Anna looked up from gazing at the floor as she yet paced before the hearth to find Davidh there.

'You were deep in thought and I did not wish to startle you,' he offered. As he walked across to where she stood, his gaze searched first her face, then the rest of her before coming back up to meet hers. 'What is in the pot?'

Anna blinked several times before she realised he'd asked her about something…something she did not remember. She turned and glanced at the pot over the fire, trying to bring to mind what she'd put in there to cook.

'I…' Anna walked over, wrapped her skirt around her hand and lifted the heavy lid to see inside. So, she'd not been as clearheaded as she'd thought. 'Soup,' she guessed from the sound and look of it. 'Soup.'

When she turned, he was there, so close she could hear his breathing. Then, he opened his arms and she walked into his embrace without hesitation or thought. Anna closed her eyes and lost herself in the warmth of him.

He'd watched her for a short while before she'd noticed him. In his experience, each person dealt with facing death or danger differently and would react in their own way. Anna had amazed him with her calm demeanour after the attack and even after panic had set in. Most women he'd seen in similar situations fell apart into hysterics or withdrew into themselves. Yet, she had maintained control over herself, returned to the village and saw to the daily chores.

As he held her now and breathed in the scent that was her, Davidh understood that a reaction could yet come. Sometimes, it was put off by duties or necessity. Yet, Davidh knew that the terror would bide its time and find its way out.

For now, though, he would hold her. He smiled over her head, accepting the very selfishness of his action. He held her because he wanted to. He wanted to hold her body next to his. He wanted to assure himself that she was well.

Though he'd tried to separate his thoughts of her from his own duties since he'd left her with Suisan, Davidh had thought of little else but Anna Mackenzie. The woman lifted her face then and met his eyes.

No tears. She'd not cried at all through this. And she did not now.

'I could get accustomed to this too easily,' she whispered.

The admission surprised her, for her eyes widened and she worried her bottom lip as though she knew she'd said too much. She tucked her head back against his chest as she had on the ride back.

'Aye.' He nodded without releasing her, realising that he could, as well. Had her words been filled with hope as he thought or with fear?

Davidh wanted to kiss her, yet he was content to just hold her in that moment. If she lifted her head and turned those green eyes to his, he would. For now, though, he would just hold her close. When the door to the smaller chamber opened without warning, they leapt away from one another as though caught in some guilty act.

Iain looked from him to his mother with a solemn expression that spoke of his knowledge of what he'd interrupted. But Colm had the innocence of a young age and did not.

'Supper will be ready soon,' Anna announced to the lads. 'Wash and get the bread.'

Iain and Colm jumped to her command, not hesitating for a moment to obey her. In such a short time—a week, was it?—they had fallen into a routine of a well-ordered household. Nay, if Davidh was being honest with himself, he saw that Colm thrived now.

He watched the boys act on her directions and Colm's ease of manner with her. His son walked to her side as she stirred the pot and tucked himself close, asking her about something. Anna touched his head and ruffled his hair as she answered and nodded. His heart pounded then, hammering in his chest, filled with both sadness and understanding.

His son had missed the warm touch of his mother for so long. Colm needed the soft care and concern that a mother gave without hesitation. Oh, the villagers, his friends, even others in the clan, had stepped forward in Davidh's time of need and helped care for the boy. Suisan was a stalwart friend who watched over Colm when Davidh was called to duty. His sister Aileen had returned for a time to help him.

Yet, from the gaze Colm directed at Anna as she answered yet another question of his, none had come close to what she had in this short time. When she had offered to care for his son, Davidh had not known how much he'd wanted this exact thing to happen. Not until now. Not until he witnessed them together like this. Anna turned in that moment and met his gaze.

Rather than the tension or fear he'd noticed in her green eyes earlier, now he saw only confidence and caring. She moved with the ease of a woman who liked what she did and was good at it. But then, she'd been a mother for nigh to ten-and-three years and had taken good care to see her own son raised. One look at the boy and he could tell that she'd put his welfare and needs above hers.

Her very presence here—returning to a place after years and with no other connection than his parentage—spoke of bravery and strength. Very few women he knew would leave their homes and travel to a distant village alone. Without a promise of marriage or other assurance of a place. Yet, Anna had done just that. And she'd slid into village life easily, making a valued place for herself.

And now, Davidh would keep his part of their bargain.

The table set, they gathered around it and began eating. Though she'd seemed unaware of what it was, the soup was thick and flavourful and filling. At Anna's nod, Iain took up the bread and broke it into four pieces, offering Davidh and Anna the larger two before giving a chunk to Colm and himself. When they'd eaten for a bit, Davidh spoke.

'I need the two of you to have a care these next days,' he said. 'You ken that outlaws have been seen outside the village.' Anna's eyes darkened as he spoke, but her gaze turned not to him but to her son. 'So, until I tell you otherwise, you are not to leave the village.' A few groans met his order, but this was necessary.

'These outlaws are dangerous. They have left death and mayhem in their path around Tor Castle and now seem to have got closer to Achnacarry and the surrounding area.'

'What about fishing in the loch?' Colm asked.

'We were to go on the morrow.' His son nodded at Iain as he spoke. 'If there are two of us?'

'Nay. Not without my permission and not without guards.' They protested with grunts and groans, but Davidh continued. 'No one leaves the village without my say so or one of the other commanders.' He put down his spoon and waited for the lads to look at him. 'Parlan returns here on the morrow.'

'Parlan?' Anna asked.

'He is my second. Lately he has been in charge of the defences at Tor Castle. Robert wishes him here now that the outlaws have become so brazen so close.' The fire crackled then and she turned to look at it. He did not miss the shiver that trembled through her then.

'We will find them and bring them to justice, Anna.' She nodded before turning back to look at him.

'Are there any other restrictions we need follow?' she asked, nodding now at the lads. 'Iain, pay heed to the commander now. Colm, you as well, heed your father in this.'

It took little time to explain the limitations in place now and until the outlaws were stopped. They were obedient lads who would listen and have a care during this threatening time. He finished with the news he wished most to share.

'On the morrow, Iain will begin working with

Lachlan Dubh. He will meet you at the stables after you break your fast and see to your training.'

'The stables?' Anna asked while smiling at her son, pleased with this step.

'Aye. He is overseeing some repairs there. He will assess Iain's skills and assign him to work in the place where those abilities can best be used.'

Iain beamed with happiness at Davidh's words and Anna reached out to pat her son's arm. 'You will do your best, Iain.'

'Aye, I will. My thanks, sir,' the lad said in a solemn tone.

'What will I do?' Colm said.

Davidh looked at the expectation in his son's expression and wondered. For the last few months, he'd been too ill to do much. He'd spent most of his time at Suisan's.

'I need your help, Colm,' Anna said. 'That has not changed.' His son's eyes filled with joy. 'And if Iain is working elsewhere, I expect to need even more help from you.'

'Truly?' Colm asked.

'Truly. Who else would help me clean out the lady's stillroom in the keep but you?'

The meal was finished in silence, but even Davidh could feel the ripples of expectation in the boys now. He caught Anna's gaze over their heads a time or two and she smiled at him. Mayhap their bargain would work out for all?

The evening had passed quickly and the two excited boys went to their pallets without argument. With the meal cleaned up and chores completed, Davidh had left for a short time to make certain the guards were posted as he'd ordered. When he returned, he found Anna seated on the steps that led up to his front door.

'Is aught well?' he asked. She did not seem upset. With a thick shawl around her shoulders and a steaming cup in her hands, she looked quite comfortable.

'They've only now dropped off to sleep. I just wanted to sit in the quiet before retiring.'

Although he would have sat at her side, the apparent dismissal kept him standing. 'Then I will leave you to your thoughts.'

'Nay,' she said.

It was not the word, but her hand on his leg that stopped him from moving. For a moment, he thought, or maybe hoped, she would slide it up on to the bare skin above his boot.

'You do not have to leave,' she whispered as she shifted aside to allow him room to join her there. Davidh stepped back down, turned and sat there at her side.

They sat in the growing darkness in silence

for a short time. From time to time, she lifted the cup to her lips and sipped whatever she'd made. Aromas of some unknown herbs wafted across the short distance to him, but he could not identify them.

''Tis mostly betony with a bit of honey added.' She laughed then and the sound of it teased him to smile. 'You were sniffing so I thought you were curious. I can get you some?'

'Nay, but my thanks for the offer.'

'Iain is very excited about the arrangements you've made for him. Anxious to get started,' she clarified.

'And you? Are you anxious for it?' he asked.

She did not respond at first. Sipping her tea gave her a moment or two of reprieve and then she nodded. 'Aye. I am.'

He thought she might explain, but he'd learned that when it came to her son, she held her confidences—and his—close. Then she let out a long, soft sigh and nodded again.

'I have wanted to return here since the first step I took away. And I've wanted to bring Iain back from the second he was born. Sometimes, Davidh, I cannot believe we are here.'

She tipped the cup back and finished the brew before standing. Davidh rose and realised she stood on the step and not the ground, bringing her face level with his. Anna leaned forward and braced herself on his shoulders then.

'I will keep Colm busy with helping me. That way he will not be restless and tempted to disobey your orders,' she promised.

His body reacted to her nearness and to her touch. Suddenly, he worried not for his restless son, but for his own restless desires. Davidh moved and met her halfway across the space that divided them. He wanted to kiss her. He wanted to know the taste of her betony tea with honey. He wanted…

And when she opened her mouth and drew in a shallow breath, he leaned the rest of the way to capture her lips. The touch of her tongue on his revealed the flavour of her tea—honey-sweet with a bitter tang. Sweet and sour. She made the most enticing sound as he thrust in to taste more of her. When she'd wrapped her arms around his shoulders, he knew not, but she held on tight now and he felt the softness of her body against the hardness of his.

How he noticed the noise of people approaching over the roar of want and need in his blood, he knew not. Davidh wrapped his arms around her waist, lifted her from her feet and carried her up the steps and into the house through the slightly open door. Still kissing the breath from her, he circled around and pressed her against the wooden door and lifted his head to look at her.

Her eyes glazed with passion, her mouth pulled in shallow, heated breaths and her hands slid into his hair and pulled him back to her. Now, she kissed him, sliding her tongue into his mouth, and Davidh let her. He pressed the length of him, and the unruly flesh between his legs, against her as she held him tightly to her body. Easing to stand between her legs, he felt pleasure as she lifted her legs and encircled his hips, all the while never taking her mouth from his.

Davidh rocked his hardness against her, wanting to be so much closer. She canted her own hips and he slid his hands beneath her to give her support. It would take little to tug the skirt of her gown and shift out of their way and do what they both wanted to do. He would fill her flesh with his and give her pleasure until she screamed.

Once more, an awareness of their precarious position—against the door—and the possibility of discovery or of being witnessed stopped him. When he lifted his mouth from hers, she pushed her head back and it met the door's unforgiving surface with a thump. One followed by her moan of pain.

'That sounded as though it hurt,' he whispered, still holding her as she slid her legs down along his until her feet reached the floor.

'I deserve it,' she muttered as they stepped apart and her skirts fell around her legs. Rubbing the back of her head, she looked up at him. Her lips were swollen from his kisses and it made him smile.

'Nay,' he said as he moved out of her way. He rubbed his hand over his face and wondered what she was thinking. ''Twas just a kiss.'

'I fear it is a sign of a bigger problem between us,' she said softly. 'And I neither want nor claim that you inflicted yourself on me. I started it.'

He watched as she moved around the chamber, putting out the lanterns and banking the fire, all the while muttering under her breath. After a few minutes of a conversation with no one but herself, Anna stood before the chamber she shared with her son. Without another word, she disappeared silently inside.

Davidh let out the breath he'd been holding. Shoving his hand through his hair, he shook his head, completely lost after their encounter. She'd kissed him...again. Oh, he'd kissed her back and would have continued this bit of love play as far and as long as she would have allowed.

Thankfully, she had the good sense to stop. He had no doubt he would have taken her against the door. A woman who had been bodily attacked by outlaws this very day and he was thrusting against her here just hours later.

She did not act as most women would if they'd faced what she had. Then the truth struck him. Davidh walked to the cupboard and found the small jug of *uisge-beatha* and lifted it to his lips, forgoing a cup that would serve to slow him down. He drew deeply and swallowed the potent liquid. As the burn spread into his gut, spreading warmth from there, Davidh understood her actions.

After such a threat as the one she'd faced, she was testing herself. Men under his command did the same thing in their training after being beaten or injured. They pushed themselves into the same activity that had hurt them, but only with someone whom they trusted to see them safely through it. One of his men had been stabbed when a quarterstaff had broken and pierced him in the leg. Once healed, it had been Davidh himself that Geordie had challenged, knowing that Davidh would see no harm came to him.

That kiss, more than the one earlier, was a test. Anna pushed against the terrors of assault she'd faced this day, knowing he would not take advantage of her weakness or fears. That he would stop when she needed him to.

His flesh surged then, aching and swollen, reminding him that he had not realised the purpose or cause of this encounter with Anna until it had stopped. He'd simply wanted her kiss, her caress, her body against his. God help him if she continued to test herself and him in this manner!

The strong spirit began to ease him then, so he took one more swallow and put the cork back in the jug. At least he was now armed with the understanding he needed to keep her approaches, and kisses, in perspective.

He told himself that all through the night and even into the next day as his body and mind seemed as agitated with anticipation as his son was. But his restlessness had little to do with the work he faced and more with the woman who slept just a yard away from him in the other bedchamber.

Chapter Fourteen

The light that pierced the darkness through a window high on the wall made the floating dust appear as burning snowflakes. They filled the chamber now, scattered by Anna's feverish swipes across the tops of the dozens and dozens of glass and glazed jars and bottles there on the long table.

The dust danced in that bright stream and then drifted back down towards the place where she'd cleaned. For a moment, she lost herself in the way the tiny specks shimmered there. As she stared at them, these sparkly bits reminded Anna of the way the lantern's light had reflected in Davidh's eyes as he leaned in and kissed her. Somehow, the flickering light of the burning lamp found shades there in what she'd thought were simply brown eyes.

Gold and silver hidden deep within the browns and the flickering light had caught the sparkles.

A long, soft sigh escaped her once more. Leaning back against the table, she shook her head and tried to concentrate on the task, the very large task, at hand. She'd lost too much time this day falling into memories of that kiss.

That kiss.

She touched her lips then, for his mouth on hers and the possessive way he claimed hers made hers swell.

It would have been a simple kiss had she not lost control of the growing desire that seemed stronger with each encounter. She had pressed against him and even wrapped herself around his tall, muscular body in a very scandalous manner. Never having been the one to initiate such things, it surprised Anna that she would have done such a thing, especially on the same day as the attack. It was almost as though the vulnerability after the attack that day had unleashed a need in her. All the while, she knew that Davidh would never harm her or take advantage or take more than she willingly offered. A strange balance of fear and comfort had urged her on to do what she'd done.

The problem was that she wanted to offer him anything she had to give. She wanted him in a way that was different from any man she'd met since Malcolm. There had been discreet and short-lived involvements in the last few years, but they'd meant nothing and were over and done quickly. What Anna truly feared was that this was more than a need to be satisfied with a few bouts of bed play.

It was also something she would need to face if she and her son would be staying here in Achnacarry among the Camerons. Particularly if she was remaining in his house. She'd never considered that being in such close quarters—something that was necessary to bring her son into closer dealings with his clan—would have been so dangerous to her own self-control.

Maybe there was something here among the good brother's concoctions and tonics that could cool her desire for the commander? Anna chose a dark brown bottle of some thick syrup and pulled the cork free releasing a terrible smell into the chamber. She quickly pushed the stopper back in and replaced the bottle in the line with the others. No matter how effective that potion might be, she would never be able to swallow it.

So, she would have to find another way to deal with this attraction to Davidh and not let it interfere with her overall ambitions. Then, a wicked thought occurred to her—mayhap it was not a bad thing after all?

He was an honourable man, one of the most honourable she'd ever encountered, and she was as certain of that as she was that he would never expect her to sleep with him in exchange for his help. From his original offer, it was clear he was trying to avoid that very thing.

Would it be such a bad thing if she did take him to her bed? The heat rose in her cheeks then as the memories of their kisses and their embraces filled her thoughts. Aye, she wanted him. Aye, he wanted her. And yet, because of his honour, he would have nothing to do with her when he discovered she'd deceived him. Would it be so terrible if she allowed herself the physical comfort he would give for the short time before he found out the true identity of her son?

Anna sighed then, unwilling to examine that too closely. Her mother had warned her there would be complications and problems if she returned here at all, but most especially if she came back with her son. The past, her mam said, did not lie still or easy when power was at stake.

Her son was at the heart of the struggle for power here.

With the right protector, he could rise to his rightful place—tanist of the Clan Cameron. With the right man guiding Iain, he could be the chieftain that his father should have been. Davidh Cameron, she was certain, was that man.

There would be time to decide all of these things and now she needed to sort through more of this chamber's secrets. Her reactions to the commander were what they were and nothing she worried over in this moment would change them.

Anna turned her efforts and thoughts back to cleaning and lost herself in her task. Colm had been sent on his way to eat and, please God, rest at Suisan's and he would seek her out after that.

When the dust swirling in the chamber brought on incessant sneezing, she pushed a small table over into a position under the window. Climbing up, she yet had to stand on her toes to reach it. It was only when she heard the door to the chamber open that she realised that Colm was returning much too soon.

'Papa!' Davidh turned at Colm's call and watched as he walked to the fence that separated them.

The colour in the lad's cheeks was a welcome change from the pallor of the last months. Davidh found himself listening to Colm's words and breathing as he approached to determine if he was doing too much.

'How goes it?' Davidh asked. 'Is Mistress Mackenzie keeping you busy?'

'Aye,' he said as he climbed up on the fence. 'I have emptied boxes and bottles all morn. Now, I am going to Mistress Suisan's to eat.' Colm frowned then. 'And to rest.' He shrugged then.

'If, if, I need to. Mistress Mackenzie said that I should think on it when I get there.'

'And what do you think you will do?' he asked. Davidh noticed the tightness around his son's mouth and knew it for what it was—his son had done too much. 'Do you think you need to rest?'

Another shrug was his answer. Davidh reached out and tousled his son's hair.

'Do not be stubborn, Colm. Mistress Mackenzie is too soft in giving you directions and letting the choice be yours. You ken what I would say?'

Colm jumped down to the ground and nodded, reluctant acceptance in his gaze. 'I should rest.'

'Aye. For if you rest now, you will be able to do more later. When your friends finish their chores and are ready to play.'

Once more, the similarity to Mara's expression—the stubborn tilt there in Colm's chin, the roundness of his eyes—struck him. Colm's illness had forced on him a maturity and a respect that Davidh wished he did not have, so when faced with decisions in his control, his son usually considered them well before acting.

Usually. Davidh tried not to think of the dangerous decision that had ended with Colm trapped on the side of the Caig Falls. At Colm's nod, Davidh felt relief.

'If I rest, if, it means that Mistress Mackenzie is left alone to work in the stillroom.'

'Does she need help then?' Davidh glanced around for a moment to see which man he could send to her. But only for a moment. The urge to find her and speak to her grew within the space of a breath to almost an uncontrollable need.

'Some of the boxes are heavy and she cannot move them without help,' his son said, puffing out his chest with pride that he'd been able to do that.

'I will send someone to check on her until you are able to return. Fear not, there will be plenty to do upon your return.'

Davidh understood well that part of the improvement in his son had to do with how needed he believed he was. Anna comprehended that, too, and her request for Colm's help was more for his benefit than hers. Giving his son the reassurance that this brief respite did not diminish that was a small thing to do. As Colm smiled and nodded, Davidh knew he'd succeeded in that.

'Go now. I can hear your stomach rumbling even from here!'

Colm walked off, chattering to himself as he did, and Davidh watched him. Anna had ordered that he not run and so the lad did not, but his pace was brisk. Davidh did not move until Colm passed through the gates.

'Going somewhere?' Damn it, he'd forgotten that Parlan was there.

'Aye.' Their assignments were complete and there was time before Davidh needed to meet with the chieftain and his son. 'Colm said...' Parlan waved off his words before he could say them.

''Tis the healer?' Davidh nodded. 'I want to meet this woman who distracts you so.'

'I am not... She does not... Robert...'

Nothing Davidh could say would either explain or placate his suspicious friend at this moment. The knowing expression in Parlan's gaze and the irritating smile on his face made that clear. And made Davidh want to punch him in that face.

'Come to supper and you will meet her.'

Then he strode away, ignoring his friend's laughter, as he made his way into the keep and down to the stillroom.

He'd not been alone with her since that explosive kiss two nights ago. Surrounded by their sons and then villagers, friends and others, they'd not spoken of it yet. But every small contact or exchange between them made his skin tight. It made his breathing race and his cock rise. No matter how incidental or innocent, his body reacted and the heat in his veins built.

Did she feel it as he did? Davidh turned into

the corridor that led to the chamber and held his breath. Aye, she did. She felt it. He could see it in her manner and in the way her body seemed to call to his. She wanted him. And though their arrangement was a simple one not involving bed play, the way he wanted her would cause all sorts of complications.

Oh, aye, there would be issues.

Letting out his breath and planning his words, he lifted the latch and pushed the door open. He lost his breath again.

Anna stood on a table, reaching up for the latch on the window that sat high up on the wall. Her hair tumbled loosely down her back, freed from the usual constraint of a braid and held away from her face only by a kerchief. Her breasts strained against her gown and his body remembered the feel of them against his chest when she pulled him to her. She glanced over her shoulder and lost her balance.

In three strides, Davidh caught her as she fell off the table. Her little scream stopped as she landed in his arms. An open-mouthed gasp was the only sound she made as he shifted his hold on her. One of his hands slid under the curve of her buttocks and she trembled at his grasp. Davidh turned her in his embrace so that she faced him and the feel of her body against his made him suck in a breath.

'Anna.'

He pulled the kerchief from her head, needing to feel the curls. She did not resist or hesitate; indeed, she shook her head, making those curls cascade down her back. Her feet did not touch the floor as he drew her closer. He slid one hand to the back of her head and he tilted her so that he could…

'Kiss me, I pray you.' Her plea was barely out of her mouth when he complied. Willingly.

He brought his mouth to hers and she opened to him, allowing him to sweep his tongue inside to taste her. No honey-sweetened betony this time, just her own flavour and just as sweet. Davidh did not kiss her—he took her mouth, he possessed her mouth, he claimed it. Until he was breathless, he did not stop. Over and over, with one hand holding her head to his and the other supporting her buttocks. He held her to him and kissed the very breath out of her. He lifted his mouth from hers and they shared the very air between them.

'Anna…' he began.

'I want you, Davidh Cameron. Damn me for it, but I want you.' A fleeting change in her gaze confused him. For just a moment, he thought he saw sadness there, but it was gone. He could see the frank desire gazing back at him now.

'And I want you, Anna Mackenzie,' he whispered back as he feathered kisses across her cheeks and on her jaw. 'I have wanted you since I saw you there above the falls.'

Her response was not in words but action. She separated her legs around his and placed her hands on his shoulders. He eased her down on to the edge of the table behind her and waited. There was a nigh unrecognisable part of him that urged him to take her, to take her now. The strength of it shocked him. It thrilled him. Yet, he waited on her word or deed.

'Touch me, Davidh. I have wanted to feel your hands on me since I watched you from above the falls.' She lifted her legs, easing her knees up until they clasped his hips. 'Touch me now.'

His cock surged then, wanting to fill that place between those strong thighs. His hands itched and his mouth watered as he watched her angle her body back, making all of her open to him. He wrapped his hands around her head and kissed her deeply, their tongues dancing and swirling and tasting. Her body arched, bringing her breasts to him and he made his way down her jaw and delicate throat towards them.

Davidh suckled the tender skin of her neck and slipped his hands down to caress her breasts. Even through the layers she wore, he felt them swell as she pressed them into his grasp. She moved her hands to the table's surface to support herself, giving him an unimpeded path to her. With her head leaned back, she gasped at each touch of his mouth on her neck and she rocked against him when he rubbed his thumbs over the now-taut nipples.

With quick movements, he tugged at the laces of her gown and then her shift and pulled the garments open until he could see her lovely breasts. Her eyes had drifted closed as he'd kissed her, though now they watched his hands as Davidh cupped her breasts. Her breaths quickened until she panted at his touch. When he leaned down to kiss there, she let out a moan that he felt from his erect flesh into the very marrow of his bones.

He drew the rosy tip of one breast into his mouth and swirled around it with his tongue. When Davidh suckled on it, Anna moaned aloud. He continued as her legs tightened around his hips. He lavished the same attention on one and then the other, gently pressing against her until she lay on the table before him. Drawing the length of her gown and shift up over her legs, he caressed his way up each one until he was so near the place he wanted to touch that he could feel the heat of her flesh there.

As he slid his fingers through the curls and touched the very centre of her heat, a wicked desire shot through him. Easing back, he guided her legs up and over his shoulders as he crouched before her. Then, with his lips and tongue and fingers, he stroked her feminine flesh, sliding into the centre of her and suckling on that tiny little bud of flesh between her legs.

His own flesh surged, lengthening, thickening and pulsing, as he tasted her essence. With long strokes of his tongue, he pushed her on. With slow and fast strokes of his fingers, he rubbed there, diving inside her as she rocked against his mouth and hands. He felt the vibrations within her begin and he pushed her towards satisfaction. He lifted his head and the sight of her—dishevelled, aroused and still in the last throes of release—nearly unmanned him.

'Davidh.'

She lifted her head and met his gaze, yet it was the throaty whisper that stirred him even more than he thought was possible. He slowly stood, keeping her legs around his waist. Grasping her hips, he tugged her to the very edge of the table and then reached down and lifted his plaid.

Anna's bones had melted. Her skin was on fire. Her flesh throbbed in satiety and ached with need. When he pulled her to him and reached under his plaid, her body arched, opening and waiting for his. She leaned up on her elbows and watched as he grasped the length of his flesh and pressed it into the swollen folds between her legs.

That initial gentle pressure changed to a powerful thrust, as he rocked his hips and filled her. It felt, he felt, wonderful there. His hardness pushed in deep and she lifted her hips to take in every inch of him. Then he eased out and pushed back in, over and over, as that tight trembling built again within her. It stole her breath and her reasoning. When he leaned down and suckled on her breast as he continued to pump into her, she knew she would fall apart. Reaching up, she tangled her fingers in his hair and held on to him. She lost control and lost herself as she fell over some unknown boundary into a full measure of satisfaction.

He lifted his head, his face tightened almost as if in pain, and then he moaned out in a deeply male, almost possessive way as his seed began to release. Only at the last moment, he pulled out of her body and spilled within the folds of his plaid. For some minutes, only the sounds of their panting breaths echoed around them in the chamber.

Anna finally came back to herself as he stepped back, drawing her shift and gown down over her legs as he did so. She took his hand and sat up, sliding from the table on unsteady legs. Davidh did not move completely away from her then. Instead, he leaned over and kissed her. This was a kiss so unlike the ones before that its gentleness made her tremble.

'I am at a loss for words right now,' he said then.

She was not certain what she wanted him to say or what she wanted to hear in this moment. He startled her when he reached up and touched her head. Holding out a feather to her, he laughed.

'I think there is even a nest of birds in this chamber,' she said, taking it from him.

'You have quite a task ahead of you,' he said. 'How long do you think this will take you?' He stepped back then and she ached for his return.

'Well, with the other things I have to see to in the village and the gardens, I planned to spend some time here each day until I finish it.' His eyes glimmered just then and she wondered at that.

He opened his mouth to say something else when his name was roared down the corridor outside the chamber. Whatever he'd planned to say was lost in a harsh curse as he walked to the door and lifted the latch.

'Parlan! I am here,' he said just as someone stopped outside the chamber. 'Anna, I will see you at supper. Can you accommodate Parlan at table this evening?'

'I will make enough,' she said.

With a nod, he was gone, pushing the man called Parlan out before he could enter. Anna could not understand what was said in the hushed exchange between the men, but she suspected that this Parlan was well aware of what had just happened here.

If they were not careful, word would spread and trouble could start. As she tried over the next hour or so to accomplish some of what she must here, Anna realised that, no matter the pleasure she'd experienced with him, trouble was not what she needed or wanted here in Achnacarry. Not until she had secured her son's place. Then it would not matter.

Chapter Fifteen

Two days had passed since Davidh had lost his mind and his control and, well, had taken Anna on the table in the stillroom. There was no excuse for such a thing other than… Well, there simply was no excuse. He would have asked her pardon for his actions, yet she had welcomed them.

He could admit to himself that entering his house that evening had given him pause. He'd even gone as far as to bring Parlan with him to avoid facing her alone. Other than a quick flashing in her green eyes at his entrance, he found no difference in her manner towards him.

Parlan served his purpose at supper, too. He'd kept the conversation lively, dividing his attention between the boys and Anna. Davidh could admit another thing to himself—Anna could keep up with Parlan's quick wit and teasing manner. Had his friend always been that way with women or only with her?

Only when Parlan asked, as he left to return to the keep after the meal, if Davidh had any claim on Anna, did his friend's intentions become clear. Parlan explained that he asked because others had asked it of him, but Davidh suspected otherwise. When Davidh quickly denied any such thing, Parlan laughed at first and then claimed it was a good thing.

The strangest of encounters and things had begun happening ever since then.

Several times now, Davidh had been invited to sup with two widows and three other families who all seemed to have daughters of a marriageable age. Then, Lilias had appeared at the fence surrounding the training yard and waited for him to approach her. He did not ever remember seeing the widow inside the walls of Achnacarry and now here she stood.

'Lilias, is there something wrong?' he asked, expecting some dire tale that needed his attention.

'Nay, Davidh. I just have not seen ye lately, with yer duties to the laird and such, and wanted to speak with ye.'

Confused even more by the way she reached up to smooth her hair out of her face and touch her lips, Davidh waited for her to continue.

When Lilias slid her hands down the skirts of her gown and adjusted her *arisaidh* around her shoulders, exposing more of her face to him, he caught on to what her true message was.

'Would ye come to supper tomorrow evening?'

And stay the night were the words she did not say aloud, but that he could hear clearly. He'd not visited her or her bed for some time and the thought of it soured his stomach.

'I fear not, Lilias. Though I thank you for your kind offer.'

Simple. Plain. Words meant to stop this before it went further. They had enjoyed the pleasure of bed play several times when the need came upon him and she was amenable, yet he knew she wanted more than that. He'd been very deliberate in his words and actions to not allow those expectations to grow. Or he thought he had. Now, Davidh stepped away from the fence and began to turn from her. The colour rose in her face and her mouth tightened to a thin line.

''Tis the witch, is it not? She has woven her spell around ye to make certain ye will not stray!' The words were uttered in a vehement whisper, filled with anger and...jealousy?

Davidh took a step closer, forcing the woman to look up at him. Leaning down so that only she could hear his words.

'Not that it is *any* concern of yours, but there is no witch and *Anna Mackenzie* is my house-keeper.'

'Call it what ye will, Davidh. Everyone kens whose bed she is sharing.' She crossed her arms over her chest and nodded at him.

'She has not shared my bed, Lilias.' For a moment, just a single one, he regretted the very fine line of truth he was standing on with his words. But this kind of talk—about Anna being a witch and about them being…intimate—could not go unchallenged.

'Och, aye, I remember yer preferences for coupling against the wall or door.' Her eyes lit then with desire. 'Yer strong body pressing mine against the door that it nearly buckled when the passion took ye.'

A memory surged forward in his thoughts, but not of this widow. Of Anna's face as he kissed her until she was breathless…against the door of his house. At Lilias's laugh, he suspected that memory must have shown on his face.

'Aye, like that. Just like that,' she said with a nod.

Correct memory, wrong woman. There had been no other woman in *his* bed since Mara.

'Well, how I swive and who I take to my bed or on my door is no concern of yours, Lilias.' Her eyes flared then. 'And the widow Mackenzie is under the chieftain's protection. So, you had better think about what lies or stories you spread about her. And what you call her.'

Now the red flushing in her cheeks drained and Lilias stepped back, lowering her gaze to the ground. Without another word, she drew her cloak around her head and stalked off, but not before muttering some words under her breath that he could not discern.

Davidh wanted to roar out his anger to the sky. Lilias meddled. It was what she and many other women in the village did best. She also gossiped. Though it was a natural thing when living in a village or kcep, he supposed. Yet Lilias collected secrets and suspicions and then dealt them out when it benefited her. He'd seen it before while it had not mattered to him.

Now, though, it did.

When he glanced around, he realised that all the small groups of his men training there had shifted away from him. Parlan, *damn* the man, stood across the yard, leaning against the fence there and listening to Athdar's counsel while watching Davidh. He could almost see the knowing smirk on his friend's face and, tempted though he was to smash it off there, Davidh did not wish to engage with Parlan in a discussion of women.

When Davidh caught sight of the men working on the stable walls, he strode off to see how Iain was doing in his new assignment there. He found the man who was overseeing the lad inside.

'He's a good one,' Lachlan said. Nodding at Anna's son, the man continued. 'Sees to his tasks and his work is strong.'

'Has he shown you his carvings?' Davidh asked. Iain was working with a few others on building an extension on to the stables at the moment. 'He is quite skilled at fine work.'

'Nay, but I have kept him quite busy with the things we need done here.' Lachlan smacked Davidh on his back. 'First what we need, then I will turn him loose to see what he can do best.'

'He has had no one to teach him.' While they were talking, Iain noticed him and came to him.

'Is aught wrong? You are both frowning at me,' the lad said. Davidh smiled and shook his head.

'Nay, nothing is wrong, Iain,' he said. 'I was telling Lachlan that you've had no teacher and yet have skills with carving and woodwork.'

'I am willing to work, sir,' Iain said, much too seriously for a boy of his age.

'A good thing,' Davidh said.

Someone called out Iain's name and he returned to the small group where he'd been working. He studied the boy for a few minutes and noticed that Iain seemed to be at ease in working with others. The lad had, without realising it, been starving for the comradery that came from finding a place within a group of men.

'For a moment,' Lachlan began, 'he looked like...' He stopped and shook his head.

'He looked like...who?'

'Nay. Seeing him next to you, I thought of...' Lachlan laughed then. ''Tis nothing. Forgive an old man's failing sight, lad.'

'He has the nose, does he not?' Davidh asked. It was one of the first similarities that Camerons shared that Davidh had noticed in Iain's features.

Davidh let Lachlan go back to his duties and returned to his. An hour or two of pounding Parlan into the dirt would feel good and would help him release some of the anger that yet ran in his veins.

Aye, smashing the arrogance off his friend's face would be satisfying indeed.

When the third man knocked on the door of the stillroom, Anna understood that there would be no peace this morn. She'd left the door ajar to help air out the mustiness and that seemed to invite no visitors *except* of the male kind.

Baen's father, Uilleam, who worked in the keep, had been first with his offer to move the heavier tables around if she needed it done.

And, would she sup with him in the hall this night? Then, Tormod, a brewer, came by, asking if she had enough supplies and if she would sup with him on the morrow. Now, Kenneth, the butcher, stood there asking if she needed any special meats to prepare her brews and broths and would she sup with him in his cottage...with his three grown sons.

Unfortunately, she'd seen this before. Though almost too young to understand it when they moved north to her mother's clan, this was wooing, plain and simple. Many village men had approached her mother, a widow, with such offers of help and requests for companionship once they'd arrived and were made known to the people living there.

A healer with skills such as her mother's would always be in demand. A widow capable of caring for and bearing bairns would always be sought out by men in need of one or the other. A woman willing to warm the bed of a man in need was always desired.

Anna let out a sigh as Kenneth nodded and walked out of the stillroom. For better or worse, she was all three of those and word was getting around. All her plans to blend unobtrusively into the people here were over. That she had caught Davidh's attentions—whether as friend or something else—gave a signal to other men. And though he had not approached her or touched her or in way showed interest in her outside the privacy of his own house since that day, word must also be out among the men that she was available.

Anna gathered up what she needed from the bottles and jars she'd checked, cleaned and organised and filled her basket. Since sweat still beaded on her face and trickled down her back from her work, she tossed her cloak over her arm and pulled the door until it was nearly closed. No one would enter without her permission or that of Laird Robert or Lady Elizabeth.

With a mind to peek at Iain as he worked, she left the keep, crossed the yard and sought a shadowed corner from which to observe him without being noticed. The men were working to expand one side of the stables and were constructing the walls now after having cleared and levelled the ground. Iain stood there in the midst of it all.

For a moment, when he turned at someone's call, he resembled his father so much it made her gasp. She covered her mouth so her position would not be exposed. Iain was adding inches to his height by the day and, with the colour of his hair growing darker each year, he looked much like Malcolm did the year they'd met.

She'd heard that Mal had had a twin, a sister, born just a few minutes before him and that their colouring was as different as two could be. The girl, Arabella, was fair-haired with light eyes and, even in her youth, her beauty and graciousness was spoken of by everyone who'd met her. Even Lara Mackenzie, the witch of Caig Falls, had been impressed.

Mal was born with darker hair and eyes and a completely different disposition from his sister, her mam had said. He relished his role as the chieftain's son and was on his way to becoming one of the best warriors in the Cameron Clan.

Then he was killed, not by Brodie Mackintosh as was first reported, but by Caelan, his cousin, who was intent on taking control of the mighty Mackintosh Clan and the larger confederation that ruled over great swathes of the Highlands.

Now, watching her son as he worked with the others, all she could see was his father in his every move and every smile. Tears trickled down her cheeks and she tucked back into the shadows lest anyone see her.

'The lifting and carrying will add to his strength.'

The soft voice surprised her, even more by coming from over her shoulder. Davidh was there, standing in the same shadowed alcove behind her. Anna did not face him.

'Each day, Lachlan Dubh will add more and more to build muscles.' She nodded.

He stepped a little to her side and she knew he saw the tears. He used the back of his hand to wipe them from her cheeks. 'A mother's tears.'

'Aye.'

'Have no fear, he is in the best of hands with Lachlan,' Davidh assured her.

'Could he be a warrior, Davidh?'

Silence greeted her and Anna wondered if that question had exposed too much. The desire to see Iain follow in his father's path and gain what his father never had filled her.

'With training and more growth, aye, he could.'

Anna waited for the words she knew were coming next. If she had only continued on her way back to the village and not stopped, she would not face this challenge now. But the sight of Iain, in the midst of other lads and young men, working and laughing, had drawn her. And filled her heart with hope that he would find his place here. She held her breath now, knowing the consequences of her words.

'Was his father a warrior, Anna?'

'Aye.' She let out her breath and nodded, her gaze still resting on Mal's son. 'Aye, he was.'

He let it rest then, not asking the next and most obvious question as she expected him to do. Instead, he let out a breath and nodded.

'We lost so many in our battles with the

Mackintoshes. Not only warriors, but women and wee ones also.' He thought that Iain's father had been killed in one of those fights!

'And now?' she asked. Though she'd gleaned some knowledge from those in the village, as commander and counsellor of the chieftain, Davidh knew much more than anyone else here.

'Those who would reclaim the clan from Robert are costing us lives and goods. 'Tis a pity when we must fight our own rather than another clan.'

'Where does The Mackintosh stand on this?' she asked. If he thought her too nosy, he did not show it. She kept her gaze on the stables to appear less interested than she truly was.

'Brodie came to the old chieftain for help when his cousin tried to destroy their clan. Euan helped him save Arabella, unseat his cousin and claim the high seat. Now, Brodie stands for Robert.'

Ah, so the formidable leader of the Chattan Confederation supported Robert's claim. But would his wife, Mal's sister, if she knew the truth of Iain's parentage? Lachlan called out to those working and they followed him away from the stables and to the keep. When they'd passed by, Anna stepped in the bright light of the sun and lifted her hand over her brow to watch them go. Davidh stepped out at her side. She began walking towards the gate, her path taking her around the side of the stables.

'Worry not, Anna. These outlaws will be discovered and defeated before Iain is trained.' He reached out and laid his hand on hers then, stroking the top of it softly with the intention, she thought, to offer some measure of comfort to her. 'All will be well for the lad.'

Every movement of his fingers was like a caress, waking her skin and making it tingle. When she stared down at the motions, he moved his fingers around her hand, rubbing his thumb into her palm and teasing her wrist with the feathery light touches. She had no idea that those places were so sensitive. Anna shivered at the small pleasure of such a thing.

The pulses spread up her arm and into her body as he drew her closer and tugged her sleeve up out of his way. Anna dropped her basket and the cloak she carried as he pulled her into his embrace and into the now-empty stables. When he found an empty stall, he dragged her to him and kissed her.

Anna lost all control as his mouth took hers and forgot every vow she'd made not to let this happen again.

Chapter Sixteen

The power of the need for his touch stunned her.

It seemed that she was fine, able to carry on as though nothing had happened between them, until he touched her. Or kissed her. She could not resist these hungry kisses, when he tasted her and invited her to do the same. She could not stand firm when his hands moved over her breasts, cupping and caressing her even through her clothing. It was when he knelt down, sat back on his heels and pulled her astride his lap that she lost all thought.

Somehow, during her path down to his lap, he'd managed to tug their garments out of the way and her aching flesh met his erect manhood. His hands seemed everywhere on her body at once. Her mind blurred as passion filled her. One arm around her waist held her off his flesh while he did not cease kissing her. The other wicked hand slipped between their bodies and caressed between her legs. Fingers, thumb, palm and the edge of his hand all became weapons in his battle to pleasure her.

She could not help it, she wanted him. She wanted this.

While his mouth possessed hers, she rocked on his hand as the tightness within her grew. Anna tried to make him touch that small place within the folds, the one that would bring her release, but he would not allow it.

'Ride me, Anna,' he ordered in a whisper against her mouth. 'Ride me now.'

He spread her thighs wider and guided her down until she felt the tip of his hardness there between her legs. She grabbed hold of his shoulders and lowered herself, inch by inch, until he filled her completely. So intent on the pleasure racing through her body, she'd not even looked at him. Now she did, their gazes meeting as she stilled, his flesh touching her very womb.

'What madness is this?' he asked, sliding his hands up and caressing her cheeks. One soft kiss followed another and another until she pushed up with her hips. He caught her and as he thrust his own hips she pulled hers down. They gasped as one.

'What madness indeed?' She echoed his words and began to enjoy whatever it was between them.

It took only a few movements before their bodies fell in the rhythm he'd asked her for. His hands under her buttocks moved her faster if she slowed. His mouth sucked in the screams of her first release. As his flesh lengthened and hardened inside her and she knew his seed would spill, he pushed up on to his knees and forward until he lay above her.

His breathing strained, his hips moved at a vicious pace, pumping into her and bringing another release, one that caused her to clench her teeth to keep from screaming. He withdrew at the last moment, reaching his own satisfaction between their bodies. Shivers racked her as her release continued, echoes of pleasure pushing into every part of her.

It took several minutes for her heart and breathing to slow. This man knew how to give pleasure. Though, with only two encounters to think about, there were many things they had not even tried yet. Her legs squeezed together as another wave trembled through her body at the very thought of those other things.

He laughed then and she felt the depth of the tone rumble through her whole body. Davidh raised his head and gazed down at her. He stared into her eyes and then at her mouth. Her lips throbbed from his kisses. He touched them with his once more before leaning back and nodding.

'Madness indeed,' he whispered.

The sounds of the real world around them seeped into this small cocoon they'd woven and Davidh eased back off her body. As he helped her to her feet, she tugged her shift down and smoothed her skirt into place. In rushed movements, he picked off pieces of straw from her hair and back. Voices could be heard growing closer.

Davidh smiled as he plucked more straw free and she wanted to outline his lips with her tongue. He stilled and met her gaze.

'I am struggling to control myself now. If you continue to stare at my mouth in that way, I will have no choice but to—'

'Lachlan!' a voice called out from just outside the stable door. 'Lachlan Dubh!' Damn it, it was Parlan again.

'Go. Use the back door,' he said, as he picked up her basket and cloak and handed them to her. 'I will stop him.'

Anna gathered her things and ran out the door, making her way around the stables and to the path that led to the gates. Her legs trembled as she walked down the steeper part, but she continued on. Unwilling to return to Davidh's house just now, she walked on into the centre of the village and sought the well.

It was a busy time of day and many gathered

at the well to fill their buckets, for cooking and cleaning and washing clothes. The women called out greetings to her as she waited her turn in the line that formed.

What she wanted to do was to douse herself with several buckets of the cold, refreshing water and ease the ache that yet filled her body. What she did was to pull the bucket, fill the dipper that was tied there and drink several times from it. It eased her thirst and did cool her. She pulled a cloth square from under her belt and dipped it in the bucket, too. After one more drink, she stepped down from the well and away, wiping her face and neck with the wet cloth.

'Are ye well?' Anna turned to find Davidh's neighbour Lilias there. 'Ye look flushed. Mayhap feverish?'

'I am well,' she answered, trying to escape the woman. Lilias watched Anna with a close attention that made Anna uncomfortable. 'I thank you for your concern, mistress.' Anna tried to walk around Lilias when the woman grabbed her arm and pulled her in close.

'I ken ye for the whoring slattern ye are, Mistress Mackenzie. Coming here when you could catch no suitable man and trying to steal one of our own. I willna let ye get yer heathen claws into Davidh Cameron.'

Anna gasped not only at the harsh words, but

at the nasty pinch to her arm that Lilias gave her.
Tugging her arm free, she was tempted to slap
the woman until she remembered her mother's
words of warning.

She was the stranger here.

The women in a village were more dangerous
than any man could be.

Pay heed not to insult the women.

Anna settled her basket and stepped back,
not missing the dangerous expression of hatred
in Lilias's gaze now. She walked a wide circle
around the woman and made her way to Davidh's house, shaken by the encounter.

'Whore!'

Lilias's furious whisper echoed across the
clearing to Anna. Then just as she thought she
could not hear the woman, Lilias uttered the
word that had the power to frighten the very
breath from her and Anna prayed no one else
had heard it.

'Witch!'

Pray God, no! Not this kind of thing and not
now. Not when her plan for Iain was moving
forward after years of waiting. It was exactly
this—women claiming witchcraft and ill deeds
on her mother's part—that had seen them leave
here before. No proof was necessary to blacken
the name of a woman other than vague suspicions and complaints.

This could not happen now!

Anna held in her tears and ran the last yards to Davidh's house. Slamming the door behind her, she leaned against it and offered up a prayer that this would go no further. If she avoided Lilias, it would go no further.

'You have a problem, my friend.'

Davidh sat at the table in the hall as Robert had requested. He'd sent word to Anna that he would not be eating with her and the lads since the chieftain had called him to his side. He swallowed the mouthful of ale and put his cup down.

'I have many problems—the outlaws, securing our keeps against them, finding out who is behind them. Which one are you talking about?' He took a bite of the cheese on his plate and chewed it, waiting for Parlan to decide that baiting him would not work.

'The one named Lilias.'

Davidh sucked in a breath and the cheese went down his throat, choking him. Parlan smacked him on the back several times until it loosened and he coughed it out.

'Hell, Parlan! Did you have to say that?'

'You were ignoring me. Got your attention, did it not?'

Davidh pushed the plate away and filled his cup from the pitcher on the table. He glanced around to see who was close enough to hear their words and then leaned over to Parlan.

'And how is she a problem?'

'I'm not certain whether it began with your conversation with the lovely widow Cameron this morn or before that,' Parlan explained. 'She just said something to the widow Mackenzie that made that one almost strike her.'

'Anna? Hit Lilias? That is absurd.'

'She didna hit her. The fire spitting from her eyes warned me. I was about to intervene, when Anna dropped her hand and fled to your house.'

'Parlan, you have the most aggravating way of telling me something. Just spit it out, all at once, and get it done!' he urged through clenched jaws that threatened to shatter his teeth. Parlan turned his stool to face Davidh.

'As I see it… First, Lilias approached you in the yard, flaunting her wares and trying to get you to buy.' Davidh let out a sound much like a growl, but it did nothing to encourage his friend towards brevity.

'Then you and Mistress Mackenzie examined the quality of the straw in the stables.' To keep from doing it, Davidh imagined his hands around Parlan's neck, wringing the life and breath from his body. 'Widow Cameron was not three yards from the open door of the stables just then, so I called out Lachlan's name to gain your attention.' If Davidh had anything in his mouth, he would have choked once again at this revelation.

'She saw us in there?' The food and drink in his gut roiled at Parlan's nod. 'But did she *see* us?' The view of the stall where he'd led Anna should have been blocked to anyone at the front entrance.

'Not certain what she saw during the act itself. She and I could see you both standing there readjusting yourselves.'

'Hell!' Those around him stopped talking at his shout. Even Robert and Elizabeth glanced towards him there at the end of the table. He nodded an apology to them. 'You disappeared after you called to me.'

'Lilias looked angrier than I have ever seen her,' Parlan said. 'So, when I saw Anna leave with Lilias stalking behind, I followed her.' His friend coughed then and took a mouthful of his own cup.

'Just tell me that Anna is well.' It was his only concern. His lack of control had led to this situation. He did not want Anna caught in the middle of it because of the possessive streak in a woman he cared little for.

'Anna went to the well and that was where Lilias caught up with her. Lilias grabbed hold of her and said something to Anna that made her angry. Then, she shook free of her and ran back to your house. When I got there, the door was closed and I heard no sounds within.'

'I will speak to Lilias,' he said. He'd never expected the widow to lay any claim to his affections or person. 'I've made my intentions very clear from the beginning.'

Parlan sat up as though struck and looked at him with an expression that mixed shock, disgruntled horror and disbelief all together.

'What?' Davidh asked.

'I do not know how it is that a man like you has gained the years you have, been educated and risen to the level of trust you have and know nothing about women. You were married which means you would have wooed your wife. You lived with her for years. Had a child. Have been surrounded by women all your life. And you know nothing.' Parlan reached out and cuffed Davidh on the side of his head when he finished his diatribe.

'You are wearing my control thin, friend.'

'See to the laird's call and then we will finish this.'

Davidh stood as Robert signalled to him to approach. He nodded to Parlan for there was much to be said about the widow's knowledge and her ability to destroy someone with gossip.

* * *

It took longer than he expected to speak with the chieftain. It took another couple of hours to sort through arrangements for a forthcoming journey that Robert would undertake to the Tor Castle, his former home. And it took more time to hunt, unsuccessfully, for his friend who had disappeared. Finally, he made his way to the village.

The house stood quiet and he eased his way in the door. It was late enough that all would be sleeping within and Davidh was practised at arriving and leaving in the dark of night. When his duties called, it mattered not the time when he must answer them. The smell of something aromatic and delicious rose from the hearth and Davidh saw the small pot at the edge of the fire.

A place was set on the smaller table that they used for meals with a pitcher at its side. As he looked around, even in the lowlight of the fire, everything was neat and clean and organised. As he paced around the main chamber, the scents of the herbs and plants she, Anna, was drying floated in the air round him. Davidh wondered if she was yet awake, so he knocked lightly on the door of the bedchamber she and her son used.

The light footsteps approaching from within made him take a breath and hold it. The door opened and Anna stood there fully clothed before him. No, not ready for sleep yet either.

Rather than closing the door behind her as was usual when she tried not to wake her son, this time she left it open as she stepped into the main chamber. Davidh could see into her room and the smaller pallet where Iain slept was empty.

'Where is Iain?'

Chapter Seventeen

'He stayed up at the keep this night. He said they begin very early in the morn and 'tis easier to be there.' With her hands clenched tightly into a ball, Anna began to pace in front of her doorway.

'Ah,' he said, watching the anxiety fill her gaze. 'You allowed this but worry over him.' He shook his head. 'Lachlan's grandson lives with him above the stables. If that is where Iain is—' she nodded '—then he will be well.'

Anna let out a breath and shook her hands to loosen them at his assurances. From the way she continued to wrap her arms across her chest and from the fact that she still paced, Davidh understood there was more to her upset than her son's first stay up in the keep.

'Anna?' She looked over at him. 'We need to speak about Lilias.'

'And I need to speak to you about your son.'

She glanced at the door to his bedchamber and nodded. 'I do not wish Colm to hear any of this if he wakes. Come into my chamber.'

Blood rushed to that part of him that he did not wish to have aroused at this moment at the innocent invitation of hers. He tamped down the growing desire within himself and swore that this would not end up as their last two encounters had.

He followed her inside and watched as she lit another tallow candle and placed it on the table that sat next to her pallet. She'd arranged a sitting area there, with a chair and a stool close to the table. A large basket filled with garments waited there, as did a smaller one of sewing supplies. He sat on the stool when she took her place in the chair.

'Firstly,' she said softly, 'we must speak about Colm.'

His son? He'd been doing so well these last weeks under her care.

'Colm? Has he misbehaved in some way?' The words no sooner left his tongue than he thought of the other, dreaded possibility. 'Is he... worse?' He closed his eyes with the pain of it.

'Aye.' The single word nearly ended his own life. His heart pounded hard in his chest as he waited for more.

'But he has not coughed. He has been playing. He has…' He thrust his hands into his hair, raking them back and pressing on his head. 'Worse?'

'The cough is not the problem, Davidh. He struggles to breathe more often. Colm will not say so, but I have observed him and he is worsening.'

'What can we do?'

His voice cracked as he asked the question and Anna's own heart tightened as she watched Davidh absorb this blow. Then she heard the question as he'd asked it—*what can we do?*

'I am changing the medicaments I've been giving him and changing the number of treatments each day.'

'What can I do?' he asked. The hunger to help in his voice brought tears to her eyes.

'I am sorry, Davidh. There is not much we can do. I think he should avoid the stillroom until I have finished cleaning it. Dusty places like that will make it harder for him.'

'There is nothing else? How can I sit by and let this happen?'

He stood then and walked to the shuttered window. Leaning his head on it, he shocked her by slamming his hand against the stone wall. She gasped as he did it again and then a third time.

'That will not help,' she said, walking to his side and grabbing hold of his arm before he could

do it again. 'Look! You have injured yourself.'
She guided him to the chair and pushed him into
it. 'Wait there.'

Anna quickly gathered some cloths and an
ointment and some warm water from the pot that
sat near the hearth. Going back into the chamber, she found him staring at the wall that separated their rooms. She dragged the stool over
and sat facing him.

'Give me your hand,' she said.

She placed his warm, strong, cut and bleeding
hand on her lap over the basin and cleaned it. If
he felt pain, he gave no sign of it. Anna understood that all the possible outcomes for his son
were racing through his thoughts right now and
he would not feel a sword plunging into his back
if someone did that.

He hissed once as she applied an unguent to
the torn knuckles, but that was his only reaction.
Once she'd wrapped a bandage around his hand,
she let it rest on her lap and placed the bowl of
bloodied water on the floor.

'Will he die?'

His usually bright eyes and direct gaze filled
now with stark grief and loss. He watched her
and waited for her to give him some shred of
hope. She had been fortunate for Iain had been
strong from birth and through his childhood. He
suffered few injuries and no illnesses, so facing

this situation was not one she had any experience in handling.

She wanted to ease his pain.

She wanted to promise she could help his son.

The sad truth was she could not.

'Aye.'

The word echoed in the silence of the chamber. A death sentence proclaimed for a young boy of eight years.

Davidh moaned then in anguish and slid to his knees. When Anna stood, he wrapped his arms around her legs and pressed his face against her. The shuddering tremors as he quietly sobbed out his grief tore her apart. She managed to guide him over to sit on the pallet and she held him until the storm had eased within him.

It was a terrible thing for a father to face and he must face it so that he could help Colm through it.

'I will do whatever I can, Davidh,' she promised. 'I will seek out knowledge about his condition and try to slow it.' She stroked his back and held him close. 'And if God wills it so, 'twill be many years before death comes.'

'Whatever the price, I will pay it, Anna. Whatever you need, I will get it,' he whispered. He lifted his head and stared at her. The devastation there hurt her.

'We will do our best, Davidh.'

When he began to stand, she took hold of his arm and pulled him back to sit at her side on the pallet. She wanted to give him comfort. She wanted to ease the horrific pain there in his gaze. He followed her back down as she laid on the pallet. Taking him in her arms, she held him close. He leaned his head down against her and did not move or speak, accepting her embrace.

Some time later, as his breathing levelled and he eased into sleep, she still held him close. And in the dark of the night, she turned on her side and he turned with her, sliding closer and closer until their bodies touched from head to toe. His warm breath against her ear soothed her and she fell deeply asleep.

'Mam?' Iain called out.

It was Davidh's daily custom to wake quickly, clear-minded and ready to see to the day. This morn was different.

His eyes felt as if someone had poured tar over them to keep them shut. With effort, he opened them to find Iain standing over the bed. Then, he felt the warm curves of a woman's body against his erect male flesh and under his hands and Davidh understood this was not his usual morning ritual.

When she shifted against him, his flesh hard

as it usually was in the morn, ached for more. His hand cupped a breast, Anna's breast, and her bottom nudged against his hardness. None of which he minded, but it should never happen in front of her son in the same room. In her bedchamber.

'Anna,' he said. 'Wake up.'

As he released his hold on her and shifted away, she moved with him, letting out a breathy sigh before opening her eyes.

'Davidh,' she whispered. Then she caught sight of Iain standing in the doorway and she froze. 'Iain.'

She scrambled away from Davidh and her tangled skirts slowed her ability to climb from the pallet. Davidh offered up a silent prayer of gratitude that they were both completely dressed even if they were wrapped around one another in her bed. He pushed off the pallet and stood next to it, nodding at the lad.

'Iain,' she said.

As she walked towards her son, she tried to gather her hair back out of her face and over her shoulders. The unruly mass did not co-operate at all. Instead it spilled over her shoulders in a riot of brown and gold and red curls that made her look as though she had been doing something absolutely decadent in bed with him.

He wished it had been something like that.

Memories of the stark grief that had filled him returned in a flood, as did the cause of that grief. He would have to handle that after they handled this situation.

'Iain,' he interrupted. 'Why are you here?'

Anna sputtered and turned to face Davidh, but he shook his head at her and looked at her son. One thing he'd learned about raising a son was that they could be simple creatures with simple needs. Trying to give too much of an explanation just made things more complicated. So, Davidh crossed his arms over his chest and waited for the lad to answer.

'Someone was hurt in the yard, sir. They asked me to fetch my mother.' Iain responded as Davidh thought he would—a direct answer to a specific question from the man in authority.

'Anna, can you gather your supplies and come outside when you are ready?' He thought she might argue, but she nodded and walked into the main room and began picking out what she thought she would need.

'Iain, walk with me.' He put his hand on the boy's back and guided him out of the house. When they'd taken a few steps away, Davidh faced the boy, leaving his hand in place on Iain's shoulder. 'Do you have anything to ask me?'

When Iain shook off his hold, Davidh thought there might be a problem. But the lad stood up straight and met Davidh's gaze without flinching.

'Nothing to ask, sir,' he said. 'Just something to say.'

'And that is?'

'If you hurt my mother, I will make you regret it.'

Stunned at the words and the tone and the vow made, Davidh nodded at the lad...young man. Part of him was proud of the son that Anna had raised. Part of him feared what would happen in such a situation.

'I will not hurt her.'

'Aye, see that you do not.'

'I am ready,' Anna said, rushing out of the house with a huge basket on her arm.

Iain lifted it easily from her and nodded towards the keep. When Davidh would have followed, Anna tilted her head at the door.

'Colm is waking and needs the first doses of the tincture in the blue jar. Mix it with heated water. He knows how to do it,' Anna directed. 'I will return as soon as possible.'

Davidh watched as they hastened along the path and disappeared around the corner. His foot was on the first step when Colm called out from within.

'Papa?'

The stab he felt through his heart as he realised the truth of his son's condition had the intensity of a true blow. How he was not bleeding out as he stood there, Davidh did not know. But his pain mattered not. Only Colm did. And Davidh refused to give up the last vestige of hope that remained in his heart.

With a deep breath taken and released, Davidh entered his house readying himself to face the biggest challenge of his life—not letting his son know the truth.

It was a simple and clean break. One of the lads working with Lachlan had dropped a beam as they were placing it. It had fallen and struck another worker, Lachlan's grandson Simon as it turned out, who had raised his arm to stave off the impact. The result was a fracture in his forearm.

It took little time for Anna to stabilise Simon's arm and give instructions for his care to his grandfather. She promised to check on the boy on the morrow. Lachlan got the group back to work. Simon, who seemed quite proud of his injury, stood with his grandfather then, directing the others and resisting Lachlan's attempts to get him to rest.

When things had settled, she looked for Iain, hoping to explain what he had seen this morning.

She nodded to him and he met her a few paces away from the stables.

'Mam,' he said before she found the words to explain, 'have a care.'

'Iain?'

'Just have a care here. We are still outsiders and I do not trust him.'

'Iain,' she said, placing her hand on his arm. 'You do not trust the commander?'

'Nay. He is loyal only to his chieftain and will not stand by you if he has to choose.'

'I have no plans to make him choose, Iain.' The lie in the words burned as they left her mouth. 'There is nothing for you to worry over, my son.' Her son's words had surprised her. Clearly, he had been more perceptive and more observant than she'd realised.

'Iain!' Lachlan called out. 'If yer mother doesna need yer help with her things, come back to work.'

'Just have a care with him, Mam,' he warned as he stepped away from her and heeded Lachlan's call.

Of all the things he could have said after finding her lying in Davidh's arms in her bed, that was not anything she'd considered possible. As she watched him walk towards the man overseeing his work, Anna wondered how much he did know about her plans for him.

She'd confided in no one back in her mother's village and no one since. How would he know she was planning to use her position and closeness to Davidh to help her son take his rightful place? Oh, she'd been clear that she was bringing him here to meet his father's clan and to find a place there among them. She'd never told him that place was one in line for the high seat itself.

Her stomach grumbled then, protesting its emptiness, so she returned to the village to begin her day again. With each step back, through the gates and down the path into the village, something told her that this strange day would get even stranger.

Davidh was at his house when she returned there, so she began as she usually did by making porridge for them. Colm sat eating, blissfully unaware of the turbulence swirling around him and his father's distress. Anna was aware of it, though.

A few brief glances from Davidh over and around his son at the table told Anna that he was being watchful, listening to every sound and breath from the boy. Just as she watched Davidh's every expression and movement. He surprised her by sending Colm to the well for water, warning him not to run or fill the bucket past the half-mark inside it.

'I wanted to…give you my thanks for telling

me the truth about Colm.' He lifted his gaze to hers and nodded. 'How long have you known?'

'From the first time I saw him. That morning at Suisan's.' He slid his hand across the narrow table and covered hers. 'I could not be certain then.'

'But you are now?' The weight and warmth of his hand on hers eased the ache in her heart as they spoke of his son.

'Aye. But, Davidh...' she covered his hand with her other and continued '...I am not the Almighty with the power to give or take lives and neither am I giving up.' The tears welled in her eyes and she blinked against them. 'I hope you ken that.'

'I ken.' Davidh smiled then. 'I did not realise that the burden of worrying over him had eased since you came and began seeing to his care. Not until now.' He stood, taking his hand from hers. 'As I said last night, no matter the cost.'

She nodded, understanding his deep need to save his son. At first, he turned to leave and she picked up the bowls from the table. Then he walked that one pace back to her and kissed her.

This was not a hungry, possessive kiss. Nor a passion-filled one.

Nay, this was the softest kiss she'd ever been given.

And yet, when he lifted his lips from hers,

she felt changed in some way by it. She opened the eyes she'd not known she'd closed and stared into his. Deep in those brown eyes was something else. Something she'd seen only once before in a man's gaze and something that shook her to her core.

Davidh stepped away. When he lifted the latch of the door and opened it, Colm came in. His stride was slow and measured as he attempted to keep all the water inside the bucket. Worrying his lower lip, he took one cautious step after another until he reached the hearth and placed the bucket there.

'My thanks, Colm,' she said. 'Exactly half the bucket!'

When Colm laughed at her words, she reached out and wrapped her arm around his shoulder in a hug. She looked up at his father and realised she wanted this boy to live. She wanted his father to never face his loss.

She wanted…

She left Colm there with a word about clearing the table and followed Davidh outside. Though her strides were shorter, she caught up to him before he'd gone far.

'I want you to know I will do everything I can to help him, Davidh.' She touched his arm. 'I will be here.'

He glanced at that connection between them and then at her face. 'I am glad.'

For a moment, the sounds of the village, its people and daily activities faded into a silent blur around them. All Anna could hear was the sound of her heart pounding in her chest. It took only that short time to realise how deeply in trouble she truly was.

She released him and watched as he covered the ground quickly, his long strides taking one for what would be every two of hers. Not until he turned the corner and walked out of sight did she turn away.

When had she decided to become involved with the boy's fate? When had she allowed anyone to impede with her true aim? She glanced back to where he'd stood and shook her head. It was worse than that for, would he want her to stay and care for his son when he discovered her deception and her real purpose here?

Iain would jeopardise the safety and peace Davidh fought to establish and preserve. Iain's existence could throw the clan into upheaval and threaten everyone. A small voice within her whispered doubt to her. It whispered about possibilities. It whispered about...love.

Anna clenched her fists, pressing her nails into the fleshy part of her palms until they left marks. Nay. Nay. She could not allow any distractions. She could care for the boy now and get him as strong as she could before the truth was revealed. Before her lies were known to Davidh.

Well, she could not stand here in the middle of the path all day. Anna would face the challenges when she must. For now, she had many chores to finish this morning. She lifted her head and took a step towards the commander's house when Lilias stepped in front of her.

Other than an angry glare, the woman spoke not a word. Anna stepped around her and walked to the door. She waited to hear the whispered insults as she pushed it open and stepped inside. Peering out through the crack as she closed it those final inches, she watched as Lilias nodded at her.

One more concern to add to her growing tally. Colm called to her and the angry woman was lost to other more pressing concerns.

Chapter Eighteen

It would seem that some ill winds had blown through the village of Achnacarry that day. The broken bone at the stables was only the first of many such injuries, illnesses and other maladies that Anna faced through the days after. Running hither and yon, from one end of the village and back up to the keep, she began to suspect that the old gods were angry with the Clan Cameron.

When the last two injured in the village—one by a spill from a boiling pot and the other in a fall—refused her help, Anna wondered if there was something more going on than just everyday wounds and ailments. It did not help when she noticed Lilias lingering outside the door of the two who'd refused her. Anna did the only thing she could—she gave what instructions they would hear and left.

Supper that evening was a quiet meal with little chatter, either from the lads or from Davidh.

The revelation of his son's true condition had shaken him and she watched as he struggled to find some balance between the need to remain with Colm and coddle him and the knowledge that he had no control over the progression of his illness. For a man accustomed to being in charge, Anna could see the toll it took on him as a man and a father.

The next morn, though everyone went about their duties as was their custom, Anna could feel something was not right. It took a few days for her to realise that Iain had not slept up at the keep since the morn he'd found Davidh in her chamber. There were other glances and glares, but Anna tried to convince herself it would all settle.

It did not.

Whispers followed her as she made her way through the village. Oh, she'd heard the names and words used in those furtive insults, for they had been used against her mother and other women who had dared upset the way things were done in a place.

The line of those waiting for her attentions had far fewer people in it than even two days before. Though a few women in the village seemed to grow more suspicious of her, the number of men seeking her out increased with each passing day. She wanted no company of that sort and she turned them down, but each day another unmarried, widowed or lonely man requested that she visit or share supper or walk with him.

There were three places where her welcome did not change—Davidh's house, Suisan's cottage and the keep. It would seem that those injured or ailing within the laird and lady's household had no hesitation in seeking her help.

The one man she wished would seek her out seemed to grow more distant. The only smiles on his face were sad ones when he thought no one was looking as he watched Colm. Was this how he'd been before she arrived here in Achnacarry?

Over the next days, he did not kiss her or even try to, whether they were alone or passing in some secluded spot. That last kiss remained in her thoughts and she both feared and wondered on its true meaning. However, she blamed him not for the quietness that now controlled him nor the lack of passion. She could not imagine how she would be if her son faced such a dangerous future. Anna wished she could change things. With every sad glance between father and son, she was forced to recognise her own limitations and that she had not the knowledge or experience to make a true difference.

Worse, Anna also had to face her own growing desire to stay here with him. To be with him.

Yet, when her son's true parentage was known and her deception was exposed, there would be no chance of that.

It took several days to pull him from his desolation over Colm. And even then, it was one of the lads who made it all so clear.

'Here now! Here now!'

Lachlan's loud shouting could be heard from the stables to the training yard where Davidh stood. He ignored it the first time he heard the man call out. And the second. The third time happened at the same moment that some raucous yelling also spilled out of the stable. It took only a moment or two for Davidh and Parlan, there at his side, to realise there was trouble.

By the time they got to the back of the stables where the work was being done, it was almost over. Two young men lay in the dirt with Lachlan standing between them. As they climbed to their feet and wiped the dust from their eyes, Davidh was surprised to see that Iain was one of them.

'I told ye that there will be no more of that!' Lachlan yelled the words loud enough that Davidh did not doubt that the laird, closed up in his chambers, heard. 'Ye are here to work. If ye canna or dinna work, ye are no' good to me!'

Davidh did not interfere. He and Parlan stood silently watching as the old man handled this situation. It was not unusual for young men to fight among themselves, but Iain being one of them shocked him. Both lads had bloodied noses and Iain's lip was split while Martyn's chin was cut. None of the damage looked serious and Davidh himself had suffered far more in his younger days. He and Parlan and Malcolm got into such trouble and fought anyone who looked askew at them. He kept his expression serious as Lachlan continued.

'Do ye go back to work then?' Lachlan's voice lowered a bit, but the anger was still clear in it. 'Iain? Martyn?' He poked each one in the shoulder until they both assented. 'Go clean yerselves and get ye back to yer tasks!'

Soon, the excitement was gone and work went on as planned. Lachlan watched, and glared at, his charges for a short time before walking over to speak with him and Parlan.

'What happened?'

'The lad, Iain, took offence over some words.'

'So he raised his fists first?' Parlan asked before Davidh could.

'Aye, but Martyn had taunted him and pushed him away when the lad walked up to him about it.'

Parlan looked at Davidh through narrowed eyes, waiting for his response. His friend let out a growl and mumbled to the sky before letting out a loud breath.

'Fine! I will ask. What was the insult over?'

Lachlan stared at Davidh instead of saying a word. As Parlan did now.

The sinking feeling in Davidh's gut told him he knew the truth of it. For, in spite of Parlan's insistence that Davidh did not know women, he had seen and heard about the approaches to Anna by men of the keep and the village. He'd heard about the insults uttered to her and the change in the way the villagers treated her.

It was in the purview of his position to know what happened throughout their lands and clan and this one woman could not escape his notice. Nor that of his men in his command who watched when and where he could not. Ever since the attack, Davidh had assigned men to keep watch over Anna.

Though the awareness that her arrival and the increased visibility of the outlaws on Cameron lands seemed to coincide, he'd been suspicious for barely a moment after meeting her. Since that first day, she'd been what she'd appeared to be. A healer looking for a place to live and a mother seeking to reunite her son with his father's people. Her compassion and assistance and efforts for so many here in Achnacarry had convinced him of her aims.

However, she was also a woman. An attractive, young widow and with her quick wit and soft smiles was a target for petty jealousies and uninvited attentions. When that woman's mother had been rumoured to be a witch, even more dangerous innuendos could arise. As he glared back at Parlan and then turned to face Lachlan, Davidh comprehended that those elements were behind this outbreak of anger between these two young men.

And so was his own behaviour.

'Just so,' Lachlan said with a nod of his head. The admission must be clear on Davidh's face. ''Twas no' the first insult.'

'Nor will it be the last.' Parlan finished the man's sentiment.

Davidh crossed his arms over his chest. 'And what do you both suggest be done about this?' Lachlan and Parlan exchanged glances before staring at him as though he'd grown two more heads. ''Tis clear to me that you have opinions on the matter.'

'I think there are a few ways to handle the situation that caused…' Parlan nodded his head towards the lads now working in the stables.

Lachlan, for his part, took his leave with a promise to inform Davidh of further problems and walked away as fast as he could without making his old body run. Davidh had the feeling that he would like to do that, as well. He could not, for he knew well that this situation and a big part of what was going on throughout the village was not only his responsibility, but also his fault. Turning back to Parlan, he waited to hear the choices he already knew.

'You can ask Anna and her son to move here to the keep. The stillroom is almost ready and you ken that Robert, and especially Elizabeth, would welcome her presence.' Parlan waited for his acknowledgement. Davidh thought his friend was enjoying this too much and set a time in his mind when his friend would face his comeuppance. He nodded.

'You could move her to one of the other cottages in the village.' Parlan glanced towards the gate, over Davidh's shoulder. 'That will cause nearly the same difficulties as you have now. You will be seen frequenting her cottage for all assorted reasons, good ones for certain, and so the rumours will continue to fly and hostilities will build.'

Davidh startled at his friend's observant assessment. Parlan shrugged and crossed his arms over his chest, mirroring David's own stance as he waited for Parlan's final choice. He prepared himself for the painful onslaught of other memories and loss at the word or very thought of…

'Or you could make it impossible for any to threaten her by marrying her.'

Images of Anna's face—in pleasure, in danger, in caring, in his house—filled his thoughts. Not the memories he'd expected to flood him. And with her face came the knowledge that somewhere along the way since they'd first met, Davidh had begun to fall in love with her.

How it had happened, he knew not. When exactly it had started, he did.

It was the moment when he'd surprised her in her cottage above the falls. When she turned and looked at him, with her green eyes flashing and her face smudged with dirt. Then, at every turn when she showed another part of herself to him, his path had been set.

The biggest shock to him as he thought about those moments was that he did not feel the pain of guilt that had assailed him before. Any desire he'd ever had for a woman since Mara's death had simply been reduced to raw physical need. He'd never wanted more than that.

Now, he wanted more. He wanted Anna in his life, in their life, and the fact that this was happening now was not a bad thing. Looking at Parlan's gloating expression, Davidh did not wish to give his friend the satisfaction that he had noticed something even those weeks ago.

So, he shrugged, much as Parlan had, and gave him as little a reaction as he could.

'So, 'twould seem that my solution does not surprise you?'

'I think 'twould be the honourable thing to do.'

'Honourable!' Parlan laughed so loud it caught the interest of those passing them in the yard. Davidh grabbed him and pulled him along as he walked to the keep. 'You want the widow Mackenzie, 'tis plain to anyone who sees you together. Davidh,' Parlan said as he stopped and faced him, ''tis no shame in this. You were a faithful husband to...'

'Parlan. There is no need to bring up Mara.'

Just then, Iain walked across near them, carrying some supplies over to the stables. Parlan stopped and stared, tilting his head as he watched the boy.

'Does he ken who his father is? Have you asked him or his mother?'

'I have not spoken of the matter. Anna has not mentioned it more than to say he was a Cameron.'

'*Was?*'

'Aye. *Was.*' Davidh glanced at Parlan. 'I think he was someone lost in the battles between the Mackintoshes and our clan.'

'I would ask her plainly before you marry. Before you do the *honourable* thing for her.'

Davidh threw Parlan a glance and made a gesture that told his friend just how much Davidh thought of his comment. 'Well, before that happens I must speak to Robert and gain his blessing. Then I will speak to the lad.'

'To Iain?'

'He was old enough to take a beating for his mother's honour, so he is old enough to be told of my plans.'

'Will she accept your offer?' Parlan asked.

'What man truly kens the mind of a woman?' he asked.

'Only a madman claims to, my friend. Only a madman.'

Chapter Nineteen

The soft knock on the door irritated her. If it was the first time someone interrupted her work there in the stillroom, Anna would not have minded. Maybe even the third or fourth. But this was…she'd lost count of how many times someone, usually a man, had knocked this morning. Tempted to ignore it, her conscience got the better of her, for it could be someone in need and she did not wish to disregard those who needed her care.

She wiped her hands on her apron as she walked to the door and took a breath. Lifting the latch, she gathered her patience to deal with whichever Cameron man stood there, hoping to help, walk out with, sup with or tup her.

'Lady Elizabeth!' Anna sank into a curtsy at the sight of her there. 'I did not mean to keep you waiting in the corridor. Come in, I pray you.' Anna swung the door open and stepped back so the lady could enter. 'What have you need of this morn?'

'You have worked wonders here, Anna.' The lady looked around the chamber and nodded. 'I have not ventured down here since you began. I could not imagine *this*—' she waved her hand at the room '—from the mess it had become.'

'I am not finished, my lady,' Anna said. 'But some of this needs a more experienced person to determine its importance. I have stored some away until one of the brothers you mentioned might arrive.' Anna pointed to the shelves beneath some of the tables around the chamber where she'd placed some of the jars and bottles and pots she could not identify. 'Will the brothers speak to me about such matters?'

One of the things that skilled wise women often encountered was the resistance and ignorance of some clergy. Her mother had spoken of such things and warned her to pay heed to any who had that attitude. If the lady insisted on bringing a clergyman here as she'd said, there would be little or nothing Anna could do about it.

'My husband and previous Cameron chieftains have been very generous to the monastery at the edge of our lands. I doubt anyone sent by the abbot would risk Robert's displeasure by insulting someone here.' Anna smiled and hoped that would be the way of things, but she'd witnessed other outcomes.

'Do you have need of something, my lady?' Anna asked. 'A potion for megrims? A poultice for some ache?'

'Nay, nothing of the sort,' Lady Elizabeth said. The lady turned and eased the door to the chamber closed. When the latch dropped, the lady faced her. 'I wish to speak on a personal matter, if you would?'

Anna pulled one of the stools over and offered it to the lady. After she was seated, Anna waited at the lady's convenience for her to broach whatever was the purpose of her visit. It did not take long and it was not a surprise.

'My maid's sister in the village told her there are some rumours making their way around about you, Anna. I have never believed that we should give gossip power over us, but it seems to do that.'

'Aye, my lady.'

'You know the rumours? Have you been mistreated then?'

'Mistreated?'

'Clara's sister overheard some whispers about you…and Davidh. Has he taken advantage of you in any way, Anna? I would ken the truth of it.'

Anna knew her mouth hung open and she

simply could not find words to make it close. Davidh mistreating her?

'Nay, my lady! The commander has not done anything but given me a place to live in his house and seen to my son's placement with Lachlan here as we'd agreed.' She did not reveal the heated encounters or the night they'd spent in each other's arms. The lady's astute gaze must have seen the blush that Anna could feel rise in her cheeks.

'Is that the way of it then between you two?'

'My lady?'

'The talk is that you share his bed, which is not my concern since you are both free to do so. The problem is that it is now known by too many to keep it quiet. And now your son has become involved.'

'My son?' Had Iain spoken to someone about finding Davidh in her bed? He would never. 'What has happened to Iain?' Anna strode towards the door, stopped by the lady's hand on her arm.

'The boy is fine. 'Twas just a tussle between him and another lad.'

'When? Where?' Anna asked. The lady did not lift her hand and so Anna stopped next to her. 'Is he hurt?'

'Nay, nothing serious. My sons seemed to get into fights all the time when they were younger and came out unscathed. It comes to my mind now that they still do. Their tempers flare and they speak with their fists.' Anna gasped then. What had happened?

'He never got into fights before, my lady.'

'Ah, but I suspect he was never surrounded by lads and young men ready to test him as he is now.' Lady Elizabeth smiled then. 'He is at that age when every word challenges and insults and needs to be met with actions.'

'How did you learn of this fight? When did it happen?' Anna worried that the lady knew of this before she did.

'Earlier this morn, over at the stables.' Lady Elizabeth met her gaze then. 'You must not make too much of his injuries—a few bruises were all they inflicted on each other—but pay heed to the reasons for it.'

'My lady?'

The knowing gaze made Anna's stomach tighten. Someone had repeated Lilias's insults to Iain. And though her son had caught them together that morn, he still defended her name. Or felt that he must.

'Just so, Anna.' The lady stood then. 'I must get back to Robert.' Anna stepped back to allow her to pass. 'I have appreciated your good works here for our people, Anna. You have a place here, in the keep, if you need one.'

'I will think on it, my lady,' Anna said. She lifted the latch and opened the door. 'My thanks for the offer.'

'Remember, the lads will fight at this age. Try not to make too much of it.'

Long after the lady left, Anna thought about her words, her advice and even the thing Elizabeth had not said. If this trouble had risen to the level when it had been brought to the lady's attention and she'd felt she must speak about it, then it was bad indeed. Now that Iain had been dragged into it, and only the God knew how that had happened, she could not ignore it and hope it would cease.

She walked around the chamber—now that the tables were arranged in the manner she liked she could pace the perimeter—thinking about her choices.

There were a few before her; all kept her ultimate aim to secure Iain's true place in the clan in mind. Those meant staying here in Achnacarry and to do so she must either admit or deny her involvement with the commander. If today's altercation showed her anything, it was that this was only the beginning of such insults that her son would face. And those insults and problems would serve as a hurdle when it came time to establish his parentage.

She'd given her word twice over that she

would continue to care for young Colm, so leaving to return at another time was not a choice. If and when the outlaws were subdued making the cottage at the falls safe once more, Anna would move there. In the meantime, though, her choices seemed to be moving here to the keep and…moving here to the keep.

If Anna accepted the lady's invitation, it would put her closer to the heart of the clan. It would put Iain here, as well. She would still be close enough to care for Davidh's son. The biggest problem with all of this would be how they would all react to the news that Iain was Malcolm Cameron's son and heir. Davidh's loyalties would be torn apart.

His position as commander of all the warriors and to protect his people would be at war with the need to also protect his closest friend's son. And that would all be complicated by his own promise to help Iain, one made without the full knowledge and based on her own deception. Anna sighed and stopped walking around the chamber.

The sting of guilt filled her then. Making her plan before she knew anyone here was easy. Now that she'd met them and knew the villagers, the lord and lady, and especially Davidh and his son, it was much harder to have faith that her son's missed inheritance should matter more than their lives and needs. Her own oath on Malcolm's murdered soul kept her moving forward with her plan.

So, she would remain here in Achnacarry and move into the keep. No sooner had she decided her path, for now, than the door opened once more and her son stood there.

His lip was torn and swollen badly. His nose was bruised, but did not appear broken. Some other bruises rose on his face and she glanced at his hands to see abraded knuckles there. Her first instinct was to fawn and cry over these injuries, but Anna held back her emotions. Her son was clearly trying to handle this situation on his own and she must honour his attempt, even if she was the cause of it all.

'Do you wish something for your lip? I have an unguent that can help with the swelling,' she said. Iain's eyes widened in surprise for he had come here expecting the other reaction from her.

''Tis well now.' Iain stepped within and closed the door. 'The commander said I should speak with you. Tell you what happened before you heard it from others.' Anna fought to control herself in the face of his words.

'So tell me how these came about, then.'

'I got in a fight with Martyn. He said some things I could not ignore.' Iain reached up, touched his nose and then smiled at her. 'I do not think mine is broken, but his might be.'

It was his smile, crooked and slight, that sent her heart racing. In that moment, with his hair pulled back as his father had worn his, and with that proud, cocksure smile sat on his face, he looked more like his father than ever before.

Anna walked to him and ran her fingers over his nose and along the bones in his cheeks and forehead. 'Nay. Nothing is broken.' Anna backed away and ran her gaze down over his shoulders and arms to his battered knuckles.

'Have you washed them?' she asked. Once more, Anna fought her initial urge to meddle because the lady had been correct—he was at an age when that was not the best course to take.

'Aye.'

So, the motherly concerns done, that left only the matter of the cause of the fight between them.

'There was no need to take offence, Iain. Not on my behalf.' Anna met her son's gaze then and waited for his own explanation.

'A man stands up in defence of those under his protection, Mam. Even the commander understands why I had to hit him.'

'The commander? You spoke to the commander about this?' What did Davidh have to do with this? Well, other than it was his name tied to hers among the village gossip. For good reason. Any attempts to be discreet had failed.

'He saw it. He came afterwards and spoke to me.' Iain's chest puffed out with something that looked like pride. 'He understands.' Anna wanted to ask questions, but her son shook his head then. 'Lachlan gave me leave only to let you see me and ken that I am well. I must return to my work now.'

Anna clenched her hands and tangled them in her apron to keep herself from pulling Iain to her and hugging the breath from him. She smiled instead, one she did not feel, and hoped did not look like a snarl on her face.

'See then to your duties, Iain. I am glad you came to me and I am glad you are well… enough,' she said.

He ran off without another word, so Anna understood that he did not fear returning to Lachlan or continuing to work with the other lad whom he'd fought. His condition did not diminish her guilt, though. Nor did it make her choices or the decision she must make go away.

This might have been the first time he'd faced such a thing. This was not the first time Anna had witnessed it or been the centre of the gossip or attention. And she knew how it would go.

She'd lived with her mother's people in one village for nigh on five years before a man's desire for her placed her in an unwanted situation. Refusal of his demands brought his fury and he began telling stories about her, about them, that had not one shred of truth in them. The resultant rumours forced them to move to another place and begin yet again.

Here, now, there was too much at stake to let this get out of control. As much as she liked living in Davidh's house, as much as she liked him, she could not risk everything that was at stake for her son. For Malcolm's son.

Anna finished her chores here and then went out to the village, taking with her various ointments and potions for ills and ails as she'd promised. The news of her son's fight spread out ahead of her every step and the whispers increased until they were not even whispers any longer. By the time she sought the solitude of Davidh's house to make their supper, her head ached from the tension of the growing gossip.

Worse, she comprehended that she must act quickly to stop this before her only choice was to leave Achnacarry completely. Anna would speak to Davidh this night, after they supped and the lads were asleep, and on the morrow she would accept the lady's invitation to move and live at the keep.

It was her only choice.

Chapter Twenty

From the strange glances directed at her by both the commander and by her son, the discussion about her move had already begun. Well, if Iain had spoken to Davidh about the fight this morning and its causes, then they had spoken also of the outcomes and difficulties that arose from it.

By the time the lads sought their pallets and she was left alone with Davidh, Anna's hands trembled and she worried that her decision was not the best one.

And yet, it was. For all concerned. For her and her son.

'Anna, we should speak.' His deep voice sent shivers through her. When he…when they joined, it lowered even more as he whispered to her. Another shudder shook her until she gathered herself and nodded.

'Aye. There is something I need to say.'

He sat across the table from her and nodded, waiting. It was one of the things she most liked about him—he listened before he spoke. Whether man, woman or child, he listened. Now, nervousness filled her as she began.

'I have lived as a widow before in other villages and it did not take long for these kinds of rumours to arise. The suspicions, the whispering and the rest. Strangers face these things and I should have kenned that simply having the laird's permission would not overcome it.'

'Anna,' he said.

'Although our intentions were the best, to aid your son and to make it easier for me to treat those in need here in the village, it has turned out differently, Davidh. I ken you have heard the whispers and the insults. Even Lady Elizabeth has.' Anna looked away from him and stared at the fire burning low in the hearth.

'And we are not blameless for the rumours,' he added. Her gaze flicked to his for a moment and the frank desire there, in spite of their present difficulties, warmed her heart somehow.

She'd been a fool to think they could do as they had without being seen or heard. His friend Parlan had heard them. Others might have, as well. Thinking about it, Anna realised that the worst of it had begun after their...meeting in the stables. Heat crept into her cheeks as the memories of that encounter flooded her thoughts. Worse, her body ached for more of his touch.

'Nay, we are not,' she said. 'Now, though, I believe we, I, must head this off before it worsens and the laird rescinds his welcome. I cannot endanger my son…or yours, Davidh.' She stood then, clasping her hands together. 'So, I have decided that the best thing to do would be to…'

'Marry me.'

Anna blinked several times quickly, trying to sort out the two words he'd said. It should be a simple thing—two words—and yet her mind could not take them in. Davidh stood and walked around to her, taking her hands in his. She leaned her head back and looked at his face. Nay, no sign of mirth or jest there. His eyes dark and piercing stared into hers.

'You were going to say that you and Iain should move out. Move into the keep?' She nodded. 'I do not think that will solve our dilemma, Anna, for as long as you are here, I will be drawn to you.' He reached up and ran his finger down the side of her face, outlining the edge of her jaw and ending on her lips. 'I will want you the same way that you want me.'

'Marriage, Davidh?'

Over the years that she'd hidden her lack of a husband by claiming widowhood, Anna had dreamt that one day she would marry. But now? Here? Davidh?

'Have you never thought of marrying again, Anna? Was that never something you saw in your life once you'd settled here in Achnacarry?'

Had she? Truly, she'd not thought much beyond claiming Iain's birthright. So much depended on her son that she had not given it any thought and she said so.

'I confess, I had not thought on it at all,' she said.

'Well, I had not thought on it either, but 'twould seem that now is a good time to do so,' he said. 'I brought you into this situation that is causing harm to your reputation and standing. I acted on my desire for you and brought you harm. It interferes with your son's efforts to know his kith and kin and I know that was an important part of you returning here.'

Anna wanted to disagree with Davidh. She wanted to point out that their actions—together—had done the harm. Though, when she thought of what they'd shared, she had no regrets about it. The one thing that struck fear in her heart was his comment about Iain. The fight demonstrated that. And it would not be the last.

But marriage?

'I know that you have not answered to a man in your life for some time,' he began, 'and I will not ask that you give up the healing skills if we marry.'

She had, in truth, never answered to a man other than her mother's laird or this one. If they married, he would protect her reputation, ease her son's way and not demand she give up the work that she loved. Honourable, which she expected. Helpful, which she'd anticipated. Reasonable, which she'd known.

So why did her heart beat so quickly, hoping and waiting for something more in his reasons to ask this of her? Why, in spite of her life of fending for herself and her son, did she wish that there was something else, something further, he wanted from her? That he wanted *her* as his wife and not just all the suitable reasons and expectations? Not because she treated his son?

'I have not considered marriage to anyone since Mara's death, Anna. Others have pushed me to do so. Others have offered.' He reached out and took her hand, drawing her into his arms. 'You are the first, and only, woman who has managed to make me care. To make me want. To make me...'

He stopped and searched her face. His arms held her tightly against his body and she wanted to scream out her acceptance. His intense gaze softened then and she recognised something deep within it that both elated and frightened her. It would make her purpose and true path more difficult. It would, he would, break her heart if he understood that he was part of her plan. It would break her heart when she revealed the truth. His next words made it worse.

'And I will protect your son as if he was my own, Anna. I swear this to you.'

Try as she could, Anna could not find the denial within her. A simple word would make all of this so much easier. A simple 'nay' would save them both from such pain. Or, by telling him the truth about Iain would stop him from this folly and this offer that was dangerous and terrifying and coveted. She drew in a breath to refuse his offer and was stopped from speaking by his mouth on hers.

He slid his hands into her hair, knocking her kerchief off and tangling those long, strong fingers into her curls. With gentle pressure, he held her there, kissing her over and over. These were different yet again from his other kisses. He'd possessed her mouth before. He'd inflamed her desire and passion with others. These kisses held out a proposal to her. They beguiled and enticed and teased her with their gentleness and underlying passion. They offered her...more.

He lifted his mouth from hers. 'Will you marry me and be my wife, Anna Mackenzie?'

In that moment, the pragmatic woman she

was disappeared into the haze of want and need and…hope. Instead, the part of her that had never had what he offered, the part that had lost everything and everyone she'd loved, the part that wanted love and to be loved, gave the answer.

'I will.'

Davidh could be quite efficient when he put his mind to it. He smiled again, for he could not help himself. He'd claimed to Parlan and even to Anna that this offer was about honour, but he admitted to himself that there was more to it. It was just not the right time to express how much Anna had begun to matter to him. To Davidh Cameron. Not to the commander of the Cameron warriors. Not to the chieftain's counsellor. Not even to Colm's father. To him.

In just over a week from his proposal, Anna stood by his side before the priest, speaking the words he never thought he'd hear or utter again. After a new outbreak of attacks, they were going to wait, but Robert, or rather Elizabeth, would have none of that. With their help, the arrangements were handled, the priest called and a supper waited for them in the lady's solar. A small ceremony as befitted them, with friends and close kin at his side.

He looked across the chamber at the lads. Iain

had given his blessing when Davidh spoke to him, but Davidh worried a bit over Colm's reaction to this. He was so young and he still missed his mother, and Davidh wondered if he would accept Anna in this role. Since they'd told both of their sons, the boys seemed to like the idea of gaining a brother. So, if this was all working out, what was it that bothered him? Then as he looked from mother to son, Davidh knew.

She kept a secret from him.

He'd asked about Iain's father, whether other kin of his yet lived here or at Tor or one of their other holdings. The only thing she would admit was that even Iain did not know his father's name. Davidh did not try to force it from her. Mayhap, once they were settled in together, she would confide in him.

Davidh brought his attention back to her now. The priest uttered the words declaring them man and wife and those watching clapped and called out good wishes to them. He leaned over and claimed her mouth in their first married kiss, knowing that the best ones would follow in the privacy of the dark of night.

The wedding supper seemed to move along at the pace of a slug on the road. Parlan nodded to him and laughed, recognising Davidh's impatience to get this part over. The laird and lady had arranged for a chamber here in the keep for this night and his body grew tense just thinking about having her to himself for an entire night.

His cock rose, pressing against the cloth of his kilt, as he realised that this would be the first time they had lain together in a bed…well, for the purposes of joining. He remembered little of that lost night, wrapped in grief and her arms, except for the comfort she gave him. And the other times… The other times had been fast and exciting and pleasurable. Once more his flesh pulsed at the memories of her body and being deep, deep inside her.

'I wonder if it will be the same,' she whispered to him from her place next to him at table.

'The same?'

'Aye. If the element of the forbidden is removed, will it be as much pleasure as those other times?' she asked. Her voice grew deeper and his body heard her arousal and responded. Then her hand drifted under the table and brushed across his thigh and his very hard member and he fought the need to lift her on to the table and take her.

Had she read his mind? It mattered not, for her own anticipation heightened his and he dearly wished they could be finished with this meal and gone now. Parlan laughed once more and Davidh dared not meet his gaze for fear that he would lean over the table and throttle his knowing friend for his impudence. The laird happened to look over just then and he took pity on his commander. Standing at his chair, he lifted his cup.

'A toast to Davidh and Anna on their marriage day. May you be as happy as my dear Elizabeth and I have been! *Sláinte!*' Robert drank from his cup and then laughed. 'Now, get ye gone!'

Davidh took Anna's hand and they stood, accepting all the good wishes and felicitations of their kith and kin. Anna stopped and spoke to the boys for a moment before walking out of the lady's solar with him. By the time they reached the stairway leading up to the chamber, they were walking faster. He held her hand and they ran up the flight of stairs and into the bedchamber.

Once inside, passion ruled them. He could not remember undressing her or his own garments being removed. He could not remember if there were candles or a fire lit for them. He could not remember if he'd slammed the door behind them. It was only as he filled her with his flesh and heard her cry out that he came to his senses.

But the tightness of her body around his, the way she moaned with each thrust, and the feel of her breasts against his chest and her nether curls rubbing his shaft sent him into the mad oblivion of pleasure. Only when she had tightened around him and then shook as she reached her release did he relent and let his seed spill. It took longer to regain their breaths than it had to claim her. Davidh lifted his head and stared down at her.

'Did I close the door?' he asked.

'Aye,' she said with a chuckle. 'The door is closed.'

'And?' he asked, hoping she would remember their discussion at the table minutes, or was that only moments, ago.

''Twas pleasurable, but a bit quick. Mayhap the next time I will be able to decide.'

'Is that a challenge, Wife?' He leaned down and kissed her, his flesh still within her and beginning to rouse.

'I did not think you feared such a challenge, Husband.'

Davidh eased out of her and then kissed and licked his way down her lovely body. It was the first time he had seen her naked and he followed her curves with his hands, touching all the places he'd rushed over in those two previous times they had lain together. Soon, her indrawn breaths and soft gasps and the way she kept grabbing hold of his head and pressing him lower told him his path.

It took three more times before she relented and admitted that laying together, in a bed, when others knew exactly what they were doing, was

indeed just as pleasurable as hasty, hidden join-
ings in stables and stillrooms.

As the sun rose the next morning, its light
waking them from their exhausted slumber,
Anna rose and dressed and suggested they return to his house in the village to see the boys.
Davidh knew he'd learned a few more things
about his new wife this night.

Oh, aye, she liked bed play. She met him,
stroke for stroke, pleasure for pleasure, through
that long night and never hesitated in accepting
his caresses and kisses or giving her own. That
did not surprise him.

The knowledge that did was the soft whisper he heard inside as he watched her worry
over their sons. A few words that echoed in his
thoughts and trickled into his heart. A heart that
had lived with loss and pain and grief for years.
A heart he thought had long ago stopped waiting for someone like her.

A woman he could love.

When she walked to the bed and tugged him
out of it with promises of fresh bread and thick,
warm porridge the way he liked it, he knew the
truth.

He loved Anna Mackenzie.

Chapter Twenty-One

Anna paused in the yard and watched the men working there. The sound of Davidh's voice could be heard over all the shouting and it had the same effect on her whether they were alone or in a crowd. Shivers raced along her spine as he called out to one or another practising under his watchful gaze. But when he called out to her son, her heart almost stopped in fear.

Walking to the fence that surrounded a training yard, she put her basket at her feet and searched for Iain in the small group of men. Anna had to grab hold of the fence post to keep from falling over when she saw her son fighting one of the warriors there.

'Raise your arm, lad,' Davidh called out as the older, stronger, bigger man swung his weapon at Iain. 'Let the targe take the brunt of his strength and protect your head!'

She felt the urge to climb over the fence and

stop this madness when someone spoke her name. She turned to find Old Lachlan walking towards her.

'Can ye help with an injury, mistress?' the man asked. 'One of the lads struck his leg instead of the beam.' He crossed his arms over his chest and shrugged. 'Ye would think they would ken the difference by now.'

Torn between protecting her own son and helping another, Anna hesitated for a moment.

'The lad asked Davidh to train him.'

'I did not know,' she said, reaching for her basket.

'Most lads that age wouldna tell their mams that they want to fight. Better to beg forgiveness in such matters than to ask permission.' Lachlan laughed then. 'Davidh is teaching him how to defend himself and will see that no harm comes to the boy.'

'Aye, I know.'

And she did. She trusted Davidh. She did. But she wished this had not come as a surprise. Seeing to his training with Lachlan and introducing him to his kin here was one thing. Battling with a sword was not something they'd talked about and yet it must be part of the life of a warrior. Inhaling and letting it out, she turned to walk away and found Lachlan standing still at the fence now.

'Sometimes, when I see them like that, it brings back memories of another lad,' he said softly. 'Davidh and Malcolm were of the same age. But ye would not ken that one.'

Anna could not breathe then. Although some in the village and keep had mentioned the family resemblance, none had made a connection between her son and Malcolm...not yet. In the week since their marriage, Anna had learned about the dangers facing the clan now and understood that revealing her son's identity at this time would add to the danger.

She did not wish to weaken or destroy his father's clan, she only wanted him to have a claim to its leadership. And knowing these people as she did now, Anna did not want to endanger them by adding to the uncertainty that flourished as the attacks and damage did. So, she had quieted the growing guilt and impatience within her and bided her time, allowing Iain to become acquainted with more of his kin.

And Davidh had not pressed her for an answer. He'd not even asked again after that one time before their wedding a sennight ago. When she'd not given him a name, he'd let it pass. Sighing, she realised that others here who'd known Malcolm would begin to see the resemblance—if not now, then with each passing day as he grew into the size and appearance of his late father.

For now though…

'Who did you say was injured?' she asked. Then she stepped away, heading towards the stables and forcing Lachlan to follow along or allow one of his lads to suffer while they delayed.

'Martyn,' Lachlan said as he rushed to catch up with her. 'That willna be a problem for ye, will it, lass?'

'The lad who fought with Iain?'

'Aye, just so,' Lachlan said. He glanced at her and when she shook her head, he pointed to the stables.

Anna found the boy in good spirits considering the bloody gash and bruises on his leg. It took little time to clean and dress the tear. Her attention was divided between the boy who was quite proud of the bandage and Lachlan who yet stared off at Davidh and Iain working together in the yard.

Lachlan was not the only one who would see it. She thought Parlan suspected something, from his hooded gaze and intense study of Iain's face. Now that Iain was Davidh's stepson and they were seen together more often, it was but a matter of time before others remarked on it.

Before Davidh pressed the question to her. Before the time he asked and did not allow her to ignore it. Oh, she had to find a way to tell him that Malcolm was Iain's father, she just did not want to see the disappointment and betrayal in Davidh's gaze when he found out.

With each passing day, she enjoyed this unexpected life more. As Davidh's wife, she found herself drawn closer to the laird and lady. Her opinion was sought and seemed to matter. Those in the village who'd begun shunning her now found themselves in peril for doing so.

The best part of this for her was the man himself.

Davidh hesitated not one bit from any of his promises—he took Iain in hand and her son embraced and was embraced by all those who knew Davidh. No longer the outsider here, being the commander's stepson brought Iain more fully in contact with his kith and kin.

His vows to her as husband also gave her a part of him that she'd not expected—the caring and respect and appreciation that she'd witnessed in so few. Being the one he regarded, Anna discovered a fuller, deeper feeling than the love she'd felt for Malcolm. That had been, as her mother had tried to warn her, the passion of a first love with none of the reality of life. This, this was more than she could have ever wanted and she damned herself a fool for it.

Unless she gave up her own promise made on Malcolm's eternal soul to claim Iain's birthright, she would lose all of this when she spoke the truth. For now, though, Anna allowed herself this respite from all of that and simply lived this life. Loving and beloved, mother, wife, healer. And she moved through her days, holding her breath, not relaxing completely, waiting for signs that it would all be over soon.

When the beginning of the end came, Anna was too wrapped up in her new life to recognise it. It began with a stranger and an angry, wrathful woman and important visitors to Achnacarry.

Davidh waited on the steps of his house and watched Anna walk down the lane towards him. Colm tagged along at her side, chattering constantly to her, as they approached. Only the growing pallor in his son's face dampened his joy.

Anna had told him that Colm was growing worse and he could see it there. No longer did the healthy blush of a growing boy colour his cheeks. He could not run as much as he had just weeks before. And the coughing had returned. Though Colm seemed oblivious to the changes, Davidh saw every one of them. As he knew Anna did.

They had not caught sight of him when Lilias walked across their path, blocking them. Anna tucked Colm behind her in a protective move that told him Lilias's words were disturbing...or insulting in some way. He'd walked several paces before realising it, moving towards them. Iain rounded the corner then and reached his mother and Colm and the lad took Anna in hand and pushed them by Lilias who would not relent in whatever she had to say. He did not know what made him look over, but something flickered to the side and he turned to see a man standing in Lilias's doorway.

It took him a moment or two until he recognised him—Lilias's brother Ailbert. He'd not seen the man in the village or on Cameron lands for some time. Davidh slowed and stared at the man, trying to bring to mind when exactly he *had been* here last. As Ailbert watched his sister and Anna, the man suddenly startled at the sight of Iain. He stared at the boy and his mouth moved in some silent word before he noticed Davidh there. Ailbert then stepped back inside and closed the door before Davidh could speak.

Torn between seeing to Anna and the lads or seeking out Ailbert, Davidh strode to them as Lilias ran off to her own cottage.

'What happened?' he asked as he scooped Colm into his arms to carry him the rest of the way. That his son did not argue only confirmed Davidh's suspicions over his worsening condition.

'Lilias is still angry,' Anna said. Then she

shook her head and nodded to the house. 'We can speak on it once we are inside.'

Davidh did not wait to speak to Iain. He let Anna go ahead and then nodded at the lad. 'You did well then, Iain. Keeping your mother from harm.'

As Davidh closed the door behind them and dropped the latch, Ailbert's presence, or rather his recent absence, plagued his thoughts. How long had he been gone was but one question that occurred to him. The other, more complex, one was what had he been doing and why had he returned now?

Anna lifted the ever-present pot of steaming water from the hearth and carried it to the table. As he sat Colm there, she gathered the usual ingredients for the treatment. He did this one twice each day. Then she would have him sip a potion which Davidh was not certain he could drink without complaining. Lastly, before he went to bed, she would rub on a poultice to ease his breathing through the night. A sense of fear pierced his heart as he waited for his son to begin breathing in the medicinal fumes and then he could speak to Anna about Lilias.

Not the boy, not my son.

The chant or prayer began again, begging God for mercy. With Anna's arrival and the success of her initial attentions to Colm, he'd thought he'd received the answer to his prayers. Now, though, it would seem the improvement was just a temporary reprieve and the words returned many, many times each day. Davidh almost wished that he'd never allowed hope back into his heart over his son. He almost wished Anna had never tried, if it meant that his son's suffering had just been prolonged.

Then, he met Anna's glance and knew his thoughts for the lie they were. He had treasured every moment that her treatments had given to Colm. Every moment he'd gained with Colm was priceless. And Anna's arrival had brought joy back to his life. He could not be sorry for that either.

She'd brought love back into his life.

Anna walked to his side now and slipped her hand in his. Her son noticed and found some chore to do that took him back outside. A perceptive lad.

'We will fight this.' Her voice was soft, but her tone was firm with conviction and promise. We. He liked having her on his, their, side. 'Lady Elizabeth said one of the healer brothers should arrive here on the morrow or day after. I will speak to him.' Davidh lifted their hands and kissed the back of hers.

'Aye, we will fight this.' Davidh released her

so she could go back to his son. 'And we will fight the other—if you but give the word.'

He had offered to see to Lilias's disrespect of both Anna and her son in a more specific way, but Anna had refused to have the woman banished to one of their other holdings. This latest behaviour coupled with the reappearance of her brother gave Davidh pause and he suspected that punishments, sharp and punitive, would be needed soon to curb the woman's vicious tongue and angry actions.

Strange, but Ailbert's return bothered him more in this moment than the malicious words of his sister. He would speak to Parlan and Athdar about the man and seek out more about his whereabouts over the last months. In his gut, he knew that Ailbert was tied to the outlaws and the attacks, and his boldness in showing his face spoke of something coming. For now, though, he turned back to Anna.

'What did Lilias say to you in the street just now?'

'Davidh, worry not over that woman and her words.'

'I worry. I saw the way she threatened you and Colm.' Davidh shook his head. 'I will see to her, if you give the word. She will not insult you again.'

Once more, she walked to his side and touched

him. Her ease with him, never hesitating to caress him and stand close or accept his attentions and affection, surprised him when it should not. Her passionate nature was there in everything she did or said…or touched. Whether practising her healing skills or seeing to his needs, Anna had taken to married life with the same zeal as everything else she did. For a woman so unfamiliar and almost resistant to married life, she had an affinity to it. Well, as he watched her gaze move back to his son even while they were speaking, at the core of it was that she cared.

'I will speak to Robert and have her—'

'Nay. Davidh, I do not want her removed from her kith and kin.'

'She continues to sow her disrespect among the villagers who listen to her opinions, Anna. 'Tis not good for them or for you. Not in this time of conflict.'

'More conflict?' she asked. She'd heard the words he had not spoken just then, but had discussed many times in the last weeks. He nodded. 'I saw the guards you added along the roads north and south.'

'Aye. And now her estranged brother has returned. Did you see him there in her doorway?' Now she nodded. 'Have you seen him before this day?'

'I think so. I have seen him elsewhere in the

village over the last few days, but not at her cottage before this.'

'Elsewhere? Alone or with others?' He kept his voice even as Anna took the tent of blankets off Colm's head. As she administered the liquid, he waited.

'Both.'

She sat now at Colm's side and helped him to drink the horrible syrup. Her hand stroked his son's head and her whispered words encouraged him on. Davidh let them be and made some of the hot drink made of betony leaves and honey that Anna favoured. By the time it cooled enough for them to sip, Colm had finished.

'Here, Colm,' she said as she drew her cup nigh. 'Take a sip of this to clear that taste off your tongue.' Davidh marvelled at Colm's complete obedience to her orders. Or advice. He took a sip out of her cup and smiled. 'Better?' she asked.

'Aye!' the boy said as he took another sip.

'I cannot mix the two, but it will help rid you of the taste.' Davidh watched as she tended to his son before asking her anything more about Ailbert. Finally, Colm had gone off to rest before supper and Davidh could finish the matter.

'Can you remember who Ailbert was with when you saw him? Or when you first noticed him?'

'God forgive me, but the first thing I thought

when I saw him with Lilias was that she'd found another lover and would leave me be. Until just now.' Anna shrugged. She cleaned up the cups and tended to the bubbling pot that she pushed closer to the flames she stirred in the centre of the hearth. 'Her brother?'

'Aye.' Davidh's gut would not allow him to ignore this. 'I must speak with Parlan. I will return as soon as I can. Do not hold supper for me.'

'I will not hold supper for you.'

They both spoke the words at the same time and it made Davidh smile. How little time it had taken for him and them to adjust and fall into a pattern of life. He did one more thing before he left—he pulled her to him and kissed her. He put his needs and wants into that one touch of their mouths, hoping she understood the promise he gave.

Then, he left, not taking the chance that he would be distracted from his duties once more.

Chapter Twenty-Two

'You will sit by my side, Anna.'

His words were not stern or harsh, yet the command in them was clear. In spite of her preference to sit down at the table where they usually sat when eating in the hall, Davidh had informed her that they would be at the high table this night.

'First, you insist I wear my best gown. Now, you force me to sit at the laird's table. What comes next?' she mumbled under her breath. At Davidh's frown and as he squeezed her hand and tugged her along, Anna smiled. 'Of course, Husband.' His laugh eased her fears.

'I am in trouble now!' he said, kissing her hand. 'Is it Brodie who you fear meeting?' Anna looked ahead at the leader of the powerful Mackintosh Clan and nodded.

The Mackintosh's expression was dark and his gaze intense at he studied the hall and everyone who sat there before him. He was a huge man, honed by decades of fighting, whose demeanour warned anyone who saw him that he would answer in kind any threat made or implied. The only time that serious visage changed was in the moments when he looked upon his wife, the Lady Arabella Cameron.

Malcolm's twin sister.

The lady's soft laughter brought a gentleness to her husband's face that made Anna want to cry. The love there was plain for one and all to see. As Davidh had explained, they had been married after the Mackintosh clan faced destruction from within. Arabella married her enemy even believing he had been responsible for her brother's death.

The words about Malcolm made her heart race as it did now. Davidh relented on his grip of her hand and she placed it on his as was befitting the wife of The Cameron's commander. Though not raised as one, Anna could act the part when needed. She did not want Davidh's reputation or standing to be ruined by her lack of manners. They were about to climb the steps to reach the dais when Davidh met her gaze. There, shining from deep within, was the same expression that Brodie had in his when he looked on his own wife.

Love.

Davidh looked at her with love in his eyes.

She stumbled then, shocked to see it there and more surprised to recognise it. He caught her up with his strong grip and led her up to the table and those already seated.

'Nothing to fear, my love,' he whispered so only she could hear. 'I am here for you.'

She just held on to him as he led her not to their seats but to stand before The Mackintosh and his lady wife. Davidh bowed and Anna curtsied, first to his own chieftain and then to their guests. When she rose, Anna got her first, clear view of Malcolm's sister.

Whenever Lady Arabella Cameron was mentioned, so was her beauty and graciousness and, looking on her now, Anna could understand the reason for such declarations. And she was just as surprised by the differences in her and her brother's appearances. Light and dark. Angel and devil. It was all true. Yet, she could see similarities in the tilt of their mouths, the shape of their eyes. Thankfully, Lady Arabella did not have to deal with the Cameron nose!

'Lord and Lady Mackintosh, this is my wife, Anna Mackenzie, lately of Caig Falls,' Davidh said. His words pulled her from her open perusal of the lady and forced her to meet the stare of her formidable husband.

'My lord, my lady,' Anna said.

'So this is the Witch of Caig Falls then?' the

lady asked. Her tone was whimsical and clearly no insult was meant. She'd also taken care to keep these words among only them. 'I always thought my brother made up stories to disguise his other antics and yet, here you stand.'

'Nay, lady,' Anna said, forcing down the panic that threatened. ''Twas my mother that was known as that. I have only followed her path as a healer and only just arrived here.'

'I pray you forgive me my jest,' the lady said. 'I think that my brother used the excuse of hunting for the Witch to give himself a way to escape the keep and his duties. Is that not right, Davidh? You knew him well.'

'Aye, my lady,' Davidh said. 'Mal always did find a way to avoid anything he did not wish to do.'

'Have we met before, Mistress Mackenzie?' the lady asked, studying her now in return. 'You have a familiar look.'

'Nay, my lady. We have not met before.'

The lady smiled and nodded and studied her more. Anna smiled in return and tried to keep breathing. She had never met Malcolm's sister and if the lady connected her with the witch or Malcolm with the witch, it would be dangerous. It would expose her secret…and, she suddenly realised, she no longer planned to do that.

'I am glad that Davidh has found *you*, Anna.

Elizabeth does nothing but praise your efforts and your knowledge of healing,' Lady Arabella said. 'They are waiting to serve supper. We can speak later.'

Anna nodded at The Mackintosh, who said nothing while he missed nothing, and allowed Davidh to lead her around the table to their seats at one end. Glad that they had been seated together and not on opposite ends as was custom, she clung to his hand as the truth of the matter struck her anew.

She did not plan to reveal Iain's secret or her own.

When her aims had changed, when she'd decided to forgo the possibility of her son staking his claim on the high seat, she knew not. What she did know was that she wanted her son, Malcolm's son, to be accepted within his family and to be happy.

And he was.

Through Davidh's ongoing efforts and attention, Iain was being trained to improve and use his woodworking and carpentry skills. With Davidh's help and guidance, he was taking his place among the young men of the clan and learning to defend himself and to fight, if needed. With Davidh's patience and good humour, Iain was finding his way through the daily challenges of being a lad growing into manhood.

Most importantly, through it all, Davidh had helped her to find a place and be accepted and valued. To use her skills. And to attain everything she'd never thought she would have. Had her original aims been wrong? Nay, they had not. But she did not see a different possibility until Davidh entered their lives and took them into his.

And she loved him more each day for all of that and more.

'Is something wrong?' he asked, leaning close to her. 'You have the strangest expression in your eyes.' He reached up and caressed her cheek with the back of his hand.

'Thank you for all you have done for my son and for me, Davidh.'

'What brought that on, Anna?' He searched her face and she hoped that love gazed back at him. If not, then...

'I love you, Davidh Cameron.'

The declaration echoed across the small space between them and in the silence that followed, she wondered if she'd spoken the words aloud or only thought them.

'I love you, Anna Mackenzie.'

The rest of everything faded away and all she could hear or feel or smell or see was Davidh. He slipped his hand under the table and claimed hers, entangling their fingers and holding her tightly. The words expressing his feelings seeped into her heart and soul and healed so much of the emptiness and loneliness that had filled her life for too long. His actions, his love, opened her to a future so different from the one she'd imagined.

Davidh touched his mouth to hers and she wanted to cry out in joy. The noise of those around them and the approach of servants with trays and bowls of food interrupted their moment and they sat back in the chairs, though Davidh did not release her hand yet.

The meal passed too slowly, for all she wanted to do was go back to Davidh's house and be with him. Young Colm stayed the night with Suisan and Iain had planned to remain here at the keep with his friends. So, they would be alone.

All night.

She shivered then, thinking on the pleasure and the love they would share. Davidh wrapped his arm around her shoulders and pulled her close to his body. The heat of him warmed her, even as he laughed. 'We will be alone this night,' he whispered, repeating her thoughts back to her.

She did not remember what they ate or the topic of the various conversations during the rest of the meal. She did notice Lady Arabella's continued scrutiny, but then the lady's husband drew her attention and Anna's tension eased over it. Soon, the laird gave them leave and they rose and walked down from the dais and through the hall.

There was only a short delay when Iain came to speak to Davidh and, after fighting the urge to coddle her growing son, then they left. Her impatience must have been obvious for a horse was readied and waiting for them outside the door to the keep.

Soon. Soon. Soon.

Her body felt tight, waves of heat coiled deep within her, and she could hardly wait for Davidh to bring her to release. By the time they reached his house and he'd tied the horse behind it, Anna's skin tingled and a throbbing had begun between her thighs, at her core.

Soon. Soon. Soon.

Arabella watched the two lovers as they sat at table. Their love was palpable, it surrounded them and was visible to anyone paying heed. She paid heed, for she knew that she'd seen Anna before. Only when they left, walking hurriedly through the tables in the hall to reach the doorway, did she remember. The lad who walked up to her was the one who tripped the memory and, as the boy stood next to Davidh and spoke with him, she remembered.

Anna's son turned and laughed at whatever Davidh said just then and, for an instant, she saw Malcolm there again. This lad was the image of her brother at an earlier age. One that she remembered clearly. Talk of marriage contracts and arrangements had sent her running from the keep in search of her brother. Mal could always settle her nerves and she sought him out.

Lately, he'd been disappearing into the woods around Achnacarry. Especially those in the direction of the falls, north of the river that fed into Loch Arkaig. Determined to escape her father's tirades and her aunt's insistence on embroidery, she'd fled, hoping to find him. And she did.

At first glance, she thought him alone and had almost called out to him as he stood deep in the shadows off the path. Then he turned, revealing a young woman in his embrace. A young woman he kissed as though she meant everything in life to him.

A young woman who now, years later, had just been introduced as Davidh's wife.

Anna Mackenzie.

Arabella stood then, thinking to follow, but Brodie's touch on her arm stopped her.

'Where do you go, my love?' he asked, stroking her arm with his hand. 'You look as though you have seen a ghost.' By the time Brodie turned to see what she gazed at, they were gone and the son had returned to his seat in the crowd.

'I see a cousin of my aunt's there.' She nodded in some direction and smiled. 'I promised to bring her word from my aunt.'

He laced his fingers with hers and tugged her to a stop. Arabella tried to keep her expression innocent. Unfortunately, no one understood her as he did.

'You are lying, my love.' She gasped, trying once more to feign innocence. He stroked his finger down her arm and pulled her in closer. She ignored the lovely shivers that his touch created in her skin and deeper still. 'Worse,' he whispered, 'you have that glimmer in your eyes that you get just before you meddle in something you should not.'

'Brodie.'

He thought to use his kisses to stop her. His mouth claimed hers then, his tongue stroking hers even as his fingers continued their caress on her arm. For a moment, she let him, for she had no defence against this man who was the love of her life and the very breath of her body.

'My love,' he whispered as he lifted his mouth from hers. 'Tread carefully. We are here to support Robert's efforts, not endanger them.'

'Why would you think...?' He held his hand up and shook his head.

'I ken you, Bella. I have seen that very look before…well, before you do something that very often I wish you had not done. Just have a care for danger lurks and threats grow by the day. What happens here could destroy your clan and your people. Our people.'

Arabella sat down and leaned back in her chair. Damn him, but he was correct. If she told herself the truth, Brodie tended to be correct in his assessments. Sometimes, it was exasperating how right he could be. And, at times like that and even now, he did not gloat. He simply pressed her to follow his guidance.

'Very well,' she whispered, acquiescing to him.

He laughed then and it echoed out to join the frivolity of those yet dining in the hall. Lifting her hand, the one with their fingers still entwined, he kissed the back of it and nodded to her.

'Now I am doubly worried. You do not give in that easily unless you have a plan in place to do exactly what you want to do.' He squeezed her hand until she met his gaze. 'Be careful, my love. That is all I ask.'

They sat in companionable silence for a short while, listening to those at table and watching the comings and goings of the hall. Mayhap if he understood that this involved Malcolm, Brodie would support her?

'I have met Anna Mackenzie before, Brodie. While my brother yet lived. She may not remember, but I do.'

Brodie turned to face her. She had fallen in love with him even while believing he had killed her twin brother. The truth was something far from that and it had brought them together. It had brought them to marriage and bairns and peace and more. But she missed Malcolm and would have faced the possibilities of other outcomes gladly had he not died.

'Then speak to her of your brother, Bella. I ken how much he meant to you and how much you miss him still. Do it privately and keep it between the two of you.'

Tears burned in her eyes then as she looked at the current laird and lady. Robert would not be chieftain if her brother had lived. The last years of strife and destruction under her other uncle Gilbert would not have happened if Malcolm had not been struck down. She blinked against the loss of what could have or should have been.

As she walked later at Brodie's side to the chamber they'd been given for their stay here, Arabella decided she only wanted to hear about her brother from this woman who had known him. Who had, as she remembered now, loved him and been with him. And she just wanted to know if Malcolm had died knowing he had a son he had not claimed.

That was all.

Brodie waited for the servants to finish and the latch to drop before he took her in his arms and carried her to bed. Arabella's last coherent thought as her husband's onslaught of love and pleasure began was a simple one.

What harm could it do to speak to the woman her brother had loved?

Chapter Twenty-Three

She dusted off the surface of the work table and lost herself as the bits sparkled in the sunlight that poured in from the window. The morning had dawned clear and warm and seemed a suitable day after the night she had shared with Davidh. Her body warmed, too, as the memories of him pledging his love and claiming hers floated through her thoughts.

They had joined their bodies and pursued pleasure many, many times. Last night was not about desire or needs to be met, it had been about love and sealing a commitment between them.

A sound echoed through the otherwise empty chamber then. Anna laughed, realising that she stood sighing to herself like a lovelorn lass. Shaking her head, she applied more attention to cleaning the table and finishing her tasks here.

The thing was… In accepting Davidh's pledge of love and giving her own, she had given up her quest, too. Yet, this morning, as that truth set in, Anna did not feel the guilt or loss she had thought to. She did not feel a failure. Instead, she felt hope that both she and her son would live here among his kith and kin and he would find his own place within the clan.

She had been wrong to want to place him where his father might have been. Anna had been so empty for so long that she thought doing so would fill her with joy. Over the last weeks here, she had learned that she'd been wrong. Her mother had tried to tell her, but Anna had ignored her words and her warnings.

Only with Davidh's love had she seen the truth and known.

Another sigh broke the silence and Anna chuckled again.

The bubbling boil of the small pot on the fire got her attention and Anna saw to making this new potion for Colm. Crouching down before the small hearth in the corner of the chamber, Anna added several more ingredients as the brother had instructed and tended to the mix as it simmered. When she heard the door of the stillroom open, she dared not take her gaze from the important task of blending this correctly.

'This will take but a few moments more,' she called out without turning away from it.

When the mixture was as the good brother

had described in thickness and colouring, Anna lifted the pot carefully from the fire and turned to place it on the table there to cool.

Lady Arabella Cameron stood there watching her.

'My lady,' she said, offering a quick and barely respectful curtsy. 'I...'

'Nay,' the lady said. 'Finish this important task.'

Anna nodded and turned back to the table. She placed the pot on the stand so she could work more efficiently with the brew. The other necessary herbs and ingredients stood waiting in small cups, already cut and pounded into the proper powdery consistencies that Brother Richard had explained during his visit last week.

'It does not smell appealing,' the lady said.

Anna laughed. 'Few concoctions that will do any good do.'

'This is for Davidh's son?'

'Aye.' Anna added the last of the ingredients and stirred it in completely. 'Brother Richard has had some success using this for ailments of the lungs. Like Colm's.' Anna finished and poured the thick, brown liquid into a clean jug and covered it to cool. 'He will return in a week or so with other treatments that we can try.'

'You have a care for the lad.'

Anna glanced up into the lady's astute gaze and nodded. 'Aye, I do.'

'You care very much for Davidh as well,' the lady said. Anna nodded once more.

'Aye,' she said. 'I love him very much.' Even speaking the words, aloud and to someone else, thrilled her. To admit the truth of her heart felt good.

'You cared very much for my brother Malcolm.'

The words, neither spoken as a threat nor meant as one, did just that. They threatened the peace that Anna had finally found. To let the past lie where it was. Meeting Lady Arabella's eyes then, the ones so like Malcolm's, Anna saw not the lady, but the sister of a man she'd loved, looking for her own peace.

'Aye, lady. I loved your brother very much.'

Lady Arabella uttered a soft gasp and laid her hand on Anna's. 'We did not meet, but I saw him with you many years ago. I followed him one day into the forest and saw you.'

''Twas a long time ago, my lady.'

'Would you speak to me of your time with him? We were at an age when we were pulled apart, each one of us being pushed on to a separate path. 'Twould mean so much to me to hear of him from someone who kenned him.'

A simple request. A sister about her brother.

Yet, did she dare speak of matters, of a person, she'd not spoken of to anyone? Oh, she'd shared some small details and bits with Iain when she told him of his father. However, he did not know Malcolm so it mattered not what secrets she shared.

This, this would matter.

'I swear I will not reveal your words to anyone, Anna. I just miss him so much and being here, where we lived and grew up together, just makes it worse.'

So, Anna did.

For the next hour or so, they shared confidences and secrets about the man they both loved. Arabella told her things that only a sister could or would reveal about a brother—his ways of avoiding duties, his methods of torment when he wanted Arabella to do something for him and his time spent with her as their father changed after their mother's death.

For her part, Anna filled in the details about those magical months when she thought Mal would be hers and she would be his. The only thing she'd not shared was the truth about Iain. When she thought to speak about him, their son, a knock interrupted them.

'My lady,' the servant said upon opening the door. 'Laird Mackintosh waits for you in the yard.' A blush crept into the woman's cheeks and a guilty smile broke out on her mouth.

'Pray tell my husband I will join him anon.'

Anna stood and waited for the lady to do so. Lady Arabella did not move, even when the servant left. Several moments passed and still the lady did not leave.

'My lady, does the laird not wait for you?' she asked.

'Oh, he very well might, but that was his way of telling me that he knew where I am and what I am about.'

'He kens?' she asked. 'About Malcolm and me?' So much for a simple talk with a man's sister. Anna should have known better than to reveal what she had.

'Worry not, Anna. He does not ken anything specific. He understands my habit of acting on my curiosity. My meddlesome ways, he calls them.' The lady stood then and smoothed her gown down her legs. 'I would ask only one more thing before I leave you.'

Anna knew the question before it happened. The lady must have seen Iain in the hall and seen the resemblance to her twin brother. She closed her eyes and waited.

'When the time comes and you tell your son the truth, will you permit me to speak to him about my brother?'

'I...' Anna could not think of a reply. To say anything was to admit the truth—the truth of Iain's life, his place, his possible future. Yet, looking at the lady, seeing the pain of loss that Anna was certain she, too, felt, she could not deny her that one connection with her lost twin.

'I do not know when that will be, but, aye, once he knows I will tell him of your request.'

Lady Arabella embraced Anna, wrapping her arms around her and hugging her tightly. Without a word more, the lady released her, dabbed at the tears in her eyes and turned to leave. When she had almost reached the door, the lady faced her again.

'Did Mal know that you bore him a son? An heir?' she asked.

'Nay, Mal had no idea.'

Some noise at her words drew her attention. Anna glanced over at the source of it—near the door—and noticed the door had been left ajar. Davidh stood there, staring at her, having clearly heard both the question and the answer she'd given to Lady Arabella.

By the time the lady turned to see what Anna stared at, he was gone.

Davidh turned and walked away, his strides growing longer and faster as he climbed the steps and made his way out of the keep and the yard.

Her words swirled around him, but he could not think on them here. Not here. Not yet. Before he reached the gate, Davidh stopped and walked to the stables.

Lachlan directed those working on the new part of the building and had not noticed him, so Davidh kept to the shadows and searched for where the lad worked. Now, knowing the truth, it was hard not to see the resemblance to his closest friend in the boy's features and stature. Looking past the nose that many Camerons inherited, now Davidh could see Malcolm there.

He turned and left then, still not allowing himself to think too closely on this. He needed to be away from this place, from the boy, from his mother, to consider what he had done. Davidh called out then for his horse and Lachlan hurried to fetch the mount. Without a word to the man, Davidh climbed up on the horse's back and he rode. He rode fast and far and without thought of destination until the horse stopped in the road.

Glancing up, he recognised that he had ridden the long way around, but had ended up there at the falls. Davidh's gaze followed the falls up past the first break to the second part of the falls and then to its highest level. Where Annà had lived.

Where the witch had lived.

'*I caught the witch,*' Mal had told him boldly on a day a long, long time ago.

They'd laughed and Davidh had thought his friend was boasting. All of the lads in the clan sought the witch—for fun, for gain, for all sorts of reasons. Yet, no one but Mal ever claimed to have found her.

Then, his friend had disappeared frequently over the next months, without word of his whereabouts or purposes. Thinking on it now, Davidh realised that Mal had not actually revealed anything to him about that summer.

That summer ten-and-three years ago.

How had he missed all the clues that pointed to the real truth—Anna had given his best friend a son?

Davidh climbed the path up along the falls, coming out at the top. He waved the guards he'd set there off and walked the area, circling her cottage and around her garden and back to the falls. He glanced at the place where Anna had been attacked. He walked the perimeter over and over, examining every encounter between their meeting and his proposal to her.

Had she known his connection to Mal all along? For what reason had she deceived him, deceived them all, about Iain's parentage? Question after question battered against his thoughts until he could not keep them all in order. Then, one memory stuck out over the last weeks— Ailbert's possible connection to the outlaws and the coincidences between her arrival and their activities and proximity to Achnacarry. Unfortunately, Lilias's brother had disappeared once more, so no answers would be coming from him now.

So, he must find out the rest of it and inform Robert of this threat.

For the boy, Anna's son, also represented a threat to the clan's hierarchy that others could exploit. If he was Malcolm Cameron's son, then he stood in line for the high seat. Malcolm would have inherited if he'd not died. Gilbert and then Robert were only eligible because their brother Euan's line had died off.

But it had not.

Now, Robert's son was positioned as heir and tanist, preparing for the time when he would inherit. Iain's claim could supersede young Robbie's. Though legitimacy was first and foremost the deciding factor in claims, that never stood against old clan loyalties. If enough of the clan believed that Iain should gain the high chair, it would threaten everything that Robert had done to secure his place and his sons there. A challenge to his right would undermine him in an already dangerous time.

He rubbed his eyes and dragged his hands through his hair then, irritated and aggravated and sorely in need of something strong to drink.

And he was desperately in need of the truth. Not the small snippets he knew along with his suspicions, but the whole of it so that he could decide how best to protect those he'd sworn his allegiance to.

His clan and chief.

His best friend.

His wife and her son.

His own son.

Protecting one or another would threaten someone else. Not upholding his promises would destroy his honour.

No matter which way he turned, no matter the path, someone would be hurt. Some could be ruined. Some could die.

Davidh climbed back down to the road and mounted his horse. There was only one way to find the truth and that was to find his wife.

Chapter Twenty-Four

Once the lady left, Anna grabbed up the potion that Colm needed and rushed after Davidh. In that moment, she'd read shock and betrayal in his eyes before he'd left as quietly as he'd arrived there at the door to the stillroom.

She made her way in haste through the keep, trying to avoid speaking to anyone. A small crowd gathered there around Lord Mackintosh, who had indeed been waiting on his wife, as his men prepared to leave Achnacarry to hunt. The lady, standing next to her husband's horse, found herself lifted and thoroughly kissed there before everyone watching and waiting. At another time, Anna would have laughed at the very public sign of affection between the powerful laird and lady. Instead, she skirted their group and looked for some sign of Davidh.

Would he have gone to Iain? Would he go to his house? Searching across the busy yard, she saw nothing of him. Rushing through the gates, she asked the guards of him and learned he had rode out just a short time ago, in the direction of the road north.

What would he do now?

Anna walked to the house and found it empty. She could do nothing until he returned and Anna knew he would not do anything rash. He would not strike out at her or her son. He would not throw them out. She gathered up her basket and the things she needed for the villagers and left.

Lilias's brother once more stood outside her cottage there. He met her gaze and nodded a greeting before going back inside his sister's home. Anna shivered then; something about his gaze made her uneasy. She would have to tell Davidh that he was back after not being seen for some days.

When Davidh returned.

She found Colm with Suisan and administered the first dose of the new concoction. The boy's usual acceptance of her brews wavered this time and it took her a long while to convince him of its importance. Anna walked the village, keeping watch for any sign of Davidh's return, and never saw him.

The day passed without him.

The evening supper was eaten by only three of them.

* * *

When darkness fell, Anna followed her usual routine, but still found herself in bed alone. Some time in the middle of the night, still awake, she heard the door open and knew Davidh was back. A short time later, he entered the bedchamber, undressed in silence and climbed on to the pallet, lying as far from her as he could. Anna reached out to touch him, but could not make her hand go those last few inches.

His breathing never fell into the pattern of sleep, so she knew they were both awake all night.

The morning arrived, grey and cloudy, which suited her. Davidh rose without a sound or word and left their chamber.

She wanted to call him back. She wanted to explain and beg his understanding. But, truly, what could she say?

I kept my son's father a secret. I brought him here as a usurper to the clan's chieftain. I intended to use you to ease his way into the clan.

Her explanation would sound as damning as the truth of it, for she had planned to do all of that. She'd used him and his honour to make her way and to place her son, Mal's son, in good stead until she could reveal his heritage.

He would never understand the whole of it.

That she'd lost her resolve because she loved him. That his love made her see a different path for her son. That she did not want upheaval and danger to face her son's clan because of his identity.

Anna rose and dressed and prepared their morning meal. Davidh spoke in his usual tone to the lads, asking the questions he did each morning and sending them on their way to their chores and tasks. He lingered over Colm, asking about this new concoction and watching his son closely as he imbibed it.

Never once did he meet her gaze. Oh, he did not speak rudely or ignore her. He just did not touch her or kiss her or even look at her directly. Her heart ached, understanding what she stood to lose now. If she had not fallen in love with him, his anger and disdain would not hurt so much.

'I will walk Colm to Suisan's,' he said, guiding his son to the door. 'Wait for me.'

That short time while awaiting his return was the longest time in her life. Anna tried to keep busy, but every sound outside, every footstep past their door drew her attention. Even her favourite tea did nothing to ease her frantic worry. Finally, he opened the door. Standing there, outlined by the light behind him, Anna could not see his face.

'So, 'tis true then? Malcolm Cameron fathered your son?' He stepped inside and slammed the door, making her startle then. 'He is the secret you kept?'

'Aye.' The word echoed across the now-great distance between them, confirming her sin against him.

'Did you ken who I was to him when we met?' He took a step towards where she sat. 'Did you ken I was his friend?'

'Aye,' she whispered once more. 'He spoke of you often.'

'And yet, he never once spoke of you.' She flinched at his words, for there was a harshness in them she'd not heard before from him. 'You kept the boy a secret from Mal as well?'

'That is not what happened, Davidh,' she said. He did not have enough of the details to understand.

'You told his sister he knew not of the bairn.' Davidh reached the other side of the table then and placed his hands on it, leaning over. 'So many secrets, Anna. How did you keep all the lies straight?'

'Davidh, I pray you...' she began.

'Does Iain know? Or was that another lie?'

'Davidh.' Anna shook her head. 'Sit. Let me explain.'

'More lies? More secrets? I think not.'

'I have not lied to you. You knew I kept the identity of Iain's father to myself.'

'Why, Anna? Just tell me why?' He sank on to the chair and stared at her.

'We have all kept secrets, Davidh. Mal kept me as his, not even telling you about me.'

She let out a breath and tried to find the words she'd practised to say. And could not. She stared at the fire, remembering the day when Malcolm Cameron came into her life.

'My mother did not want my presence known to anyone here, so I stayed up above the falls, out of sight. I've come to believe that she feared exactly what happened—that I would meet a lad, fall in love and want to be with him.' Her eyes burned with tears then. 'I fell in love with him the first time I saw him. 'Twas the foolish first love of two people too young to ken better. Or to realise all the problems they would face.'

Davidh shifted on the chair, drawing her attention for a moment. He was uncomfortable, it seemed, with her explanation about loving his friend. Anna looked back at the flames in the hearth.

'We hid from everyone. My mother had no idea until 'twas too late.' She looked at him. 'I saw you then. Those times he led you away from the falls so you would not use your cleverness and find the way up. So that you would not ken that he had found the witch's daughter. That he had caught me.'

'You were carrying?'

'Aye. I was pregnant within weeks and my mother knew it by the time I was three months.' Anna let out a sigh. Smiling then at the memory of the moment she'd realised she was carrying Mal's bairn. ''Twas wondrous and frightening and a miracle. But Mam was a practical woman who explained the hard truth of the situation to me.' She faced him then.

'You see, Mal told me that he would convince his father to let us marry in church.' Davidh's snort at those words gave her pause. 'All I needed to do was wait until he could.'

'No one ever convinced Euan Cameron of anything the man did not want to do,' Davidh said softly.

'Aye. That's what my mam explained. We left and returned to her clan up north. Iain was born six months later, hearty and hale and wonderful. I'd always planned to tell him of his son. Then word came of his death.'

She stood then, for this would be the harder part to tell him. It would expose her pettiness and need and…greed. Anna took her cup over to the hearth and filled it from the pot simmering there. He shook his head when she looked at him to offer him some. Returning to the table, she took the stopper out of the small jar of honey and let a dollop drop into the cup.

'His death changed me, Davidh. I'd always harboured a hope of being reunited with Mal. That I would send word to him of his son and he would force his father to accept him, to accept us.' She shook her head sadly, seeing the truth of it so clearly now. 'Knowing he was dead, I grew resentful. There was a time then when I hated Mal for never searching for us, for me. And then for abandoning us.'

'His father sent him away.'

Anna glanced at Davidh. His expression was empty. 'What do you mean?'

'At the end of that summer. His father sent him away, to the south, to another of his holdings. To Robert, if memory serves me.'

'Without word, I grew bitter. I decided that, at some point, when Iain was of a certain age, when my mother no longer fought me on it, I would return here and claim Iain's birthright. I made a vow on Malcolm's soul that I would not fail his son.'

'So, you came not as a healer, but on your son's behalf?'

'Even then, 'twas both. Things had become

difficult in the village after my mother's passing. A woman, alone, with a son.' She shrugged, remembering the few choices facing her over the last year. 'I had heard stories about Gilbert, so I did not think about moving here then. But when word spread about the upheaval and that a new chieftain sat in the high seat, I thought 'twas time. I had something to offer in exchange for a place here.'

'You came and bided your time. I guess I was a convenient addition to your plan? Offering to bring you to Robert. Offering my help. Protecting you.' His words ended with the same bitterness that she'd felt all those years before. She would not lie to him now, no matter how hard it was to admit the truth.

'At first, aye.' He slammed his hands on the table and pushed back, pacing around the chamber, but never close to her.

'When I asked you to marry me—was it for your purposes then, too?'

She closed her eyes, unable to see the pain the truth would cause him. 'Aye. But…'

'Nay! Make no excuses. I would hear the truth and ken the extent of your deception.'

''Tis no excuse, Davidh. I was still on my path when you asked me to marry you. But, *but* I was losing the heart and commitment to my original plan even then. For the first time in my life, I had the opportunity to have what I'd always wanted. Not for my son. Not for Mal's memory. Not to prove my mother wrong. For me. Just for me.' The tears spilled now, down over her cheeks. She dashed them away with the back of her hand.

'And still you did not trust me enough to tell me.'

The silence between them grew as he stared at her from the corner of the room. As he waited, he already knew the answer. She had refused to tell him, even when he'd asked her directly.

'What did you think I would do? Tell Robert? Harm the boy somehow, Anna?' Her eyes widened and he knew he'd struck the truth. 'He is the son of my best friend. I'd promised you I would protect him.' He let out a breath, remembering earlier words than the ones he had given Anna. 'I'd promised Mal to be at his side and be godfather to his son. A blood oath, made by two lads who thought they would ever be friends.'

The small scar on his hand itched then, reminding Davidh of the words spoken as their blood mingled, sealing their boyhood promise. He rubbed at it with his thumb now.

'Aye, I thought you would tell Robert. I ken where and to whom your loyalties are, Davidh. But I never suspected that you would harm my son. Though what others may want or may do, I ken not.'

He let out the breath he didn't know he held in at those words. If she'd thought he could harm her son…

'So, now that I ken about the boy, tell me the rest of it. You ken the dangers of trying to claim his birthright now. How will you do it?' He crossed his arms over his chest, trying to harden his heart against her. She'd claimed to love him. She'd given herself to him. All of it a lie.

'I did not know about the outlaws until I arrived here.'

'Wait!' He strode across the chamber until he stood before her. 'Truly? Or are you in league with them?'

'Davidh!' she cried out. 'Nay! I have no part in their mischief. They attacked me.'

He had struck out at her with that accusation. It was not good of him to say such a thing. But he was angry. Angry at her for deceiving him. For deceiving all of them. For using him. All of it. He glanced away from her, the pain in her gaze too much for him to look at.

'I came here for all the wrong reasons, Davidh. I admit it. I give you my word that I never acted on them. Once I met you, met Colm and the others, and they let me in, I weakened in my resolve to see my plan through. I could not carry it out, for I fell in love with you and them. You had given me everything I'd ever truly wanted in my life.'

He wanted to believe her. He wanted to believe that her words of love were true. But if she could not trust him, how could she proclaim to love him?

Davidh glanced at her for a moment and knew that they'd said what they had to say to each other. Could they go on? Together? If they did not trust each other, could they truly love one another?

'I must go,' he said. He walked to the door and lifted the latch. 'I have duties.'

His duties had kept him sane through the years of loss and pain. They had been the one thing he could count upon to remain the same.

He left without another word to her, trying to sort through his choices now. His first loyalty was to his clan and chief and he should report this to Robert and let him decide. He climbed up on his horse and touched his heels to the horse's sides.

Instead of the keep, Davidh took the horse to the stables and left it there. He found himself wandering over the next hours, watching the men training, observing Lachlan and his lads building, and even just standing there and watching as life moved on around him.

His place among all of this had always been

settled. He was a man serving the Cameron Clan, serving its chieftain, protecting the chief and clan from dangers and attacks, from within or without. He selected the most able to guard and protect his clan and to fight for their causes. He protected those unable to fight.

Now, though, one of the most dangerous attacks had slid past his guard. She'd distracted him by caring first for his son and then for him. She'd brought in her own son, a young man who threatened not only the peace that Davidh fought to maintain, but also the very hierarchy he'd promised to defend.

More than that, she'd raised the spirit of his dead friend from his grave, reminding Davidh of the first promises he'd ever sworn.

When the training was done and the evening meal called, Davidh was no closer to sorting it all out. What should have been a clear choice—to honour his vows to his chieftain—somehow paled when he considered the effects that would have on the woman he loved.

He walked through the gates this time, returning to his house, his son, his best friend's son and his wife. As he lifted the latch to find them all there, he was no closer to a decision than he had been on learning the truth.

Chapter Twenty-Five

Anna stood there, in his house, before the hearth, trembling. Great shivers shook her body. All the colour had disappeared from her face and the ghostly pallor made him think she was getting sick. Who treated the healer when she needed help?

Davidh closed the door behind him and looked and listened for the boys. No sign or sound of them. He had to fight the urge to take her in his arms and kiss her. When she still did not speak, but only stared with a horrified expression in her green gaze, he went to her.

'What is it, Anna? Are you ill?' He lifted his hand to touch her brow much as she did when inspecting someone who was fevered. 'Is it Colm?' His worst fear was for his son. Had it happened? Had his lungs finally given up their struggle? Was he...? 'Dead?'

'I did not know what to do, Davidh,' she whispered. She held out her hand and in it he saw a folded piece of parchment. 'You are the only one I can ask for help.'

Davidh opened the note and read it. His blood froze in his veins and he understood why Anna was so shaken by it.

Unless she brought whatever proof she had to make her claim for Iain's rightful place, those who had taken him would kill his son. Then, if she still did not, they would send her pieces of her son until she relented.

'Dear God, who has them?' he asked. 'Where did you find this? When? Was anyone around? When did you see the boys last?' At her rapid blinking, he realised he was rattling off questions and giving her no chance to answer them. 'When were the boys last seen?'

'I asked Iain to remain here with Colm. He was not feeling well and I wanted him to rest. Suisan went to visit her sister, so I could not send him to her. That was just before noontime.'

'Iain stayed here?'

'First he went to speak to Lachlan and then he returned. I fed them and went to see those who were ill.' Anna glanced around. 'I came back to begin cooking and the house was empty. Before I could go search for them, something hit the door and I found this tied around a rock.'

He examined the note once more, looking for

anything he might have missed the first time. The instructions told him that these people had knowledge of not only how things were done here in Achnacarry, but also what was going to happen. So, they had spies here. Her hand on his arm surprised him. It was the first contact between them since he'd learned the truth about Iain.

'You must save the boys, Davidh. If you do, I will destroy the proof and take Iain away from here. He will never be used to threaten the Camerons again and you will be free of us. Just save them, I pray you.'

'Why did you not come and find me when you got this?'

'They are watching. They know you are to escort The Mackintosh and his wife to their lands on the morrow. It says not to tell you about this and if I did something wrong…'

'You did well.'

His thoughts spun rapidly then about what he could do, what these outlaws must know and what they wanted. They would keep his son alive as long as he was needed—if the very actions of kidnapping him had not harmed him already. Iain had been their true target. Somehow they had learned of his identity and were pinning their hopes of uniting the Camerons behind themselves, ridding themselves of Robert and his sons and placing Iain as the rightful heir.

'What will you do?' she asked. She wrung her hands, clenching and unclenching them ceaselessly. Her eyes were wide with worry and fear.

'On the morrow, we will follow their instructions. I do not ken what proof you have, but take it and leave it as they demanded you do.'

She turned then and walked to her sewing box. Opening it, she searched for something and lifted it out. Anna walked back and gave it to Davidh. He held it up and examined it.

Malcolm's ring.

The clan crest carved into its dark jewelled surface, this ring had been made for him by his father and given to him on his twelfth birthday. A chieftain's gift to his heir to mark his position as tanist. Anyone who'd been alive at the time would remember the ceremony, the festivities and the pride that Euan Cameron expressed in his son as Mal took his place as the heir to the clan. As Davidh recognised it.

He also remembered when Mal claimed to have lost it. The punishment was swift and terrible for The Cameron did not forgive the loss of something so valued easily. Not even for his only son and heir.

Not lost at all, it would seem. Given to the woman Mal loved as a pledge and sign of his promise. Davidh glanced over at that woman now and knew he loved her. What a strange irony this was—to love the woman whom his best friend had also loved. He smiled at her and handed the ring back.

'In the morn, I will leave for the keep and escort The Mackintosh and his wife back to their lands. You will wait and take this to the place they say and leave it.' Anna began to speak, to question him, but he stopped her with his finger on her lips. 'I ask that you trust me, Anna. Can you?'

She searched his face and nodded.

'Good. Then seek your rest, for the morrow will be a long and tiring day.'

'Will they harm them?' she asked.

'The lads are valuable to them. Nay, I do not think they will come to harm.'

At first, Anna took a step closer and he almost opened his arms to her. She looked away then and went off to their chamber as he'd instructed.

He got no sleep that night and was certain she did not either. Davidh sat on Colm's pallet and wondered if his son was frightened. He thought on Iain, who most likely had no idea of why they'd targeted him or of his value to them. What a terrible way to discover the secret of your parentage.

* * *

When the sun rose the next morning, Davidh had thought out his plan and was ready. It all depended on trust, his trust in others and Anna's trust in him. He prayed as he walked out the door that he would not be shown a fool for having misplaced his.

Anna could not speak to him. The terror almost overwhelmed her as the morning came and it was time to play her part. Only his quiet, confident words, urging her to follow his instructions and trust him kept her from screaming like a *ban-sidhe* through the village.

She fought the urge to beg his forgiveness and to throw herself at his feet. She'd offered what she could in return for his help and Anna prayed that their sons would not pay the price for her lies and betrayal.

After putting the ring around her neck and tucking it inside her shift, Anna followed the instructions and walked to the edge of the village and turned on to the east road, the one that would lead to the loch and then south along it. She counted the large boulders at the side of the road and stopped at the tenth one. Lifting the ring over her head, she asked Mal if he was listening to ask the Almighty to protect the boys.

Then, she wrapped the ribbon around the ring and left it there on top of the rock.

Anna closed her eyes and listened for a moment before turning back and walking away. It was one of the hardest things she'd ever done, but Davidh had promised he would rescue the boys. She just had to trust him.

When the boys were safely returned, as he'd promised, she would take Iain and leave. They would find another village, far away, where they were not known and make their life there.

Anna spent the rest of the morning helping Suisan with laundry and trying to behave as if it was just a customary morning for her. Suisan had so much gossip to share from her visit with her sister that the woman hardly paused long enough to take a breath. Which was fine with Anna.

Minutes passed like hours and, by the time it was midday, Anna felt as though she had lived and waited a week. She begged off of staying longer and walked back to Davidh's house to wait…and to pray…and to hope. Once she latched the door, she realised that she would have to pack once more. She had moved more times in just the last three months than she had in almost the whole of her life until now.

Standing in the middle of the chamber, she

turned round and round, taking in all the baskets and bowls and jars and pots. With summer's approach, the gardens near the top of the falls would begin to yield up their growth and there would be herbs and leaves and plants and stems to cut and dry and store. The stillroom would be stocked and the supplies would last through the coldest part of the next winter.

But she would not be here. Her gaze fell on her mother's basket. It was the one that Anna used to carry supplies as she made her way through the village each day. She would take that and some of the basics that she'd brought with her. Cuttings from various plants that she could plant at her new home.

Lost in thoughts of leaving and losing everything here that she'd begun, the clatter outside grew louder before she took notice. Yelling, horses stomping, and then loud footsteps had her pulling the door open just as Parlan reached it.

'Parlan? What is it?' Anna said.

She barely stepped out of his way as the large man came running at her, his arms full of a blanketed bundle. She could see only hands and feet sticking out as he pushed his way past her and ran for one of the bedchambers.

Only when he laid the bundle down on one of the pallets did she understand that it was a boy.

An unconscious boy. Parlan tugged the blankets free and stood away.

'Davidh said to bring him to you and you would save him.'

Dear God in Heaven! It was Colm. He looked a ghastly grey shade and she was not certain he yet breathed. She reached over and pinched his leg sharply to elicit a response. She cried out as he gasped slightly at the pain of it.

'He is alive,' she said. Leaning down, she placed her hand on his chest and listened close by his mouth. 'Barely breathing,' she said. Touching his face and neck, she found his skin cool and damp. 'No fever.' Pulling her attention away from the sick child, she looked to Parlan. 'Iain? Did you find my son?'

'Nay, only Colm. But Davidh is yet tracking them,' he said. 'He will find him, Anna.'

She tried to believe Parlan's words and to keep the terrible fear in her heart at bay. The only thing she could do right now was see to Colm and pray to God that both lads would survive. Apparently, the clamour of Parlan's arrival had drawn Suisan's attention and she pushed her way into the bedchamber and knelt down at Anna's side.

'What can we do? What do ye need, lass?'

Anna called out orders—heat the water, find this herb and that, pour this, blend that—and they were done. First, she had to stimulate his breathing with one potion. Then, she must have a care for the cough that would happen. Next there would be cramping in his muscles and possibly convulsions.

And at each step, the boy could die.

Not his son. Not his son. Not his son.

Under her breath, constantly throughout the next hours as she fought for Colm's life, she prayed and bargained with the Almighty, much as Davidh had confessed that he did for his son through the last years of tending to his illness.

She did not leave the boy's side, not through that day or the night that followed. Suisan and Parlan were her constant companions and other villagers and kith and kin stopped to see if they could offer her help as she fought to save Davidh's son.

Only the next morning, as Colm opened his eyes and met hers, asking for his father, did she take a moment and ask Parlan what had happened. When the man began to explain, Colm interrupted him several times, taking long, measured breaths in before speaking in a low, slow pace.

'Iain told them that my father would slaughter them if I died. He told them they did not need the trouble that I would bring.'

'Bold words,' she said, her heart proud of her own son no matter what happened now. Another silent prayer in her son's name floated up to the heavens.

'Aye, he told me to wait for his word and then pretend I was sick. He said to cough and then lie on the ground as though dead. So, I did just that.'

'Colm!' Anna shook her head while Parlan called out 'good lad.'

'He told them to leave me where I was so I would not slow them down.' Colm shrugged. 'I knew he was protecting me, for he'd said we were brothers and that's what brothers did.'

'Your son managed to leave a trail behind them. Davidh and the others were following to find their camp while I brought Colm to you.'

'When his pretending became too real,' she finished. 'But wait? The others?' she asked.

'Aye, love. A good commander always takes enough men to carry out his mission.'

Anna turned then to find Davidh there, in the doorway of the bedchamber, covered in mud and dirt, a few leaves and a good amount of blood. A quick glance told her it was mostly not his. She stood then and watched as he stepped aside, revealing Iain there behind him.

Anna crossed the short distance and clutched her son to her, wrapping him in her arms and hugging the breath from him. For the first few

moments, she controlled herself, but then realising that she could have lost him, lost Davidh
and Colm, Anna broke into sobs that would not
be held within.

'Commander?' her son said, over her shoulder as she cried.

'Here now, my love,' Davidh said, as he eased
her off Iain and into his arms.

'I thank you for bringing my son back safely,'
she whispered.

'And I thank you for saving mine. I thought
him dead in that moment when we found him
by the road.'

'I told you, Mistress Mackenzie,' Colm called
out. 'I played dead just like Iain told me to do.'

Davidh released her and went to his son,
kneeling at his side and whispering to the boy.
She wanted to cry more, to ease the sadness that
filled her, but there was too much to do now.
Davidh had fulfilled his part of the bargain and
now she must do as she'd promised.

'I would like to stay just one more day,' she
said. 'To make certain his breathing is back to
what it should be.' She wiped away her tears and
smoothed her hands down over her skirts and
apron. 'Then we will leave.'

'Leave? I do not wish for you to leave, Anna.
I never asked that of you.'

'But I promised I would.'

'I think we should stop making promises we cannot keep and only make those we can.' Davidh took her hand in his and entangled their fingers as he liked to do. 'I promised to love and cherish you. That is where we can start.'

'And I promise to trust you, Davidh.'

He kissed her then, promising her in that quick touching of their mouths that his love was hers for always.

When the murmuring and whispers around them grew louder, Anna realised that they were not alone. Well, only a few people were inside the house, but the sounds from outside made it clear that others were waiting and listening. She walked to the doorway and looked out.

There in the road, a large group congregated around Davidh's house. Not only Camerons, but Mackintoshes, too. Warriors on horses and on foot. Both of the chieftains, along with their personal guards and more. Villagers and those from the keep stood watching and waiting.

'You went to the laird?' she whispered to Davidh.

'Aye. I have faith in my chieftain and kenned I could ask for his help in this. He did not fail me.'

'Does he ken the truth of it?'

'Aye, mistress,' The Cameron said with a nod as he'd heard her question. 'I ken.' The Mackintosh nodded as well and Anna wondered at that.

'The boy is my kin, too, Mistress.' The Mackintosh glanced down the road towards the keep. 'Damn it,' he swore aloud. 'She cannot stay where I put her. I will try to slow her down.' Swinging his long leg over, Brodie Mackintosh climbed from his horse and walked off towards his wife who was running towards them.

Iain was the lady's nephew, the son of her twin brother. But did her son know that? Turning away and leaving The Mackintosh to see to his approaching wife, she looked at Davidh.

'Does Iain know?'

'Aye. The outlaws told him when they tried to convince him to play a part in their uprising. They promised to support him if he claimed his rightful place,' Davidh explained.

'Iain, I beg your pardon for not telling you first.' Anna walked to her son. 'I should have told you long ago about your father.'

'You did, Mam,' Iain said. 'The commander and I have been talking about him. You told me so much about him and the commander added more.'

Before she could say more, the laird dismounted and walked inside alone. She curtsied to him as he approached.

'Davidh's son is well?' he asked.

'Improving, thank God.'

'I would speak to you about a private mat-

ter,' he said softly. 'To put your mind at ease, if
I can, mistress.'

They walked to the other side of the room
and she reached out her hand to Davidh, invit-
ing him to join them.

'Davidh told me a little of the story, but there
is more that I can tell you.' She felt Davidh's arm
encircle her waist, holding her close. 'Malcolm's
father kenned about you,' the laird said. 'I do not
believe he kenned about the bairn, but he took
you as a threat to his control over his son and
the plans he had in mind for the boy.'

'He did? How?'

'There was not much that Euan did not control. From what he told me when he sent Malcolm to me that summer, I think he threatened
your mother to make her take you away.' Anna
gasped. 'Then he sent my nephew to me with
orders to send him south and keep him away
for months.'

'Which you did,' Davidh added. 'Mal did not
return until the middle of winter.'

'When he returned here, my brother supervised him more closely and tasked him with
more responsibilities to prepare him as his heir.
Malcolm never had much time after that for mischief, as my brother called it.'

'Why do you tell me this?' she asked the laird.
'Is Iain not a threat to you?'

''Tis no secret that I came by this seat late in my life and how it happened. Though I want my eldest to have it after I am gone,' he said, 'life has a way of interfering with plans we make. And I have learned that it is not good to tempt the fates too loudly.'

The laird nodded at her son. 'I am pleased that Malcolm's son is here now. He will learn and train and, if called to serve, will be chosen and placed on my seat.' Robert nodded at her son. 'He has a good teacher in Davidh,' he said as he took her hand. 'As he had in his mother.'

Robert reached inside his tunic and brought out Malcolm's ring. 'His father gave this to you in pledge and his son should have it. We got it back when we took the camp.' He gave it to her. 'I have had them struck for my own sons.' Robert Cameron cleared his throat and spoke so all could hear now.

'Elizabeth will be waiting at the keep. I should go to her and tell her before she, too, comes running.' He pulled open the door, glanced down the road and laughed. 'Too late, I fear. I think The Mackintosh's wife might be a bad influence on mine.'

He pulled the door closed behind him and quiet descended within the house.

Chapter Twenty-Six

When the laird left, the crowd outside began to disperse, too. Word had spread that young Colm was on the mend and so the usual demands of life called them all back to their work and duties. And the promise of a feast to celebrate the defeat of the outlaws two days hence gave everyone something to cheer about.

Soon, only Anna and Davidh and their sons remained there. Colm was sleeping now, for his battle to breathe and the medicaments and concoctions she'd given him had tired him. When he'd handed the boy to Parlan by the road, Davidh did not know if he would see his son alive when he returned. So, for now, he sat by his pallet, holding and rubbing Colm's hand, as he offered up more prayers.

Davidh could hear the quiet conversation between Anna and her son out in the main room. Iain had acted with courage and intelligence these last days. His quick thinking about Colm had, Davidh did not doubt, saved his son's life. And Iain had sorted out where the outlaws camp was and left good signs of their trail so Davidh could follow.

They had attacked swiftly and the outlaws were, to a man, destroyed. Ailbert, Lilias's brother, had been their spy and had met the same fate as the others. As Davidh considered what had happened, he only then noticed he yet wore the grime of the road and the blood of their enemies. Many had died this day, but only one of his men.

He watched Colm sleep now and slowly released the boy's hand on to the pallet. Standing, he tucked the blankets around his son's frail shoulders to keep him warm. He left the bedchamber and found Anna alone.

'Where is Iain?'

'He wanted to see his friends. He was not hurt and seemed more excited to speak with them, so I saw no reason to keep him here.'

'Iain looks at this as an adventure. He now has a story to share with the others.' Davidh waited for her to face him, but she did not. 'He is like his father in that, Anna. Mal could not wait to tell me of his travels when he returned to Achnacarry.'

He saw her head nod in agreement and realised that Mal had done the same with her all those years ago. The well-educated, travelled son of the chief telling the woman he loved about his adventures. They had shared the same friend.

'I am heating water so that you can wash.' She stood there by the hearth. 'And there is porridge in the pot. I thought it would be something hot and filling if you hunger.' Her voice was halting and she did not look at him as she spoke.

Something was wrong.

He walked over to her and turned her to face him. She shook in his grasp. Her eyes were wide and haunted and her skin cool and pale. Davidh had seen this many times, even felt it himself, after facing danger. He rubbed his hands down her arms from her shoulders to her elbows and back, trying to bring some warmth into her.

'This is just a reaction to all you have faced this day. The fears you controlled so that you could do what needed to be done. The worries over my son as you fought to keep him alive. Even watching your son turn into a young man who is new to both of you. You fought a great battle this day, my love.'

He leaned down and pressed his mouth to hers, the tip of his tongue touching her lips, tasting the remnants of her fear. She leaned into him and opened to his kiss. He tasted her, sliding his tongue into the heat of her mouth and finding her own. Rubbing his against hers, Davidh felt her body relax against him. Her arms slid around his waist and she held him close, disregarding the filth he yet wore.

'I should have trusted you, Davidh. I should have told you who he was as soon as I knew who you were.' She lifted her head and looked up at him.

'I should have trusted you, Anna. When you explained. When you said that you had changed your mind. We could have introduced him to Robert together, made him known to his kin without making him a possible weapon to be used against them.'

'Mistakes.'

'Aye, mistakes. I do not plan on making them again.' He watched her face as a smile filled it then.

'I am not accustomed to answering to a man,' she whispered. 'I have been on my own, seeing to my needs and my son's, for so long, 'twill take some time for me to learn to depend on someone else.'

'We have that time now,' he said. 'Now that we have got over the dangerous parts, it should be much easier.'

Anna laughed then and his heart warmed at the sound. He wanted to hear that always. For so long his home had been filled with sadness and grief and worry. Now, with her, it would be filled with warmth and joy.

And two sons to raise together.

He held her then, in silence, simply enjoying the possibilities that now lay spread out for them. As he did, a strange thought occurred to him.

One day long ago, his friend Mal had asked him to stand as godfather and protect his wife and heir. The request came unexpectedly and Davidh thought it strange how Mal was making such plans for his future wife and son. As he thought on it now, Davidh remembered when they had spoken of such a thing.

It had been a year after that summer. The summer when Mal had met and loved Anna and created Iain. Had Mal known all along, then, of the son Anna gave him? He looked down at Anna and wondered if he should tell her.

One day, he would sort it out and speak to her about it.

For now, he would stand as guardian to her son. For now, he would hold her and protect her and love her. Everything else would follow.

Two days later

'Lady Arabella has invited us to visit Glenlui.'

Anna watched as her son spoke with the chieftain and his wife—his aunt. Brodie Mackintosh apparently was quite impressed by Iain's actions in the rescue and battle that followed and had spoken to her and Davidh of fostering him. As her son talked with the powerful chieftain, Anna smiled. Clearly, Iain was pleased and the smile on the lady's face as she met her brother's son told Anna that they would have a care for the boy if the offer was accepted.

'She said we could visit at any time.'

'So, Wife,' Davidh whispered as he slipped his hand around hers, 'have you decided then?'

'After hearing your counsel and kenning it would not be until next year, I think we should accept. Iain will benefit greatly from it and he will get a chance to meet his Mackintosh cousins and other kin that live there.'

'*We*, is it, then?' He laughed from behind her and the warmth of his breath tickled her skin there. 'I am so glad that my wife pays heed to my words and my orders.'

His words teased them both, for he was thinking of the hours they'd spent in bed together this morn and the *orders* he'd given her. She shivered as her body remembered some of the most pleasurable ones.

'But, certainly, my husband. I would always obey your commands.' She pressed back against him and felt his male flesh hard against her buttocks. He let out a groan as his body responded to hers.

Anna laughed then, stepping away and trying to stop teasing him. If she was not careful, he would find a place—a closet or alcove—and pull her in there. Oh, she enjoyed those encounters and would not deny it to him, but she had something to tell him and it seemed like the right time. Anna smoothed her hands over her skirts, trying to find the words.

'Iain's journey to Glenlui might be perfectly timed,' she began. Anna turned slightly so she could see his face. 'I will be quite busy next spring.'

'By then, your gardens should be well in hand,' he said. 'Are you expanding them?' She laughed then at the words, even though he did not understand…yet.

'Well, Husband, the gardens are not expanding, but I suspect I will be.'

One moment passed. Then another and another. Finally, his eyes widened and he sucked in a deep breath.

'Truly?' he whispered. She nodded. 'When did you ken?'

Anna shook her head and leaned closer. 'I thought that all the…upheaval had caused my courses to be late. Then, this morn, I did not keep my porridge down.' He smiled wide—

a daft reaction to someone heaving up their morning meal. 'When I thought more on it, and counted back, I realised I have not bled since...' She felt the heat rise in her cheeks. 'Since you... Since we used the table in the stillroom.' His actions to prevent such a thing that morning had clearly been unsuccessful.

He laughed loudly then and drew the attention of those around them. Then Davidh took her into his arms and claimed her mouth. One kiss, after another and another, until she was laughing and gasping for a breath. Then he dragged her away from those before the dais and...into a curtained alcove near the corridor.

'Are you well?' he asked. 'Other than losing your porridge?'

'Aye. So far, I am well.'

'Are you pleased? We never spoke of having a child.' His worried gaze stared into hers.

'I am shocked and overwhelmed, Davidh.' She smiled then. 'But I am well pleased.' He'd taken hold of her hands and entwined their fingers. 'Are you?'

'Aye, love. I am pleased at the thought of our own child.' He kissed each of her hands. 'And Colm will be thrilled to gain another brother...'

'Or sister,' she added.

'Or sister. When shall we tell him and Iain?'

'I think we should tell him when we discuss

The Mackintosh's offer. Then we can tell Colm he is to be a big brother at the end of winter next.'

A few minutes later, Anna and Davidh returned to the festivities. As she sat at table, she realised that her life had come fully around from when she'd met Malcolm Cameron.

Now, as she'd hoped and dreamed, their son was accepted by his clan and he would live and grow among them.

Malcolm Cameron might have died, but the best of him yet lived in his son and heir. Whether he sat on the high seat of the clan or served in some other way was yet to be seen.

* * * * *

COMING SOON!

We really hope you enjoyed reading this book. If you're looking for more romance, be sure to head to the shops when new books are available on

Thursday 29th November

To see which titles are coming soon, please visit
millsandboon.co.uk

MILLS & BOON

Coming next month

A SCANDALOUS WINTER WEDDING
Marguerite Kaye

'Kirstin.'

He blinked, but she was still there, not a ghost from his past but a real woman, flesh and blood and even more beautiful than he remembered.

'Kirstin,' Cameron repeated, his shock apparent in his voice. 'What on earth are you doing here?'

'I wondered if you'd recognise me after all this time. May I come in?'

Her tone was cool. She was not at all surprised to see him. As she stepped past him into the room, and a servant appeared behind her with a tea tray, he realised that *she* must be the woman sent to him by The Procurer. Stunned, Cameron watched in silence as the tea tray was set down, reaching automatically into his pocket to tip the servant as Kirstin busied herself, warming the pot and setting out the cups. He tried to reconcile the dazzling vision before him with Mrs Collins, but the vicar's wife of his imagination had already vanished, never to be seen again.

Still quite dazed, he sat down opposite her. She had opened the tea caddy, was taking a delicate sniff of the leaves, her finely arched brows rising in what seemed to be surprised approval. Her face, framed by her bonnet, was breathtaking in its flawlessness. Alabaster skin.

Blue-black hair. Heavy-lidded eyes that were a smoky, blue-grey. A generous mouth with a full bottom lip, the colour of almost ripe raspberries.

Yet, he remembered, it had not been the perfection of her face which had drawn him to her all those years ago, it had been the intelligence slumbering beneath those heavy lids, the ironic twist to her smile when their eyes met in that crowded carriage, and that air she still exuded, of aloofness, almost haughtiness, that was both intimidating and alluring. He had suspected fire lay beneath that cool exterior, and he hadn't been disappointed.

A vision of that extraordinary night over six years ago flooded his mind. There had been other women since, though none of late, and never another night like that one. He had come to think of it as a half-remembered dream, a fantasy, the product of extreme circumstances that he would never experience again.

Continue reading
A SCANDALOUS WINTER WEDDING
Marguerite Kaye

www.millsandboon.co.uk

LET'S TALK
Romance

For exclusive extracts, competitions
and special offers, find us online:

- **f** facebook.com/millsandboon
- 🐦 @MillsandBoon
- 📷 @MillsandBoonUK

Get in touch on 01413 063232

For all the latest titles coming soon, visit
millsandboon.co.uk/nextmonth